DAWN OF THE HYBRIDS

J D Curtis

Acknowledgements

To the lady who encouraged me to write many years ago and sadly is no longer here to see the completion of my first book, I am truly grateful. Thank you Mum for your love and wisdom.

To my daily inspiration and the love of my life, my beautiful wife, Corrine. Your belief in me, support and your words of encouragement when I needed it most, were the wind beneath my wings. Your unconditional love inspires me every day and I am so excited to share the success of this book with you and live out our wildest dreams together.

To my dear friends John and Dawn Ward: I am so humbled by the effort you put in to help me complete this book, even when you were busy with your own commitments. You picked me up at a very low point and with your help and enthusiasm was able to push through to the end. Through life you truly see what people are made of and your magnificence has shone through. I will never forget your help and long hours of tireless editing and looking forward to celebrating all that life has to offer with you both.

Thank you Mitch and Caro for your help, I really appreciated your input. Amy and Lauren, thank you so much for all your help in editing. To all my children Amy, Mitch, Lauren and Jesse, I am so proud of you all and I am blessed beyond words to have you as my family.

To my spiritual advisors Francesca and Angie, for always listening to me and offering your guidance. Francesca your help and support will never be forgotten, and I am forever grateful. To Angie, thank you for always listening and encouraging me. To a beautiful soul, you know who you are, thank you so much, I am so grateful for your help.

I would also like to thank Annie Turkington for your gentle critiquing and turning my book in a new direction with your kind help. A big thank you to Reece, Rachel and Kasey, thank you so much for helping me with the photo shoot.

Contents

Chapter One: Birth of the Freak Show

I'm not sure why I feel so screwed up. My self-esteem is below zero and I just don't seem to fit in. I'm like the square peg trying to fit into a round hole. I have grown my fringe trying to hide behind it and I spend my days at school blurring into the background and hiding from my bullies. Is it all because my one and only older sister took her own life a year ago? It has sent my life into the darkest place you could ever imagine. I hate her for what she has done and the fallout and vacuum it has created in my life. It hasn't just been the last year of dealing with the aftermath. I have watched my parents paying for hours and hours of counselling, exhausting every effort to take the pain away from their first-born daughter. We all watched on helplessly as her precious life force drained from her body.

My parents have aged so much through all this they look more like my grandparents now compared to the other kids' parents in my class. I'm sure they don't even know I exist anymore. They are so fixated on clinging to the memories of my sister and blaming themselves for not doing enough or somehow preventing this tragedy from happening. Their way of dealing with it is by not talking about it. Pretending it's all just going to go away. The silent treatment sends my mind into over analysing and relentlessly beating myself up. Blaming myself and reinforcing to myself that I am damaged goods. To compound my pathetic life, I get to watch their lives fall apart more every day. Mum cries every morning and continues throughout the day, while dad has recurring nightmares. They usually walk around the house like zombies, numb and having no idea how to heal and move on from this nightmare. To say I hate my sister, is being completely selfish. She was my best friend in the whole world. She got me. We laughed and giggled for hours when we were kids and then came high school. She was a little different from the average teenager. She was quirky and at times a little zany. Her tormentors started the bullying slowly, then, one day, she made the fatal mistake of retaliating to a comment on social media and that was it. It exploded. She picked the biggest bully to upset, who had an army of try hards on her side, desperate to be liked and would do anything to please her. They blasted my sister day and night on social media. They were relentless, publicly shaming her about her looks, weight and having no friends.

It never stopped even when they found out my sister stopped eating. Due to the anxiety and stress, she began to fade away and spent nearly all her time hiding out in the safety of her room. She stopped talking to my parents and I was shocked when she even stopped talking to me. We all watched on as she slowly withdrew from life, powerless to stop the barrage of torment and bullying at school. Social media was the scourge of our existence. She suffered alone, never knowing who could help end the humiliation.

My parents tried by constantly changing schools for both of us; speaking with the authorities but nothing ever changed. Social media just followed us. New school, different bullies. No one really knew how to stop it. I was the unlucky one who found her hanging in her room that day. She succeeded this time after she botched her last attempt with an overdose. That memory of her hanging there haunts me every day. A stain I can never remove from my mind. She wrote my parents a letter saying sorry and uploaded a video on YouTube. She showed large cards in front of the camera telling the world she was going to end her life as she couldn't continue to go on under the barrage of cruel and merciless bullying.

Then she did it. The video of her last minutes went viral. Then I became the target.

"Are you going to cop out too like your sister Larkins?"

"What's wrong, don't you have any friends either?"

"Don't upset her now... she's fragile too you know!" they would mockingly shout at me sending their group into laughter.

I have grown up witnessing the ugly side of humanity. I'm not sure which is more painful, being bullied and humiliated or the isolation of having no friends. How can I be so alone with this many people on the planet? God I wished she was still here. I hate what she did but I miss her so much, it aches. I wish I had friends and wasn't so alone. I wish I was pretty, had no acne and didn't have to wear these geeky glasses. I wish I had clothes that fitted me properly and had a boyfriend like most of the other girls. I wish I had a friend who would protect me from my bullies. Finally, I wish I had parents who knew I was still alive. I wish, I wish, I wish.

The strangest thing is... all of this hurt and pain has galvanised an inner strength within me. I will not quit like my sister and I won't let them beat me. Besides, nothing has really changed from my sister's death anyway. Promises made by the school to change things never happened. Within six months it was all forgotten. Just a little picture in the school library with a number for those in need of help is all that remains.

"You're not alone. Yeah right!" I thought to myself.

They don't know how to stop it. They don't even notice I'm being bullied now!

There are often times I think this nerdy, pimply-faced girl with baggy rags was destined to be a loser. The cards have always been stacked against me. Every morning my stomach is in knots at the thought of having to go to school. Every moment drags on in slow motion. I detest school. Even something simple like being asked to read something out loud in front of the class, is torture for me. My face turns so red with embarrassment that I need to pull at the collar of my shirt to let out some heat. My heart pounds like a drum. I'm sure the others could see it and hear it pounding in my chest. In a timid voice, I stutter the words out, hating the sound of my own voice as it shakes and trembles. All the while hearing the laughter and sniggering of all those around me. You know it's bad when the teacher has to stop the class from ridiculing you. There are no fond memories here.

The siren sounds for the end of lunch, time for my next class... basketball! I detest sport more than reading out loud. At least I have some protection in the classroom but out on the basketball court, I am 'free game.' My skinny body doesn't stand a chance against these strong athletic girls. I've tried everything in my power to get out of it but I've used up all my excuses and sick notes from mum and the other teachers. There's just nowhere to hide. It's time to face the music yet again.

Reluctantly, I make my way out onto the court, only to hear the cutting and hurtful taunts as they poke fun and laugh at me. We split off into teams, the bitches take turns lining me up and taking me out, usually by tripping me. I hit the court hard, time and time again. I grimace every time as my skinny body hits the floor. Sometimes I get winded, other times my knees knock together hard, it's always painful. Doing my best to ignore the pain, I manage to peel my body up off the floor as I scramble to find my glasses and rearrange them back on my face. The coach side-tracked by all the young pretty girls, just simply 'turns a blind eye'. He shakes his head and shouts at me.

"Come on, Larkins. Is that the best you can do? Try a little harder."

Try harder? I don't think so. With the ball in hand, I dribbled the ball down the line doing my best to dodge all the blocks but then it happens again. One of the more popular bitches stuck her foot right out in front of me which sent me plunging face first onto the gym floor. I picked myself up again after finding my glasses. As usual, they were all enjoying my misery.

"Alright! Alright! That's enough you lot. Penalty shot Larkins. You okay to take it?" yelled the coach after blowing his whistle.

"Yes," I mumbled in a pathetic and wimpy voice.

"Speak up, Larkins. Can you take it or not?"

"Yes, coach", I replied a little louder, "I can take it."

My knees were stinging and every muscle in my body ached. I fought back the waves of nausea at the realisation that I had to take a penalty shot in front of everyone.

All eyes were on me. Burning red with embarrassment and feeling repulsed by the attention, I walked to the line to take my shot.

As I turned around to receive the ball, I felt the full thrust of the ball hit my stomach, thrown with so much power that it took my breath away and left me doubled over in pain. I fell to my knees, winded and desperately trying to breathe. It was then that I began to hear the blood-curdling screams of all the girls around me as they recoiled in horror.

Everything was moving in slow motion. I cradled my stomach trying to ease the unbearable pain. That's when I first saw the blood. A pool of blood that was spreading around my knees and something was lying within it. What was that? Light-headed, I did my best to focus on it. I was staring at this thing in complete disbelief. It looked like a small fetus but was mutated beyond belief. It was moving around in the blood gasping for air, trying to breathe. What the fuck! That blood is coming from me! Which means that thing... came from me... I have only just begun to get my period... this can't be happening. Confused and in a state of shock, trying to understand what was going on, the deafening screaming in the background was turning hysterical. Still dazed, I slowly looked up and caught sight of the bullies, seeing the horror in their eyes. As I gazed beyond them, I could see the stands emptying fast in panic as some other onlookers were frantically running towards me with their phones in hand. I swayed, almost unconsciously as the crowd moved in on me but due to my heavy blood loss, my dizziness spiralled and I fainted.

That's when I saw him for the first time. I looked behind me thinking he was staring at someone else. Was he looking at me? Nobody looks at me like that! Looking at me as if I was the only person in the world who ever mattered, I couldn't move. I could barely breathe as his beautiful eyes stared straight into my soul.

I could feel his presence all around me. I wanted to reach out and touch him. Was he here to protect me, to watch over me?

I was feeling tingly all over as his smouldering eyes still mesmerised me. They were the purest blue I had ever seen. I was under his spell and could not stop staring into those eyes.

He then moved closer to me, sending my pulse into overdrive. Edging closer he leant forward to kiss me but paused for a second. The anticipation was excruciatingly exciting.

My first kiss!

I closed my eyes to etch this memory into my mind forever. I felt his warm, soft lips caress mine. I didn't feel awkward or shy... just connected to his love and compassion radiating from his body into mine.

I was floating on air and my body tingled with excitement. My senses were dancing with delight. I loved it. Is this Heaven?

"Come on now sleepy head. Gotta wake up sooner or later."

Who was that? I heard a voice but couldn't see anyone.

Then a series of loud noises jolted me back into the present moment. With squinting eyes, I tried to regain focus. I could see a nurse fussing over me, checking my condition and making notes on her clipboard.

"Where am I? What happened?" I asked. My throat was sore and croaky.

"It's good to see you've returned to the land of the living! Do you remember anything? What happened Samantha?"

Her question sent my brain diving into my memory bank, searching for answers.

"I was playing sport... basketball, I think... and then... I must have passed out."

The hospital nurse walked around my bed, stood close to me and then gently took hold of my hand to check my pulse. She was mature, motherly and had a kind face with a gentle manner. I felt safe with her.

"Is that all you remember dear?" she asked.

"Wait a minute! There was blood. Lots of blood," I struggled to piece it all together.

Fragments of my memory were returning, as the incident began to unravel in my mind. I sat upright on the bed and grabbed at the nurse's uniform and desperately yanked it.

"Please tell me what happened. Why am I here? Are my parents here?" I asked pleading.

"Your mother has been here all night. She just ducked out for a coffee and your father was called into work early this morning. If I were you, I would use this time to get my story straight," she said with a raised eyebrow.

"What? I don't understand. What do you mean 'get my story straight'?"

"You don't remember anything... at all?" the nurse quizzed with a curious look on her face.

"I've already told you that all I can remember is the blood and then fainting."

"Samantha... you have had a miscarriage," the nurse explained.

"What?! Are you insane? I haven't even had sex yet! Where's my Mum? I need to speak with Mum!"

"Calm down, calm down. It's okay. I didn't mean to upset you. I'll go and find your mother. Now lay back down and rest."

She left the room and returned a short time later with Mum.

"I'll give you two some alone time," the nurse said as she left the room and closed the door behind her.

Mum shuffled towards me. She had aged so much in the last year it was frightening. I looked pleadingly into her sullen face.

"Mum! What's she talking about? What's going on?"

"I was hoping you could tell me, Sam."

"All I can remember was playing sport... basketball, I think... I got hit hard. There was blood... lots of blood all around me and then I must have fainted."

"You miscarried, Sam! How could you do this to us, after everything we have just been through with your sister?" her sad eyes looked tired and were swollen from crying.

"No, Mum... no! I swear. I'm a virgin! I promise I'm not lying. Please believe me! What do I have to do for you to believe me?"

"Then how do you explain what's happened, Sam? I just don't understand."

"It's not what you think Mum. I promise! I would never do this to you after what happened to..." I didn't want to say her name. It would have pushed her over the edge, "Mum I swear I couldn't be pregnant, I've never even had a boyfriend!"

Mum just stared at the floor, she wouldn't even look at me. I knew I would never convince her. There was no way she was going to believe me and I could feel the shame emanating from her. She didn't need this especially since my sister's suicide. I could feel the tension rising between us by the second and I didn't have a logical reason to explain what happened.

"I need to go home and cook dinner. We'll talk about this when you get home," she said in a serious tone.

Clutching her handbag, she left without looking at me and even saying goodbye. I knew in my heart things would only get worse from here.

I stayed overnight in hospital due to losing so much blood. While I was there, they ran some precautionary tests on me. HIV and other sexually related diseases. The nurses were doing their best to make me feel cheap and dirty with their cold and judgemental stares and looks of disapproval. They made no attempt to conceal what they were thinking.

The hospital finally released me when they were happy with my results. Dad picked me up on his way home from work. After exchanging somewhat formal and awkward greetings, we didn't say another word to each other the whole drive home. I just stared out the window and watched dark clouds descend on us, which said it all.

Who was I kidding? Why would I expect them to believe me? The facts are the facts. In their eyes, I am just another teenage girl sleeping around and simply too scared to face the consequences of my actions, so I'm pleading ignorance.

They have both been burying themselves in work to help cope or run from their pain brought about by my sister's death. Mum works tirelessly at the local church, leaving her no spare time, whilst dad avoids coming home if he can, taking all the overtime he can find.

They barely talk to one another. They come and go like ships through the night. Too proud to ask for any help or counselling, they forge their way through their pain blindly.

I always found it difficult to relate to my parents and after my sister's death, it's become almost impossible. They didn't understand that I was also hurting, she was my sister, goddammit! They were so buried in their loss and in their own separate worlds, they assumed I was coping. It was so long ago since they were at school and things have changed so dramatically.

Drugs are rife at my school and apart from the physical bullying, there was now cyberbullying. People online, whose sole purpose was to make your life a living hell – publicly posting lies and trashing you for the whole world to see. As a coping mechanism, I studied hard and buried my head in learning as much as I could. I wanted good grades as I was determined to be a lawyer. I wanted to bring in my own style of justice to the world and right as many wrongs as I could.

Mum was always concerned with what others thought of us. She was always seeking everyone's approval, spending much of her time 'keeping up appearances.'

Even before Lizzie's death, Dad always had trouble expressing his affection to me but he always looked upon me kindly with loving eyes. He'd give me a big warm smile and a cheeky wink, as if to say, it's going to be alright Sammy.

I used to be the apple of his eye. Now all I see is the hurt in his eyes and with this latest disappointment, no amount of saying, 'I didn't do this' will change that look. That's what hurts me the most.

So, where to from here I thought? I will die if they make me go back to school. It's bad enough that my parents are ashamed of me and now I'm officially known as the town slut. My head hurts trying to understand what happened and my mind is exhausted figuring out what to do next.

I have this sense of knowing that what happened to me was not going to be a 'one-off incident.' I had no control over what had just happened to me and I feel that it is going to happen again. It's a very unsettling feeling.

I slid into my bed that night and the tears rolled down my face. I thought they were never going to stop. I feel so alone, so afraid and have no idea what to do. Praying for answers, praying for help, I drifted off to sleep.

I woke in the morning feeling a little unsettled because I had a dream during the night and I knew exactly what I had to do, which scared the crap out of me.

I told Mum I was feeling sick and didn't feel up to going back to school today. She took a deep breath, ready to challenge me but then paused and reluctantly agreed. She knew if I returned to school all the tongues would start wagging again and she wasn't coping well with the gossip-mongering from her church friends about her promiscuous daughter.

I had to remind myself that Mum was now also carrying the weight of this burden on her shoulders. Ever since my sister's suicide, I've seen her sneak around town with her head tucked into her chest, covered with a shawl in disguise, doing her best to avoid any contact with anyone who might recognise her and now she has the embarrassment of my dilemma.

Mum finds it difficult to make eye contact with me now and when she does manage to look at me, she only sees the person who is responsible for all her extra troubles and pain. Her excuses are always the same, errands to run, food shopping to do and of course, the church.

I feel a stranger in my own home. The awkward silences are unbearable. My parents make small talk purely for the sake of ending the awkward silences.

It was time to put my plan into action. As terrified as I was there was no point putting it off any longer. As soon as Mum left, I frantically stuffed as many clothes and snacks as I could fit into my backpack and what money I had saved.

It wasn't much but at least it will get me a bus ticket and a few dinners. I was getting anxious and didn't want a panic attack to come on. I've been having panic attacks since my sister's death and they really freak me out. Anyway, I'm finished with school. I've suffered enough and I'm not going back to endure any more ridicule or bullying.

I scribbled a quick letter to my parents explaining my actions.

Mum and Dad,

I'm so sorry for the pain I've caused you both. I don't expect you to believe me but I promise you I didn't do this. Mum I prayed for help and received it in a dream, that's why I'm leaving. I have been tormented and bullied to breaking point and with what happened the other day, it will only get worse. You have already lost one of your girls so please forgive me, Mum. I wish I could take all your pain away from Lizzie's death. I miss her so much too Mum. I love you both and will come home when all this blows over.

Love Sam xx

I grabbed my backpack and remembered my phone was on the counter. Mum had put it on charge. I turned it on and unlocked it. It lit up like a Christmas tree filling my phone with messages and photos. My entire body felt nauseous as I looked at one of the many photos. It was me kneeling in my own blood, surrounded by girls filming it from their phones and falling from fainting. I was hurt beyond comprehension.

"Fuuuuuck!" I yelled as I hurled the phone against the lounge room wall and watched it smash and disintegrate into pieces. No more phones! No more social media! I thought as I picked up the broken pieces and binned them.

There was no choice now. I had to leave and run away. Knowing that my parents would report me as a missing person and being a young female; everyone would be out looking for me. I knew my appearance had to change!

I went into Mum and Dad's bathroom scrambling through Dad's bathroom drawer. I managed to find his hair clippers. I plugged them in and turned them on. I took a big breath and started. Shaving as close to my head as possible, I watched my blonde hair fall to the floor. The clippers struggled to cut through my thick long hair. I watched in the mirror as I metamorphised right before my eyes. It was bizarre, looking at the new me in the mirror as my old identity lay on the floor.

Turning the clippers off and closing my eyes, I ran my hands over my head, removing any remnants of loose hair. When I opened my eyes slowly, I didn't recognize myself. The reflection in the bathroom cabinet revealed a courageous and tough-looking young woman ready to face all her fears.

Leaving no evidence of the 'new' me, I swept up all my hair and put it in a bag to take with me. After pulling on some old jeans and a hoodie, my transformation was complete. The timid and shy girl had been slain. I cringed at the thought of her existence now, walking around too afraid of looking up in fear of attracting attention. She was pitiful and pathetic.

Now that I had shed my old skin, my new identity needed a name. Sarah, Sarah O'Connor. I kind of looked like Sinead O'Connor now, but my heroine was Sarah Connor from the Terminator movie.

It was so liberating watching myself evolve. New name, radical haircut, different clothes and for the first time in my life I felt confident, alive, free and that I mattered. I wasn't invisible anymore.

It was time to leave as Mum would be home soon. I pulled my backpack on, slipped my hood over my head, and made my way outside through the front door. I slammed it shut and locked it, along with my past.

In purposeful strides, I walked down our street heading towards the bus station. I stopped dead in my tracks. Mum was walking straight towards me, though buried in worry and she seemed a million miles away, as usual.

I reached into my front pocket and grabbed the sunglasses I had taken from Lizzie's room. I quickly replaced my glasses with Lizzie's and continued walking again. The dark shades gave me cover and I felt unrecognisable and even walked differently. I continued with my head down. I could feel my anxious heart beating faster and faster, as I walked right past her nervously without even a look from Mum.

Relief swept through me as my heart slowly returned to its normal rhythm again. I was bold enough to glance back at her through my dark shades, knowing it could well be the last time I might ever see her again. Her head was still down and her drooping shoulders and snail-paced walking just wanted to make me cry.

The reassuring thing about moving to a new town is people won't recognize me or judge me. People don't know anything about me. It would only be a matter of time before my parents would report me as missing.

Then a sad realisation dawned on me. Perhaps they might not report me missing. Would they let all the pain, rumours and suffering quietly disappear? Reporting it would bring more unwanted attention to them, inflaming all the gossip-mongering. The story could drag on for weeks, perhaps months. I don't think my parents would cope with that pressure right now.

Here I am, taking on the blame for something I haven't even done. But one thing is for sure. I don't want to be looking over my shoulder every minute worrying if someone has recognised me and perhaps reported me as the missing girl.

I began to over analyse again which only made matters worse. I had so much internal conflict but I knew I had to leave.

"Keep walking Sam... I mean Sarah. It's Sarah now. Got it! Stay strong. You can do it. Keep walking to the bus station and get on Sarah. You can do it. That's it, keep walking. Nearly there, now deep breaths." Speaking out loud was the only way I could drown out the loud mental noise in my head. I arrived at the bus station, relieved. Thankfully, I didn't have to wait long before the next bus pulled up.

After paying my fare, I made my way to the back and slumped into an empty seat. The bus was nearly empty with only a handful of passengers on board, who all seemed distracted in one way or another. They were either staring out the window with emotionless faces or had cords dangling from their ears, isolating themselves with a 'do not disturb' look on their faces. That suited me just fine.

I relaxed enough to pull back my hoodie and put my glasses back on. After the last person boarded, the doors were closed shut and the driver began turning the large steering wheel and navigated the bus on its designated journey. The trip gave me some much-needed processing time, as I was still in free fall from the decision to leave.

For now, I was in a safe place and would be for several hours. My school days and all that misery were now behind me. I could walk into a new town and not feel judged or have anything to hide. I felt newfound freedom and even some excitement filling my body. The question still remained. How did I get pregnant when I haven't had sex? I mean, hello! If you took a look at Sam Larkins, you'd know why. I've only just turned 15 and I don't even have one female friend, let alone a boyfriend! Not like Jessica Hawley. The boys were hypnotised when she walked into the room. Their minds propelled into their dark, brooding fantasies. The girls would turn green with envy and start whispering to each other. If Jessica Hawley got pregnant, you wouldn't be surprised. But me?!

As the bus continued, I began to let go of my past and turned my attention to looking out the window. The warm sun coming through the window transported me into a daydream. That's when the visions of my past dreams came flooding back to me.

My dreams felt like they had been physical and I had this strong feeling that I had been visited. The beings in these dreams were always loving and kind but they needed something from me, though I was never sure what that was exactly. I could never make out their faces and it was just these strong feelings and weird sensations that they were doing things to me. Perhaps I wasn't supposed to remember.

Were these dreams somehow connected to me? Did these beings have sex with me in my sleep? It just doesn't make sense. Surely, I would have known if they'd had sex with me? I thought about mum not understanding and realised she would have read my letter by now and would be worried sick. Well, Sarah O'Connor, you wanted a new life and something tells me you're going to get a whole lot more than you bargained for.

A couple of days ago I was worried about having acne, no friends and playing sport with bullies. Today, I don't know where I'm living, sleeping, or where my next meal will come from.

The drone of the bus engine lulled me into sleep. I only remember waking up when we reached the end of the line. My eyes struggled with the bright daylight as I stood up and stretched my aching body that had been stationary for too long.

Hurling my backpack over my shoulder, I made my way off the bus nodding at the driver to say thanks. Stepping off the bus and into a new reality, I needed to appear grown-up and in complete control of what I was doing. On the inside, I was shitting myself.

I was becoming self-conscious and paranoid, as my mind ran from one scenario to another. Not knowing where I was going to stay and sleep for the night was making me anxious again.

'Get your shit together Sarah... do you hear me?' I spoke those words to myself and it calmed me almost immediately. Sarah O'Connor would not allow herself to weaken like Sam Larkins. She would be planning her next move and then taking action.

The frightened voice of my inner child began getting louder and louder and overriding Sarah O'Connor who had it all sorted. She was tired, hungry and scared and as nightfall approached, she needed a safe place for the night.

I got my shit together and my eyes were frantically scanning shop windows for any information that advertised accommodation. I ignored my tired legs and continued to search for a safe place to crash for the night. Finally, exhausted, I asked for help and was given directions to a backpacker's hostel a little out of town.

After walking for what felt like hours, I eventually found the hostel. It looked old, run-down and badly in need of some maintenance, but I'd hoped that also meant it was not going to be expensive.

As I pulled the front door open cautiously, its old and rusty hinges squeaked as I entered sheepishly.

On the left-hand side of the entry, a long-weathered office desk stood proud. Above it was a large blackboard displaying prices for accommodation untidily scrawled in chalk. I sighed a sense of relief as I had enough money for one night. To the right of the blackboard, another sign was stating all the rules and regulations of the establishment. No drugs or alcohol allowed on the premises. Keep your rooms tidy and locked at all times. It went on and on - rules, rules, and more rules. A teenager's worst nightmare. The last one stated that failure to comply with any of the rules would lead to eviction without notice.

Straight ahead I saw a hallway with lots of rooms leading off from it. My eyes wandered back to the front desk spotting a service bell that had escaped my notice at first glance. I pushed the button, keen to negotiate a room so that I could have somewhere to crash for the night. It was my first day on the run and I was mentally and physically exhausted.

Waiting in anticipation, my mind continued to predict who would appear and my paranoia forced me to put my guard up and be ready on alert. Was this place safe? Taking deep breaths and preparing answers in case a barrage of questions came at me – regarding my age, was I running away, or was I that missing girl on the poster?

All my assumptions were completely misguided as a punky, spirited young girl appeared before me. Her bright red hair was cut very short on both sides of her head, a trendy shave cut with three or four white lines of skin and an inch of very short hair in between the lines. Her ears were heavily pierced and her arms were adorned with intricate and colourful tattoos that easily caught your attention. She had artistically applied her makeup and was oozing attitude.

"One, two or more? Prices up there," she said in a 'whatever' voice.

"Ah, I'll just take one night to start with and see how I settle in," I replied.

"You can stay as long as you like, you're paying," she said nonchalantly, as she chewed gum noisily.

As I handed over the money I asked, "Who owns this place?"

"Why's that, yah wanna buy the place?" she replied with a smart-arse attitude.

"No, no I was just curious, that's all," I said politely.

"That would be Francesca, you'll see her around soon enough."

"Francesca, okay thanks, I'll keep an eye out for her."

"You look kinda young to be running around on your own!" she questioned.

"Something tells me you would know all about that." Going on the attack seemed like my best form of defence.

"Whatever, there's your key. Any questions, I'm in 21 and by the way, people call me Red."

"No questions and thanks Red."

I grabbed my key. It was large, old and rusty with a weathered metal tag attached to it, displaying 'No. 7'. Slinging my backpack over my shoulder, I dragged my weary body down the hall. I could not get into my room fast enough.

Hurling my belongings on the floor and locking the door as fast as I could, I fell onto the old creaky bed, grateful for a safe room for the night. Curled up in the foetal position and checking out the room, I took stock of what I had done and where I was. I wiped a few tears from my tired eyes. I was 15 and all alone.

The tears continued to fall and soon turned into uncontrollable sobbing. My body shook and spasmed as it went about releasing an overload of emotions. This wasn't just about the miscarriage, all the bullying and leaving home. I had never grieved my sister's death. Cautious not to let anyone hear me, I buried myself under the blankets, my head under the pillow and continued to release the emotional overload from my body, eventually crying myself to sleep.

A loud passionate conversation coming from another room woke me early the next morning. My annoyance soon turned to gratitude because the interruption was my alarm clock and time was against me. I sat upright on the bed, still dressed from the day before, planning my next course of action. Showering was my first priority, then to find Francesca and negotiate a solution to stay here longer. If I couldn't, I would have to keep moving and I needed to know my fate now, rather than later.

I got distracted by the front desk bell being constantly pressed and I was becoming increasingly more agitated. Someone was clearly pissed off and continued to press it, in frustration of being unattended to. Then it dawned on me that Red wasn't answering the reception bell.

Curious, I wandered off to investigate. Entering the reception area, I found a young Asian couple pointing in a very animated fashion to all the prices and rules on the boards.

"Ah, hi. I'll go and find someone for you, take a seat," I said as I pointed to the chairs.

They just smiled back at me, doing their best to understand me, as I went in search of Red. Most of the doors were closed as I walked down the hallway. I couldn't find her. Acting on an impulse, I entered the shower block and looked around anxiously in search of Red. I called out for her but there was no reply. There in the last cubicle, I could see a body on the floor from under the shower curtain. My heart was racing as I pulled the curtain across to one side. Curled up in a ball in the corner of the shower, was Red. Water flowing freely from the shower hitting her naked, tattooed body. Her head was buried in the corner. She was incoherent and mumbling, in a state of shock as bloody water puddled around her, before making its way down the drain hole.

Unable to hear Red from where I was standing, I moved closer.

"Get that thing... away from me! Get that fucking thing away from me!"

"Red... what thing? What are you talking about?" I asked.

Red's blood-soaked towel was covering something on the shower floor, which was moving.

"Fuck!" I jumped back.

"Get that fucking thing away from me! NOW!" she shouted, still hiding her head in the corner of the shower.

"OKAY! OKAY! I got it!"

I was nervous now. Whatever it was, it had freaked Red out.

I slowly moved in and carefully grabbed a corner of the towel and nervously peeled it back and then screamed. I let go of the towel and jumped up and away in shock. I ran around in the bathroom as if I had just felt a spider crawling on me, trying to shake the images out of my mind.

"Fuck! Fuck! Red. Did you just... did that come from you?"

There was no response from Red. It was useless trying to talk to her. She was in shock, shaking and mumbling.

"Someone help me. Please help me!"

I turned off the water and helped Red to her feet. I turned her head to face mine and held her head in my hands.

"What do you want me to do Red? Tell me!" I said firmly.

"Get me out of here," she insisted, "and get rid of that fucking thing!" Red began to collapse. Snap out of it Sarah and think. Quick, before someone else comes in.

Quickly composing myself the best way I could, I knew I had to deal with it. Red was incapable of anything now and with no time to spare I had to act. This thing was still alive. Something had gone horribly wrong with this thing. **It was grotesque.** It had a very large head compared to the tiny arms and legs, which were twisted and stumpy. It looked pink and its distorted face was desperately gasping to breathe.

"Oh Fuck! Fuck! What the hell is this thing?!"

It then finally stopped gasping for air and was motionless. I quickly grabbed a fresh towel and wrapped it around the other blood-soaked towel and picked it up. I was shaking and disgusted, as I walked around the bathroom deciding where to put it. I then dropped the lot into one of the bins near the sink and covered it with some paper towels, deciding to come back and deal with it later. My priority was now to get Red dressed and back to her room but before that, I needed to flush away all the blood. I turned on the taps and squeamishly used my foot to push the blood clots through the narrow slits in the drain hole. I fought back waves of nausea.

"Red... you okay? I'll be with you in a sec. Just hang on. I'm nearly done here okay?"

I managed to flush most of the blood away.

With some cooperation from Red, I managed to towel her cold shivering body dry. She was reeling in shock. I then remembered the young Asian couple was still waiting to book a room in reception.

"Red listen to me," as I shook her firmly several times, "Red you need to get dressed. There are people waiting in reception to book a room. Red what are we going to do?"

Her vacant eyes stared at me. Her blue lips moved as she mumbled, "This is the fourth time. They won't leave me alone."

"What are you talking about?" I asked.

She looked straight ahead in a trance-like state. Frustrated with my failed efforts to get her dressed, I decided to walk her back to her room, wrapped in a few towels only. Her body slumped onto the bed and I threw a blanket over her, closed the door and went straight back to the office to cover for her.

Upon entering the reception area, I saw an older woman checking in the Asian couple. They received their key and were about to head off in search of their room.

"Can I help you?" she asked me, straight to the point in her strong accent. I guessed she was in her 60s. She wore modest clothes and I noticed her hands were rough, cracked and scarred, I assumed from years of hard work.

"No, I booked in late yesterday. Red served me," I said.

"Where is that little bitch? That was her last chance. I'm done with her," she angrily exclaimed.

"Ahh... Red's not feeling well... she has a migraine and asked me to find you to see if it would be okay If I filled in for her," I said nervously.

"Oh, did she now. She is always sick or going missing that one. Can I trust you with my money?"

"Yes, yes, of course you can. I won't let you down," I reassured her.

"If you only knew how many times I've heard that over the years. I'm Francesca... what is your name? You look very young. Are you a boy or a girl?"

"Sarah... ahh... gggirl."

"You're not in trouble with the police, are you? Are you on the run?"

"No... not at all. I'm 18 and just travelling about. You know?"

"Well... you'll have to do if that little bitch can't do her job. Not the first time you know. Young people today have no idea how to work. Come with me I'll show what to do... if you can keep up," she said in her no-nonsense way.

Francesca spent the next fifteen minutes showing me what to do.

"Don't let me hear that bell ring more than three times. Do you hear me? If you work out, we can come to some arrangement, for now, you can work for free board. What do you say?" Francesca said with a raised eyebrow.

"Yes, that would be great. Thank you Francesca," I said, trying hard to contain my excitement.

As Francesca left, I slumped into the chair behind the front counter with sheer relief. In all the panic and chaos, I hadn't had time to process what had just happened to Red.

I am not alone! This has happened to someone else! Is this is happening to others?

My mind was hurling flashbacks of that horrific thing in the shower and I couldn't get the image out of my mind! Was that the same thing that came out of me as well? I really needed to speak with Red. She had information and I needed to know everything about what had happened to her previously.

I quickly got up and returned to Red's room. I opened the door to reveal she was gone. Blood-stained towels a testament she had been there. Why has she gone? She's weak and needed the rest. Red was hiding something.

"Damn you, Red. I could have helped you and you could have helped me, too."

"Who yah talkin' tah, missy?"

Startled, I jumped in fright. When I turned around, a scruffy, unshaven man was standing in the doorway. He was not someone you wanted to cross.

"Shit! You scared me," I paused, "ah, no one. I wasn't talking to anyone. I was just thinking out loud," I replied, regaining my composure.

"Yeah? Well if yah see that bitch Red, tell her that I want Lenny's money and I want it now! I'm tired of her games! Pay up or she'll wish she never met me."

The bell rang at the front desk.

"Got it. Gotta go. Duty calls!"

I squeezed past him to attend to the bell ringing at the front desk and check-in new guests. After showing them to their room I returned to reception and sat down and began to think about what had just happened. God, I felt so much better in myself - I'm not a freak. That thing wasn't normal at all. Why us? What's happening?

Dammit! I should have stayed with Red and gone with her. I've got a room but no money and I'm stuck here listening out for a bell all day. How's that going to work for me?

By late afternoon Francesca took over the front desk so I decided to take off and look for Red. There was still no sign of her anywhere. I checked the local hospital, the chemist and even the doctors but not a sign of her.

As I couldn't find Red, I had decided to stay on at the backpackers for the next few weeks, hoping Red would come back. Nearby was a soup kitchen for the homeless, which kept my ever-rumbling stomach quiet. I convinced Francesca into some much-needed painting around the place which gave me a couple of dollars. I was surviving and it felt good to be stable for a while. It was far from perfect but it worked for the time being.

Just when everything settled down for a while, my dreams began again. They were so vivid, I would swear they were real. It felt like these beings were doing tests on me like they were taking blood or tissue samples. They would appear, carry out what they had to do and then leave. It was like being operated on and as the drugs were wearing off, I got to experience a little of what was happening to me. It was bizarre but I never felt threatened.

The next morning, I made my way to the bathroom early, so that I could shower in peace and have my little private time before the bell would start to ring. As I was drying myself, I felt sore on the side of my body so I went to the mirror in the bathroom and took a closer look. I could see two puncture marks on the side of my body. They were small, like snakebites.

Then I recalled my dreams. 'FUCK! What the fuck!'

These marks were not just in my dream. This was happening! It was real! I could also see purple fluorescent-like marks near the wounds, like fingerprints.

As I was finishing dressing, I heard the bell ringing and was grateful for the distraction, my mind was taking me places I didn't want to go. I marched quickly to the front office and I was in for more surprises, as I could see two men in police uniform waiting at reception. It was a holy fuck moment. Are they here for me? What am I going to say? My mind was in overdrive again and I was extremely anxious. They saw me approaching; it was too late to turn around and do a runner.

"Get your shit together Sarah O'Connor - do you hear me? Grow a set and take control," I gave myself a serve just before I got to the desk.

"Hi. I'm Officer Tomlinson and this is my partner, Officer Harris. We are looking for Racheal Matthews. We believe she is working here, or possibly staying here?"

My heart was racing.

"Racheal Matthews! I'm sorry. I don't know anyone by that name," I stuttered.

"She has short, red hair and lots of tattoos. Shortish girl, about 17 years of age."

"Oh, sorry you must mean Red. I never knew her real name. Yes. She was here about three weeks ago but she just upped and left. No idea where she went."

"Are you okay? You seem a little nervous?" questioned Officer Harris.

"Ahh not at all. Sorry it's been a busy morning and I'm a little flustered, that's all. Is there anything else I can help you with? I'm rather busy this morning and the boss is on my back; you know how it is."

"Sounds familiar. Listen, if you hear of anything or she comes back, please call me. And thanks for your time. We'll let you get back to work," said Officer Tomlinson, as he gave me his card.

"Is Red in any trouble?" I queried. As much as I wanted them gone, I just had to ask that question.

"Not that we are aware of. Just following up in relation to another matter. Don't concern yourself. I'm sure it will be fine. Thanks for your time."

They were not telling me the whole story. Where was Red? What had she done? I thought to myself.

The next few days passed without incident. Things were looking up. I had even managed to persuade Francesca to pay me a regular wage on top of my room. It was either that or leave. She had quietly admired all my painting and hard work and was also fed up of losing staff. With the extra money, I was eating better and even managed to buy some clothes down at the local second-hand shop.

Occasionally, one of the backpackers I could trust watched the hostel for a couple of hours, giving me some much-needed freedom to get out and live a little.

On returning to the hostel, one particular night I found someone waiting for me. She had sat down in the chair and had fallen asleep. It was 7:00 pm and usually, things were quiet by then. People had already found where they were staying for the night.

She looked Italian with jet black hair, which was greasy and unbrushed, olive skin, very pretty and about the same age as me. Her clothes were dirty and smelly. Her graffitied backpack was attached to her hand with a chain. I gently tried to wake her.

"Are you okay? Can I help you?" I whispered.

She woke up with a fright, "Oh, I'm sorry. I had nowhere else to go. I rang the bell and when no one came, I sat down and must have fallen asleep."

"It's okay. What's your name?"

"Maria."

"Hi Maria, I'm Sarah. Do you have any money? You know, to stay here, I mean?"

"I used my travel card for the bus fare. I don't have any money," she tried to keep it together explaining her story but it wasn't long before she broke down and started crying.

"My father is very strict. Something happened to me and he didn't believe me, so he kicked me out of home. I have younger sisters. I am so scared for them."

"Okay. Here's what we are going to do. You can stay in my room tonight with me until we can figure something out. Would you like to have a shower first? I'll get you some of my clothes, I reckon we're about the same size. Then come back to my room and we'll talk about it more."

"That would be great. I would love a hot shower and some fresh clothes. Are you sure though? I don't want to get you in any trouble," she said.

"It's no trouble," I said warmly.

"Thank you so much. I am so grateful," she leant forward and stood up and gave me the biggest hug.

"Thank you. You are so kind," she gave me a beautiful, warm smile as we headed to the showers.

"You may have to return the favour one day Maria, who knows? Here take my shampoo, conditioner and soap and here's a fresh towel. You won't find them in the showers, they tend to go missing very quickly in hostels so please bring them back."

"You have my word and thanks again, Sarah."

After twenty minutes, Maria returned and looked like a different person.

"Wow, you look so different!" I said.

"I feel like a new person. Oh my god, that was the best shower I have ever had! I swear."

Maria sat on the edge of the bed next to me.

"So, Maria what happened to you?" I asked sincerely.

We faced one another. She placed her hands together in her lap, as if she was praying, looking down, as if too ashamed to look at me.

"I am the eldest of seven children, six are girls. My parents are Italian and are strict culture Roman Catholics. I don't know if you know what that means but marriage and sex is a very sacred thing," she began to cry softly.

"We were at Sunday church for the 10:00 am service, some time ago. My family attended every Sunday and Dad would walk in so proud, showing off Mum and all his kids, he loved us all. We were not rich but dressed immaculately and we always sat up the front and filled the entire church pew. All of a sudden, I began having these stomach cramps and was not feeling well at all. I forced myself up to receive Holy Communion. Of all the times and places! Can you believe it?" she broke down and wept inconsolably.

"It's okay, Maria. You're safe here. It's okay," I reassured her and she continued.

"I was making my first Holy Communion. We usually make it at age nine or ten but due to falling numbers and fewer priests, they now do a combined service, so there are kids from 17 down to seven years of age."

Maria was shaking. She paused to try and calm herself and continued again.

"So, there I am in this pristine white gown, that looked more like a wedding dress. I'm standing there with my arms out in front of me, hands cupped to receive the Host. The church was so full, people were standing outside who couldn't even get in. Then I felt my stomach contract and began to feel dizzy and as I looked down, I saw my dress stained red and a pool of blood at my feet. It was horrific. Still feeling light-headed, I watched the priest faint, after that, I must have gone into shock and passed out because the next thing I remember is waking up in a hospital bed. Mum was beside me and I didn't think she would ever stop crying."

"Why Maria? Why? How could you do this to us? You're a smart girl, top of your class. I thought you would know better!" she cried.

"Mum," I pleaded with her, "what are you talking about?"

"The doctor said you had a miscarriage. How could you do this to our family? Maria."

"Mum I didn't do anything. You must believe me please!"

"I have been up all night praying to God for answers Maria. Your father is furious. You embarrassed him in front of the whole church, full of his friends and family. It's not a good time for you to come home right now Maria. I have spoken with Aunt Rosa and she has agreed to let you stay with her for the time being."

"That's it? You're kicking me out without even talking about this Mum?"

"It's in everyone's best interests. Please don't make this any harder than it is Maria."

"So, you're calling me a liar?" I said angrily.

"Aunt Rosa is coming to pick you up from the hospital. She is on her way. I love you, Maria, I hope you understand in time. I will see you soon."

She leaned forward kissed me, blessed herself and said, "Please watch over her My Lord and keep her safe," and then walked out crying.

"That was it. My mum and family just abandoned me. Left me in shame and I didn't even do anything. God! I've never even kissed a boy. Can you believe it?" Maria said frustrated and then continued.

"I wasn't waiting for Aunt Rosa and living in this shame for something I didn't do. I got dressed and caught the first bus out of town and ended up here," Maria wiped her eyes trying desperately to be strong.

"I understand Maria. No one believed me either. No one understood. I did exactly what you did and here I am."

"Did I just hear you right?" she was staring at me in disbelief.

"Are you serious?" she said shocked.

"Well I'm not here by choice, that's for sure."

I paused slightly, "That's not all. There are others, you and I are not alone," she looked at me with a puzzled face.

"What are you talking about Sarah?"

"I have seen another girl, our age, go through exactly the same thing as us!"

"Oh my God. You're serious. Shit! Sorry. What are we going to do?" Maria asked, worried.

"I've been trying to find a girl that used to stay here. She said it's happened to her four times now. She has information and I have to find her. I'm hoping she can give us answers," I explained.

"Sarah, how long can I stay here with you?" Maria asked in a pleading voice.

"Good question. As long as you want but we can't let Francesca find out just yet."

"Who is Francesca?" Maria asked.

"She's the owner. She's tough but fair."

"You must be so strong to go through all this on your own," Maria said.

"The day I got off that bus I was so scared but with each day I got a little stronger. Today I feel like the oldest teenager on the planet," we both laughed.

"Well, Sarah, someone must be watching over me as I found you. I wasn't ever going to tell anyone what happened to me. I really thought I was going out of my mind. I thank God I found you, Sarah. Thank you," she leant forward and hugged me again.

"Oh, you've got to be joking," the bell was ringing in the reception area again.

"What is it?" Maria asked.

"Someone needs a room. I thought I was finished for the day. Just stay here and be quiet, I'll be back as soon as possible," Maria nodded her head in agreement.

Locking the door behind me, I made my way up to the front desk. After tending to a new guest and showing her to her room, I sat down in the office chair and pondered my position. I could already feel the extra weight on my shoulders – what was I thinking? How am I going to hide and feed Maria? My 'one day at a time' strategy was working for me and was all I could cope with at the moment. I needed to find a solution.

Another girl who experienced the same trauma. What do we all have in common? I thought. We are young and we haven't had sex and yet we are all miscarrying. We've all been impregnated without knowledge or consent and from what I have seen from the miscarriages, those things scare the living shit out of me. From my dreams though, they do not appear to be hostile. I began to feel a little anxious thinking about it, so instead began to focus on what to do next.

I feel my time at the hostel has come to an end. I have regained my composure and I need to move on. I need to find Red; that is my number one priority. I had made my decision I was going to leave.

Maria and I slept head to toe, it wasn't comfortable but we managed. When I woke in the morning the decision I had made to move on felt right. I trusted my gut feeling and was going with it.

"Maria, are you awake?" I said quietly.

"I am now," she laughed, "what is it?"

"I've been thinking and although I have been here for weeks now, I feel it's time to move on. You can come with me or stay. If you want to stay, I can talk to Francesca about you taking my job. It's totally your call."

"Do you always wake up like this? I'm still trying to open my eyes. Can I think about it first?" as she yawned, rubbing the sleep out of her eyes and squinting at me.

"Of course, you can. I'm sorry. I know that's a lot to take in. I'm going to go for a shower so you can think about it. I'll see you in a little while," I grabbed my towel, soap, and fresh clothes and left.

I made a point of really enjoying my shower, knowing full well it could well be my last for a while. I savoured every second as I washed myself and my short hair which had grown back a little. My stomach was full of butterflies over the decision to leave but I knew I was doing the right thing. My body was never comfortable with change. When I got back to the room, Maria was sitting upright and looked very decisive.

"Sarah, I'm going to stay, if Francesca will give me a job. I have no money and I'm not going to take yours. I think I need time to gather my inner strength, just like you have. I've spent years mothering my sisters and I don't want to be a burden on you. I hope you're okay with that?"

"Of course, Maria. I completely understand and that makes perfect sense. I'm sorry to have to leave you so soon. We could swap numbers if we had phones, right?" we both laughed as I suggested we go and find Francesca.

The meeting was quick. Francesca took an instant liking to Maria when I introduced her. She was sorry to see me go, as I had proven myself a hard worker and won her respect. She didn't give out compliments too often, but I managed to land one. She said I was the best worker she had ever had.

It didn't take long to pack. Within minutes I was ready. My backpack once again was filled with some clothes, food and some much-needed money I had saved working for Francesca.

After giving Maria a big warm hug, my eyes welled up, it was an emotional goodbye. We had only known each other for a short time but there was a really strong connection and it felt like we had known each other for years.

I walked off feeling proud for pushing myself. It would have been much easier to stay.

I feel like I'm being drawn north and I needed to trust my intuition and follow it. I feel like Alice in Wonderland going down the rabbit hole but how far was I prepared to go?

Chapter Two: Wardens Woes

"I want all those security cameras checked, frame by frame and second by second. I want the man who did this! Do you hear me, Hames?! Do I still see you standing in my office Hames? Are you deaf?!" I shouted as my blood pressure soared sky-high.

"No. Going now, Warden," Hames replied as she scurried out of my office.

"Barbara, can you organise Tyson to meet me in the interview room," I yelled from my office, "also I want the night rosters for who worked solitary over the last four weeks, ASAP!"

"Will do, Warden. Is there anything else?" she asked in her efficient, secretarial voice.

"Did I ask for anything else?!" I replied sharply.

"No sir, I'll have those for you shortly."

My name is Joe Walsh. I started here as a guard and have been Warden of this women's correctional facility for the last 25 years. I am six months away from retirement. Grumpy, impatient, sarcastic, rude, bad-tempered and just plain mean is how I have been described by the staff here. They think I don't know.

Are they correct? Absolutely! Frankly, I don't give a shit. I am fed up with the system. It's failing and I'm fed up with the prison board forcing their constant changes on us. My staff are incompetent and don't even get me started on the inmates. That's a whole story on its own. I am nearly 65, overweight, I smoke, eat poorly and drink way too much. My blood pressure is through the roof, my cholesterol reading is nearly double digits and if that's not enough, I am type two diabetic.

I hate this job! Over time, I have allowed it to consume my life… my hobbies… my interests and finally my marriage.

In six months, if I am still alive, I will be heading off on a world cruise, by myself, leaving all of this behind me. Then after 12 months of holidaying, I might come home.

I was hoping for the next six months to pass without trouble, commotion or scandal. In this place, that's a big ask.

I sat in my chair, hands behind my head and closed my eyes for some insight into this latest incident. Opening my eyes again, I noticed line one flashing. Reluctantly, I hit the button.

"Yes, Barbara."

"Tyson is ready for you in the interview room sir."

"Good. I'll be there shortly," I said abruptly.

After collecting the prison doctor's report off my desk, I straightened my tie, then angrily walked down that old, pale green lino floor. My shoes squeaked on the freshly polished floors, as they have done every time I've made my trip into this interview room.

On entering, I could see Tyson in her orange overalls, sitting there with a smug look on her face. Tyson is a 35-year-old former drug addict with white skin and long, ratty blonde hair. She is in here for a range of offences. A real tough bitch.

"Well, looky here! What do I owe the pleasure of the prison's finest on this beautiful Monday morning? I have always liked going straight to the top," she laughed and flirted with me at the same time.

"I have your routine blood tests back, Tyson," I replied ignoring her unwelcome advances.

"Oh, I do like the way you look after us here, Warden. You are so sweet," she replied sarcastically.

"A very serious matter has come to my attention Tyson," I said seriously, "did any guards enter your cell while you were in solitary confinement last week? Be careful how you answer that question."

"Why, I do detect a little hostility in your voice this morning Warden. Now let me think, um... aaah... that would be a no!"

"Are you absolutely certain? No doubt at all? Any chance someone could have drugged you and then come in later?"

"Ohhh, sounds saucy. You're getting me all wet, Gov! But that's still a no, unfortunately. Why? What's all this about?"

"Pyke, we're done. Take her back to her cell. Ahh... actually on second thoughts, make that solitary. Give her some time to rethink her story."

"Hahaha... solitary doesn't bother me, you know that Gov... I love getting time away from those noisy bitches. I love my solitude but I thought we had so much more to talk about... you had me all wet. Well, you know where to find me Gov if you change your mind.

Don't wait so long next time, you hear me? I'm all alone in there. I won't tell if you don't!" she kept up the pretence but I knew she was pissed off.

Still annoyed, I headed back to my office, slamming the door behind me. On my desk were the rosters I requested.

"Barbara, get me Hames again. Pronto!"

"Yes Warden, oh and you have a meeting at 10:00 am with-"

"Cancel it, just get me Hames," I cut in and then hung up the phone.

After doing background checks on the two male guards, I am more confused than ever. The silence in the room is broken by a timid knock on my door.

"Come in Hames and close the door behind you."

Hames entered sheepishly and then stood in front of my desk.

"What can you tell me about Johnson and Myles?" I said firmly.

"Both excellent men, sir. No problems with either man to date. They are both reliable and trustworthy," Hames replied with conviction, "have they done something Warden?" she questioned.

"There has been an incident involving Tyson. They were the only male guards on night shift in the last four weeks... correct?"

"That's correct, Warden. We only put the best on at nights to eliminate any possible mishaps. It's our most difficult period, Warden."

"I know that, damn it! How many years do you think I've been doing this job for Hames?! I want you to stand them both down immediately, until further notice. Is that clear Hames?!"

"With all due respect, sir, I would personally vouch for both those men. They would not have set foot inside her cell. I can guarantee it!"

"Until further notice Hames! That is all," I replied abruptly.

"But, sir, there's got to be a mistake. Something doesn't add up," Hames questioned.

"I have a pregnant inmate who was in solitary for the last three weeks. Her previous blood test clearly showing she wasn't pregnant before solitary. That means she had no access to anyone, Hames. Are you keeping up with me so far? We have two male guards on night duty. With a skeleton staff, there is an opportunity for things to happen. You know how it is, Hames? Men working long hours, late nights, stale marriages and cameras conveniently stop working at certain times. Oh yes and a female on her own in a cell. That has got to be one hell of a temptation, wouldn't you say?"

"I agree, sir but not these two. They are good family men. They wouldn't do this."

"Until further notice, Hames. Now, I have work to do."

I watched the disappointment fill her face. Her shoulders dropped and she slumped as she closed my door and left. I knew she would have been dreading having to tell the Officers.

Something still didn't add up. Tyson has no idea she is pregnant and I believed Hames that they were good men but I still have to be seen to be taking action. I'm the one who answers to the board and I do not intend to have my reputation tarnished with six months to go before I retire. Besides, I have an inmate now pregnant that I must get to the bottom of and I need to ensure that this will never happen again.

Rumours spread through the prison like a virus. You just couldn't help but catch them sooner or later. There was lots of whispering, guards were looking over their shoulders and morale was low. Good Officers should never be punished as scapegoats. I knew that and they knew it too but then there's the correctional facility board that I answer to and they don't listen to hunches or gut feelings. They just go by the facts.

I continued looking at Tyson's file. The board will want answers and I have nothing for them. She had no visitations for months and yet according to the doctor's reports she is three weeks pregnant. Hames swears her men wouldn't have done it and I do believe her but Tyson would have a field day with this if she knew. She never even caught on what the talk was all about. It just doesn't make any sense.

I continued looking at her file, turning page after page. I went back over her complete health history even before she entered prison.

There it was! That's why she had no idea what we were talking about. You've got to be kidding me! Someone's fucked up here big time. There it is in black and white. Tubal ligation at 29 years.

"Tyson had her tubes tied at age 29, following a miscarriage," I read it out loud to myself.

Her case file explains everything. She was sexually abused from six years of age by her stepfather, in and out of foster homes and juvenile prison where she was sexually abused even more. Finally settles down for a while and marries a loser who beats her. Has a kid, who is then taken from her at 25. She goes on the run, continuing to find losers who beat and rape her. She had two more miscarriages until the operation at age 29.

To smooth out her ride a little, she does some drugs in between and gets hooked. One thing is for sure, she is one resilient woman.

I rang the hospital where she had the operation.

"Yes, can I speak with Doctor Olsen, please? Yes, I understand. Would you have her call me back then, please? It's Warden Walsh at the Benson Prison Facility. Thank you for your trouble."

"Barbara, get the prison doctor in here as soon as you can, please."

"Yes, Warden. I'll page her right away."

I stood up from my desk and went to the window. The inmates were outside smoking, walking, talking and playing sport. Everything looked normal out there. Just another day in prison.

My thoughts were interrupted by a knock on the door.

"Come in."

"You sent for me Warden?"

"Yes, Doc. Have a seat. Now, Lesley Tyson... you did her medical report the other day... yes?"

"That's correct. Is there something I can help you with?"

"Is there any way you could have made a mistake? Got the samples mixed up with someone else's or anything of that nature?"

"I was as surprised as anyone Warden. So, I ran the same test three times and I can assure you there is no mistake. I can run some more if you like?"

"So, you are absolutely certain, beyond any doubt, the test results are correct?"

"As much as it makes no sense whatsoever, the results are correct. There is no doubt in my mind that Tyson is pregnant. Do you want me to re-run the tests?"

"That won't be necessary. You can get back to your rounds, Doc. Thanks for your time."

"Warden, Line 3, there is a Doctor Olsen on the phone for you."

"Thanks Barbara. I'll take it."

"Putting it through now Warden."

"Doctor Olsen. Thank you for returning my call. I'm calling regarding an operation you carried out on Lesley Tyson about six years ago. She asked you to perform a tubal ligation. Apparently, she was a drug addict at the time and in a bad way. Can you recall her at all?"

"I see a lot of patients, Warden. That's a long time ago."

"Okay, well according to her personal records you did perform the operation. I was wondering, is there anyway, in your opinion, that these types of procedures can be ineffective and women fall pregnant after they are performed?"

"That's impossible, Warden. This type of operation renders women sterile. It's fool-proof, Warden."

"Thank you, Doctor!"

"Is there anything else I can help you with Warden?"

"No, there isn't. You have answered all my questions. Thanks for returning my call, Doctor Olsen."

"Barbara, how many male guards do we currently have on-call here?"

"Just checking my records, sir. Let's see. At present, we have nine including Johnson and Myles. Five full-time workers and four casual workers on staff."

"How many female casuals guards do we have on standby?" I asked.

"According to our records, we currently have six casuals."

"Okay great. Can you get Hames back in my office ASAP?"

"Paging now, Warden."

Within minutes line one was flashing. I pressed the button.

"Hames is outside your door Warden."

"Hames come in," I said, "take a seat."

"I'm fine standing thanks. You called for me Warden."

"Yes Hames... I want you to stand down all the male guards for the time being, until further notice. Find some more female casuals.

Call temp agencies, pull them from another prison, get them out of retirement I don't care, just get it done."

"But Warden, they are good men... and-"

"I don't remember asking for your opinion Hames. Let the other guards know I am cancelling all visitation rights, until further notice."

"That's going to make a lot of people unhappy, sir. Morale is already low," said Hames in a surprised tone.

"Tell all visitors we have a suspected viral outbreak and it's in the best interests of everyone to take this action at present. As soon as we know it's safe again, we will return their visiting rights."

"I'll let everybody know. Warden, if this is about Tyson-"

"If I want your opinion, Hames, I'll ask for it," I cut Hames off with a stern response, "I'm not leaving here looking like a fool. No one knows how this happened but it did and I don't want it happening again. I'm not taking any chances."

"But Warden-"

"That'll be all Hames. Close the door on your way out," I said abruptly.

No sooner had Hames left my office when there was another knock on my door.

"Come in, it's officially insane day. Feel free to jump in."

"It sounds like you're having my kind of day, Warden."

"Huh! If only you knew. How can I help you, Doc?"

"Hmmm! I'm not sure how to tell you this. I'm afraid it gets worse."

"Oh, I do love a good surprise, Doc! Hit me, I'm up for anything today."

"I've just carried out further tests on two more inmates who were complaining of stomach cramps. Turns out they are also pregnant and about three weeks along, the same as Tyson."

"Jesus! What the hell is going on in here?"

"There is no mistake. I have checked and double-checked these Warden. They are definitely pregnant."

"Who else knows about this? Have you told anyone else?" I snapped back angrily.

"Just the clinic nurse, that's it. I checked up to see if either of the two women had conjugal visits in the last month."

"And did they?!" I shouted.

"No. Neither of them. Plus, both women are in their fifties and I know these two would not be wanting a baby by choice. It doesn't make any sense at all."

"I need you to keep this completely confidential. That includes husbands, boyfriends and mothers, everyone! Do you get the picture, Doc? Tell your assistant she can't tell a soul or I'll fire her arse out of here in a second and I'll make sure she never gets a job anywhere else. Also, I want those women escorted to quarantine. Tell them they may have a suspected virus and it's for everyone's protection. Make sure they know they are not being punished."

"Okay. I know you really don't want to hear this right now but I think there is more."

"What do you mean, there's more?!" I shouted back.

"The women I have tested all have small puncture marks on their sides of their stomach area. I have noticed these for a while now but there was no wound as such and the women weren't complaining, so I didn't think it necessary to test them. The two pregnant women have the same marks. The big issue is I have seen these same marks on most of the inmates, Warden."

"Fucking hell! Sorry Doc excuse my language. I've had one of those days. I can't believe this is happening! It's bizarre." I paused for a moment to think about this latest news.

"Okay, Doc. This is what I want you to do. Test every woman in this prison. Tell them we are just taking precautions about a virus. Make something up, anything. Just get me those results ASAP! Please close the door behind you."

She nodded back at me and left.

Chapter Three: Immaculate Conceptions

I was doing my routine daily walk through the grounds of Saint Theresa's Convent. The grounds were beautifully manicured. The scent from the rose gardens was heavenly and the roses bloomed profusely. The lawns were evergreen, cut weekly and the hedges clipped so accurately. The edges perfect and the brick-paved pathways weed-free. Some plants were so perfect I often touched them to see if they were real. Walking in these grounds was a form of meditation for me, I loved it.

"Sister Mary Ellen! Wait up, if you would. I need to have a word with you."

"Mother Superior! Yes, of course," I turned my head to make sure, though I would recognise her voice anywhere. She spoke in a deep, stern voice which always commanded respect.

"You have been here now for 10 years and I am very impressed with your faith and dedication. They are extremely difficult virtues to master and practise, as you know."

"Thank you, Mother Superior. Yes, they are. They both require a strong will and patience. Neither can be rushed and there are no short cuts."

"Which is exactly what brings me here child. I am putting you up for promotion. I have already spoken with the Archbishop. Keep up your dedication and you will receive it."

"I don't know what to say. I wasn't expecting this. I am delighted, Mother Superior. That's wonderful news."

"Are you okay, Sister? You look a little pale."

"Yes, I do feel light-headed, come to think of it."

I watched as the image of Mother Superior slowly blurred. I could only hear her mumbled words as the vision of her was now completely distorted and I felt myself falling in what seemed to be slow motion. I don't remember hitting the ground.

The next thing I recall was waking up in the infirmary room with the doctor undertaking a series of tests on me. I slowly gained my focus and fought to sit upright in the bed.

"What happened doctor? I don't remember anything," then I saw Mother Superior in my peripheral vision on the other side of the bed.

"This is Doctor Patell, she has been looking after you," Mother Superior said in an angry, blunt manner.

Doctor Patell was young, seemed polite and gave me a warm smile which put me at ease. She looked to be Indian, with long, jet black hair clasped in a ponytail and a beautiful smile.

I looked over at Mother Superior. She was not smiling and was clearly angered with a look of disgust on her face. I had never seen this look before.

"Mother Superior, you look angry. Have I done something wrong?" I asked quietly.

"Don't come at me with that pretence and innocent act. I wasn't born yesterday. How long have you known? For the record, you can forget that conversation we had this morning, Sister. Or should I now call you Jane? That was your name when you wandered in here all those years ago, was it not?"

"Mother Superior, I don't understand... what are you talking about? What has happened?"

"You're pregnant, Sister. You can drop the act now. The vows too much for you, were they, Jane?"

"Sister Mary Ellen, you didn't know?" questioned Doctor Patell, in her diplomatic and polite manner. She was feeling awkward with the tension in the room.

"Pregnant? There must be a mistake. Ah, no, no, no. To the best of my knowledge, one still must have sex to get pregnant and I most certainly have not signed up for any IVF program either. I will swear on the Holy Bible I did not do this, Mother Superior. There has to be a mistake with the tests!"

"How dare you use the Lord's holy book to clear your name, you little charlatan! I will not allow you to bring shame to Saint Theresa's Convent. So now you're telling me this is some kind of Immaculate Conception? My, my, we have risen up the ranks quickly."

"As far as I can tell you are three weeks, Sister. Is there anything I can do for you or help you with before I leave?" said the doctor.

"Can you run some more tests, please doctor? This must be a mistake. I have not had sex, doctor. I know how this must sound, but it's the truth. I swear."

As I pleaded with Doctor Patell and Mother Superior to believe me, our conversation was cut short from cries of help outside the room.

A frantic Sister burst through the doors yelling, "Doctor please come quickly! It's Sister Francis! She has passed out in the kitchen. Please come quick. There is blood everywhere and-"

"Now it's time to use your skills on someone truly deserving of your time doctor. Wouldn't you agree, Jane?" she snarled with precision and venom.

Doctor Patell grabbed her medical bag and looked back at me with a smile of reassurance.

"Please take care and be kind to yourself, Sister. I'll come back and check on you later," Doctor Patell said as she was ushered out of the room by Mother Superior, towards the kitchen.

I felt remarkably well considering and decided to get up and follow them, as they rushed to the kitchen. I walked a lot slower but knew where they were going, so it didn't matter.

When I entered the room, the air was thick with judgement and condemnation. The doctor was doing her best to wake Sister Francis up.

Mother Superior was kneeling over Sister Francis as if she was covering up something.

Her habit was soaked in blood. Mother Superior had already sent for two more nuns to clean up all the blood.

Doctor Patell was busily trying to revive Sister Francis who was still unconscious. She saw me in the corner of her eye.

"What are you doing out of bed Sister? We can't have you jeopardising the health of your baby."

"Will she be okay, doctor?" I asked desperately, "there's so much blood."

"Leave Sister Francis to me. You should be resting, Sister Ellen," her soft, kind words were comforting.

"When she wakes, please tell her I'm praying for her, won't you?" I asked.

"Of course. I'll come and check in on you tomorrow, Sister."

"Thank you, doctor. You are most kind."

I saw Mother Superior still kneeling over Sister Francis.

Her position looked awkward and it was obvious she was doing this for a reason, as her holy garments were now covered in blood. What was she hiding?

As promised, I went back to my room and prayed with great compassion for Sister Francis. She had tremendous faith and enormous compassion for everyone else and still so dedicated to the order, even at fifty years of age. She had always inspired me.

I cannot believe the change in Mother Superior, nor can I fathom the way she is treating me. She has judged and already sentenced me to exile without even listening to me. I knew she was firm but I would have thought all those years of prayer would have somehow softened her and prepared her for dealing with unusual circumstances such as these.

Mother Superior's dark side seems to have revealed itself. I must admit I'd prefer to keep out of her way. I fear this side of her.

I am so eager to speak with the doctor again, to check on Sister Francis and to see if she can re-examine me. Time seems to go so slow when you really want it to go fast.

I spent the remainder of the day in deep prayer for Sister Francis and the rest of us, including myself.

I began to question how did I get pregnant? It's impossible. How did I not even know until now? I just don't understand. I prayed for more understanding and insights into what was happening. I prayed for compassion from Mother Superior and for calm and peace amongst us all.

I cannot begin to imagine how much conflict and tension this will cause in the convent. I already feel ostracised and no doubt Sister Francis will not fare well with the rumours and innuendos. This will test our faith. The ultimate sin; nuns becoming pregnant. Mother Superior will turn this convent into a quarantine camp in the grip of a deadly virus. No one will be allowed in or out.

The media would have a field day with this story. What a trashy headline it would make. Mud sticks unfortunately and some stains never come out. Permanently etched scars that will never heal.

Prayer settles my overworking mind from trying to solve the question of how this happened and why. I am so exhausted from the day and the emotional toll on my body, I fell asleep almost as soon as my head hit the pillow.

I had a bad night's sleep but woke mid-morning as Doctor Patell entered my room, hopefully with some good news. Her lovely warm smile lifts my spirits.

"Your smile fills my room with sunlight doctor."

"Thank you, Sister. You are so sweet. How are you feeling?"

"It's difficult to answer that question. Physically, I feel fine. Emotionally and mentally? I'm struggling."

"I completely understand. I can't begin to imagine what you must be going through."

"Doctor, there is something I must ask you, if I may? Sister Francis, what happened to her yesterday? Mother Superior was clearly hiding something. What was it?"

"I am not at liberty to say, Sister. Patient confidentiality, you know how it is?"

"Yes, I do understand doctor but if I am not alone in this and if this is happening to others, I want to know. The shame alone is eating away at me. Did you see the way Mother Superior looked at me? Like I'm the devil's spawn."

"I don't know what to say, Sister. I am truly sorry for your troubles however, apart from my own code of silence, Mother Superior made it very clear to me that this incident was not to leave the room. I am truly sorry."

"I understand doctor. You don't have to apologise and thank you anyway."

She looked at me compassionately and then walked out of the room, closing the door behind her.

I needed answers and I was going to get them. Feeling quite well, I left my room and slowly made my way to where I believed Sister Francis would be recovering. I was anxious about bumping into Mother Superior, so I was scanning the rooms and often looking behind me as I walked.

When I found Sister Francis, she was alone resting. No sooner did I slip into her room, her eyes opened.

"Oh dear, Sister Mary Ellen! You startled me. Where did you come from, sweet child?"

"Sister Francis, it's so good to see you. I have not stopped praying for you. Are you feeling better? What happened to you?"

Her head turned away from me immediately.

"I don't wish to discuss it," she responded quickly.

"Sister Francis, please listen to me. I believe the same thing has happened to me. You're not alone in this nightmare and I feel certain there will be others."

"This also happened to you?" she asked very surprised.

In that split second her entire body language had changed. She sat upright and with pleading eyes and desperation in her voice, she begged me for more information.

"It has! Please tell me what happened. I'm so scared. Mother Superior is very hostile towards me. Please help me!"

"I am not sure if I can Sister, to be totally honest with you. I find myself in the same difficult position."

I began to tear up. I paused, gathered myself and after taking a few deep breaths continued, "I feel so ashamed and yet I have done nothing wrong. I have no one to talk to and no one will believe me. You see, I fainted Sister Francis, just like you but in the grounds. The doctor examined me and when I woke up, told me I was pregnant," I said sobbing.

"It's okay, child. You know I won't judge you," Sister Francis said in her kind soft voice.

"I'm pregnant!" I cried.

I looked down as I spoke the words. Even though I am innocent, I felt the guilt from Mother Superior's judgement begin to take over my thoughts.

"Then, amidst all that hysteria and drama, they ran out of the infirmary to attend to you, because you had collapsed," I paused again to check her reaction.

"I heard all the commotion and got out of bed and went to see what was happening for myself. That's when I saw all the blood and Mother Superior kneeling over you, doing her best to conceal what I am now guessing was your miscarriage? I'm sorry. I know that's sounds awful, Sister Francis."

"Unfortunately, it's the truth. I have no idea how this has happened. I do not believe it. But the facts remain: I am a 50-year-old nun and I just miscarried. That's all Mother Superior sees and knows and now I am an outcast. I am too ashamed to look anyone in the eyes, Sister," Sister Francis put her hands up to her face concealing her tears. I placed my arm lovingly around her.

"Believe me, Sister Francis, I know exactly how you feel. However, you miscarried and I am still pregnant. I do not know how or why this is happening and like you, I have been exiled. Don't you find it interesting Sister Francis, we pray every day for compassion and understanding so that we don't judge others and yet after 60 years or more, when tested on all these virtues, Mother Superior has condemned us to hell without even letting us speak? What if this happened to her?"

"Oh, come now child. Do not speak these evil thoughts. We must continue to practise these same virtues ourselves. Mother Superior is consumed with how the outside world will judge us and her. She is beside herself with worry and feels responsible for this."

"As always, so diplomatic and understanding of others, Sister Francis. You inspire so many of us here. Your faith is so strong. You are truly blessed," I said warmly.

"I do not like being treated like this any more than you do but can you imagine what the outside world will think if this gets out? If you were Mother Superior, what would you do?"

"I see your point. I honestly do not know what I would do. However, I would like to think that I would at least take the time to listen to what they have to say, to gain a better understanding of what is happening."

"Ah, wise words indeed, child. It's easy to think so clearly when you're not the one in the firing line, in the midst of the heat, so to speak," said Sister Francis with a wry smile on her face.

"I would have thought if you were going to lead, you would surely have to be able to withstand the heat?"

Sister Francis simply replied, "I'm a nun and I am pregnant at 50 and I still can't believe it."

"But it's not your fault, Sister Francis. I believe something is happening out there, way above our comprehension and intelligence and I am sure in time it will be revealed to us."

"Do you really think so, Sister Mary Ellen?" questioned Sister Francis.

"Yes, I do. We just need to be patient. My intuition tells me, there are other women in the same situation as we are."

"Oh, dear God, pray for us," she blessed herself and went into deep prayer.

I disappeared back to my room through the back rooms to avoid the wrath of Mother Superior again. It's difficult enough dealing with my own predicament. I didn't need to hear more humiliation and shame.

Chapter Four: In Search of Answers

I was drawn to a town, five hours north of where I was staying at Francesca's. It was a beautiful little town nestled amongst tall, rugged mountains. Beautiful trees adorned the streets. It was an old town and the buildings were dated, everyone seemed to have time on their hands as they went about their business.

After leaving the bus I made my way to the backpacker's hostel which was visible from the bus depot and then paid for a room. It was much the same as the last one. The layout was similar, the rooms about the same size, though this one was more run down.

I threw my backpack on the floor and locked the door to my room before taking a stroll around the town to get a feel for the place.

As I looked for casual work on the shop windows, I spotted some flyers about a women's refuge centre. I asked for directions and a short walk out of town led me there. On approach, it looked just like any other boarding house.

There were women scattered about, some in groups, some alone. Several were smoking on the front veranda of the old weatherboard house while others were reading a book alone. Others were lying in the sun having a nap. I had a strong gut feeling about this place and decided to stop and say hello.

As I got closer, I was confronted by an overly protective woman who looked to be in her 50s. She was well dressed, average size with a strong presence. Her hair was long, mousey brown in colour with some grey showing through. The way she stood and presented herself was quite fearsome. You wouldn't want to be on the wrong side of this woman! Her facial features were strong, with high chiselled cheekbones, but her weathered face had obviously seen harder times.

"Can I help you?" she asked, straight to the point.

"Yes, I hope so. I'm looking for a friend of mine. She goes by the name of Red. She has short, vivid red hair and she is about 17."

"No. I can't say I recall anyone fitting that description. Is she in any kind of trouble?"

"That's a long story, maybe!" I replied, not wanting to go into details.

"They always are. It just depends how deep honey."

"Have you had a lot of young girls staying here lately? A bit of a spike, perhaps?"

"Why do you ask?" she replied in a guarded tone.

"Just curious."

"As a matter of fact, we have but they don't stay long and they keep moving on. There is something unusual about them. I've seen a lot of young girls pass through here over the years but there was something different about this lot. They were very secretive, kept to themselves. Not the kind of girls you would expect to wind up homeless. They wouldn't open up about anything either. They'd come here in twos and threes and whisper to each other all day and night. Then as fast as they arrived, they were gone. No word, no warning- just gone, like they were running from something or somebody."

"Anyone like that here now?"

"As a matter of fact, there is. A young girl called Tina. Seems smart, quiet, can't get "boo" out of her. Took days to finally get her name but that's all we got. Looks really troubled but she won't talk to anyone. She just sits in her room staring out the window all day."

"Would I be able to see her? Sorry, I mean would you let me see her?" she hesitated, looking at me intensely the whole time.

"Sure. I can't see why not; you don't look like you're out to hurt anyone. Follow me," she instructed.

She turned and headed for the front door of the old run-down house. As I followed her, I fended off cold and curious stares from the women and girls who were sitting and standing around.

She led me into the house and down to the end of a hall which had a closed door.

"Are they always this friendly?" I asked sarcastically.

"Honey, if only you knew the half of what some of these women have been through. Let's just say they don't trust easily now," she replied.

"Knock, knock, Tina... it's me, darling. I have someone here who wants to see you. I am opening the door now, okay," she said softly.

As the woman gently opened the door, I could see a young girl about my age sitting on a bed staring outside, just as the woman had said.

I quietly went in and sat on the bed next to her. She continued staring in a trance, out the window, as if she didn't even notice me.

I just sat and looked at her and let her get used to me sitting there. She was tiny and looked very timid. She wore a white crocheted beanie which really suited her. She was very attractive and I could tell she looked after herself. Long, wavy brown hair fell out below the beanie and down past her shoulders. Her eyes were filled with pain and her drooping shoulders and sullen face told quite a story.

"I'm sorry I didn't get your name?" I politely asked the woman.

"Mrs Henshaw. My apologies! And yours?"

"Sarah, Sarah O'Connor. Would you mind giving us a minute Mrs Henshaw?"

She hesitated again. Then trusting her instincts nodded and left saying, "I'll just be outside Tina, okay?" then closed the door behind her.

"Hi, Tina. My name is Sarah." I paused for a few seconds so I knew she was listening, "something happened to me recently and I think it may have happened to you," I paused again waiting for her reaction. She looked at me, checking me out. "Can we talk about this?" I said softly.

That caught her attention and she slowly turned around to look at me. All the tell-tale signs were there. The frustration and sadness. Being exiled from your family. Having nothing left.

I slowly began to tell her my story. She listened to every single word. Watching the expression on her face soften was encouraging. I watched her tears run freely down her cheeks, then she nestled into me. She wrapped her arms around me and wouldn't let go. Then Tina began to tell her story.

"My father hit me and called me a slut. I explained it the best way I could to mum that I hadn't had sex but she couldn't bring herself to believe me either," she sobbed gently over my shoulder.

I could see her internal struggle. She was trying her best to be understanding but her face told another story.

"We were best friends, Mum and me," she continued, "until I miscarried. I didn't even know I was pregnant. Have you ever heard anything more absurd in all your life?" she said as she sat back in front of me.

"It happened on the school bus in front of everyone," she continued.

"I have never been so humiliated in all my life. Nowhere to hide on a bus now is there? The bus became some freak show. I sat there screaming as blood ran down my legs and then miscarried. Girls were screaming, while others filmed the whole scene on their phones, some were even laughing, can you believe that? Then in amongst all that ugliness, something kind happened?" the words were tumbling out of her quickly. She paused to catch her breath.

"What happened Tina?" I asked curiously.

"The driver stopped the bus with all the commotion going on and walked down the aisle to see what was going on. He looked at me kindly and said,

"It's okay, I'll drive you to the hospital."

"Then he told all the girls to get off the bus there and then and drove me to the hospital. It was so nice of him and I was so grateful to be alone on the bus to sit in silence, trying to understand what just happened. I'll never forget what he did for me that day."

"When word got out at school, they graffitied my locker, bags, and clothes. I was trashed all over social media as a slut. I copped it all. I tried to end it but failed, twice. After a couple of months, I decided enough was enough, so I got on a bus and ended up here. Why here? I don't know, it just felt right. I just wish I knew how this all happened. I didn't do this, I swear. No one believes me... no one!" she cried.

"Tina, I absolutely 100 percent believe you!" I said with conviction.

It was like she was still in shock. I gave her another hug her as she wept inconsolably.

"Tina. I believe every word you're saying. That's exactly how I felt. Listen something really weird is going on and we seem to be right in the middle of it. Why? I have no idea. What I do know is that a few girls who have never had sex before are now pregnant or have miscarried. Once again, I don't know why but I'm doing my best to find the answers. Anyway, I can't stay here long Tina. I must keep going. I need to find answers to lots of questions and to also find a friend. I was hoping she was here. I keep getting pulled in this direction. That's why I'm here."

"Please don't leave me, Sarah. I don't want to stay here anymore. You're the only person who understands me and I can't tell you what that means to me right now," said Tina begging.

"Okay. Listen to me. Stay here a couple more days and think about it. It's a big decision. Don't forget you are being looked after here, fed and housed and that's not always the case on the run, believe me. Besides, I'm curious to know if any more girls like us will turn up here."

"I don't think any more will show up. I haven't seen any new faces for days, apart from you."

"Yeah, well, let's just see anyway, okay?"

"Okay, sure," she leant forward and hugged me again. She was leaching my energy and I could feel myself getting drained. She didn't seem the strong type and I feared for her.

"I'll come and see you tomorrow. Okay, Tina?"

She nodded, then went straight back to looking out the window, however now she looked a lot more settled.

As I walked back to my hostel room, my mind was busy thinking up possible scenarios of what to do next.

Then something caught my attention. I could hear people frantically yelling and screaming. I walked briskly over to the commotion. I heard, "Someone call an ambulance!" "Oh god she is dying! Someone do something quick!" it filled me with anxiety and got my heart racing. I could see a middle-aged man pushing his hands repeatedly in sequence into a young girl's chest. He only stopped to pinch her nose and breathe into her mouth at short intervals.

"Oh my God!" my hand automatically covered my mouth just like some of the onlookers, who had gathered around. They looked stunned and watched with worried faces, desperately hoping that the man's efforts would be successful and that she would gasp some air and wake up and become conscious.

As time passed, so did her chances. Another person checked her pulse and then put their hand on the shoulder of the now exhausted man who was performing the CPR.

"She has gone... you have done all you can," said the concerned person.

He continued to carry out CPR, convinced she would wake up. Then, as those words must have slowly registered, he stopped.

Exhausted, he collapsed over the girl, crying out loud, "I'm so sorry...
I'm so, so sorry I couldn't save you."

The stunned crowd was silent and in shock upon witnessing
the passing of the young girl. They began to console one another;
some broke out in loud grieving sobs. I squeezed my way through the
onlookers to get a closer look. A young girl around my age and clearly
pregnant had died in front of our eyes. I pushed my way out and
made my way back to my room.

Was she one of us I thought? I will never know the answer to
that question. My gut instinct tells me she had taken her own life. To
go through this at our age was difficult. All the judgement and stigma
attached to being pregnant so young can be too much for some. Or
had she miscarried a monster like Red and she couldn't go through it
again on her own? If she had I didn't blame her at all. I am just angry
I didn't find her in time. I know I could have helped her.

I wish I hadn't seen that. I was already struggling. I collapsed
on my bed, feeling empty inside. I couldn't even cry, I was beyond
that. I stared at the ceiling and after some time, drifted off to sleep.

I was in a deep dream state, the ones that feel so real that you
can't tell if you're awake or still sleeping. Then, it happened again.
The dream had become a familiar one, where everything seems to
move in slow motion. I could see beings around me, hovering above
me. I am being impregnated. Somehow I know and yet I'm not scared.
The feeling is inexplicable.

I was woken early that morning by a loud argument between
two backpackers. They were so loud, it sounded like they were in my
room. Their accent sounded Scottish. They were arguing over money,
who was to pay for the accommodation. I sat up quickly to gather my
senses.

I began to remember my dream but only vaguely. I could
almost feel several beings hovering over me. They were gentle and
careful not to hurt me as they went about the procedure. It was
meticulously performed and I could feel it was carried out with a lot
of love. Even though I was asleep, I could see them blurring around
me as they moved. But that was it. It's as if you're not supposed to
remember. I instinctively knew beyond doubt, I was pregnant again.

Waking up hungry, I made my way to the local bakery. The
smell of cinnamon buns, pies, and freshly baked bread had my
stomach rumbling and my taste buds dancing.

A bus pulled up not far from the bakery and as I ate my
breakfast, I watched the passengers file out onto the street. I always

enjoyed people watching. The last person to get off the bus caught my attention. She threw her backpack over her leather jacket with attitude, looked left, then right and then walked off. Her hair was long, jet black and parted down the middle into a slick ponytail. I rushed through the rest of my breakfast. Something compelled me to follow her. Her long deliberate strides had others side-stepping, getting out of her way before she even approached them. She loved it and it gave her power. I wasn't sure if she was just really confident or just very arrogant. Her body swayed noticeably from side to side as people even apologised for getting in her way. I continued to follow her as I wanted to know where she would stay tonight and if she was alone. I was also curious why a girl like that was doing in a very quiet country town like this. She seemed out of place here.

She didn't look like a team player, just looked like she gave orders, not take them. I watched as she walked into some fancy motel units. She had style and it looked like she had money. She wasn't dimming her shine for anyone. No dingy backpackers or refuge centres for miss attitude. I wanted to talk to her but she looked intimidating. What was I going to say anyway: 'Hey, you ever had a weird pregnancy, lately? Cause I might be able to help. Here's my card if you wanna talk.'

Well, at least I knew where she was staying. I decided to leave it for now. I was behind a bus stop where I could just see over the road where a teenage girl caught my attention. She was acting suspiciously, constantly looking around to see if she was being watched. I saw her make her way to a large commercial waste bin with a grocery bag in her hand and she walked as if she was in pain. She was still looking around slowly, then making sure no one saw her, she lifted the large lid and then tossed the bag into the dumpster. She dropped the lid then went on her way, constantly looking behind making sure no one was following her. I managed to get a good look at her and would easily recognise her if need be. I had a horrible thought and as grossed out as I was with the idea, I made my way over to the bin. I had to be sure. Maybe I was being paranoid.

Lifting the lid, I managed to stretch my arm down deep enough to retrieve the bag. The bin was almost full which made my job easier. My stomach was doing somersaults and my heart was pumping furiously with anticipation. I couldn't stop, I needed to know. I carefully lifted out a small blood-soaked parcel wrapped in newspaper and placed it on the ground. I began to feel nauseous and almost heaved as I unwrapped the package. There it was. I gasped and jumped back in shock. I quickly turned away and threw up.

What I saw scared the living shit out of me. It was a small fetus that was severely deformed. Its head was abnormally large, yet the arms and legs were tiny. The deformities were incomprehensible. My heart went out to that young girl. She must have gone through this horrific experience, all by herself. I bet she's traumatised trying to understand any of this.

Then it hit me like a hammer to the head. One of these things was now inside me again and I too had miscarried a monster, except I wasn't awake to see it. This was bigger than the one Red had miscarried. Was that why that young girl took her own life yesterday? Perhaps she saw what she gave birth to previously and couldn't come to terms with going through it again.

I couldn't look at it any longer and before someone else saw it, I quickly wrapped it back up and placed it back in the bin. I feel like this is only just the beginning.

"Oh my God! Tina!" I yelled out loud. I told her I would see her today. I had totally forgotten. She would never cope with this on her own. Then again, how many 15-year-olds could? I felt compelled to try and protect her. She is like a younger sister, small and needing protection. I headed out to the refuge thinking about what to say to her. What I've seen here in the last two days is enough. Should we just leave now?

I started taking deep breaths. I needed to calm myself. I had to keep it together especially around someone so fragile. I composed myself as I swiftly walked back to the refuge centre. As I approached the front veranda I was greeted by the very protective Mrs Henshaw.

"You like the place that much, hey?" asked Mrs Henshaw.

"Yep! You can't keep me away!" I said, smiling back at her.

"Trust me, it has that effect on most of them."

"Is it okay to see Tina, again?" I asked.

"Of course it is. She is expecting you. She seems a lot happier since you visited her yesterday."

"That's great. Glad I could help."

I went to Tina's room; the door was already opened. She still looked worried.

"As promised, here I am!" I said with a little drama.

Her face broke out in a small grin as she sat with her legs crossed in a yoga-like position. She had pulled her long sleeves down over her hands.

"You look like you're meditating," I said.

"No. I always sit like this. I've been doing a lot of thinking."

"Yeah? What about?" I smirked to lighten the mood.

"You know what you were talking about yesterday. If you go, I want to go with you. I'm absolutely certain," she paused then asked. "If you don't mind, that is?"

"Well, I'm glad you brought that up because I'm not staying here any longer. I've decided to move on sooner than I thought and yes you are more than welcome to join me."

"I don't have any money for the fare and I really don't want to be a burden on you."

"Don't be silly and as far as the fare goes, my shout, okay? I've got it covered."

"Are you sure?" she asked, with her face screwed up in doubt, "I'll pay you back as soon as I get a job, I promise."

"Listen, why don't you grab your things and come back with me? We can hang out together where I'm staying until the bus comes. It leaves in a couple of hours and that suits me fine. Wadda ya say?"

"That would be awesome. I'll just be a sec. I don't have much to pack. I need to thank Mrs Henshaw for looking after me and tell her my plans."

"Of course. I'm sure she'll understand."

Tina thanked Mrs Henshaw and we said our goodbyes. She has a heart of gold and does a miraculous job watching over these lost souls I thought.

As we reached the gate, Mrs Henshaw shouted, "Take good care of her now, won't you?"

We both turned around and waved again.

"She really understood me and as much as my own mother. I didn't think that was possible."

"She isn't emotionally attached, Tina. It's easier to be more objective when you're not. Mothers are supposed to worry. It's their job."

"By the way Sarah, how old are you?" asked Tina.

"Just turned 16. Why do you ask?"

"You seem so much older and wiser than 16."

"Oh great! Cause it feels like I have just aged 10 years in the last few months. Trust me!"

We talked, non-stop, all the way back to my room. She was easy to talk to. She had opened up to me and that made me happy. It will be good to have a travelling companion.

When we arrived at my room, I went to unlock the door with my key but the door was already opened. I went in cautiously.

"What the hell are you doing in my room?" I demanded. Tina did not enter.

"Calm down, Pimples. Easy now. Don't wanna go upsetting anyone now do we?"

It was her, the black-haired girl that I saw get off the bus and go into the motel. What the hell was she doing in my room?

She had large round angry eyes but a really pretty face. Above her lip, on her left side was a horrendous scar with lots of stitch marks in it. The wound was big and it's all you saw when you looked at her. You couldn't help but look at it. It was like staring at a beautiful painting with a huge, black mark right in the middle of it.

"I'll ask again!" I demanded, "what the hell are you doing in my room? I'm going to start screaming if you don't get the hell out of here, right now! Do you hear me?" that's all I could think of under pressure. "Is that how you pay for your fancy rooms? By stealing from others?" I said angrily.

"I have no idea what you're talking about Pimples. I must have the wrong room but I'm going now. See? I'm leaving, slipping right out of here. We will see each other again I can promise you that!"

"Not if I have anything to do with it," I tried to sound tough.

"So hostile! You need to chillax a little Pimples. Be seeing yas," she said as she pushed past Tina.

My clothes were strewn all over the floor with my backpack empty and its contents out on the floor. Luckily, I left my money in a deposit box at reception. That bitch! I was livid.

"Who was that Sarah?!" asked Tina, "she looked really scary!"

"I don't know but I saw her get off a bus. She just got into town."

"She looks like trouble. I'd stay away from her, if I was you, Sarah."

"Don't trust anyone. Not anyone, Tina. You won't last five minutes on your own if you do. You hear me? No one!" I made sure Tina listened carefully.

I had become very distrustful, since flying solo. I had no one to watch out for me. It was the new normal for me.

"Let's get out of here. I can't leave this place fast enough," I withdrew my money from reception and we headed for the bus terminal, where I paid for our tickets.

We chatted until the bus arrived. It was on time to my relief, so we boarded. The driver waited patiently for any stragglers and when he was satisfied there weren't anymore, he proceeded to close the doors and drive off.

The bus hadn't gone far when the driver slammed on the brakes, sending our heads and bodies lunging forward.

A loud burst of air could be heard as the doors opened, letting someone on. She boarded panting heavily. Annoyed by the delay, everyone looked up to see who had caused it. I guess some people just love attention.

It was her again. The black-haired bitch with the scarred face that was in my room. She paid her fare and then staggered down the aisle, still short of breath as the bus sped off in a hurry. She was checking out the passengers as she continued to make her way down the bus.

We were halfway down the bus.

"Well, well! If it isn't Pimples and Mousey Mouse. We meet again. I knew I was gonna love this ride. That's why I just had to catch it."

She had a smart arse look on her face. She clearly thought she was a force to be reckoned with.

"The back is empty. Go and join all your friends Scarface," it felt good giving her one back.

"Ohh! Do I detect a little tension in your voice, Pimples?" as she staggered towards the back seats.

The trip went smoothly, once we got going again. Damn her! I wanted a clean break from that place. Tina was a great travel companion and it made the trip go so much faster. We never heard a sound from Scarface.

We arrived at our destination five hours later. We filed off the bus, grateful to stretch our legs once again and we meandered off to find somewhere to stay.

"Wait up, Pimples! We still have unfinished business to take care of."

I turned around and in a loud annoyed voice yelled, "What do you want?"

"It's not what I want it's what I've got," she said teasingly.

"Dream on. There is nothing you have that I would ever want."

"You sure about that now Pimples?" she slid her hand into her trendy ripped denim jeans and pulled out the necklace belonging to my Mum.

"You thieving bitch! Give it here!" in my haste to leave that day, I didn't check to see if anything was missing.

"So hostile! I would never have guessed you had this side to you, Pimples."

"That's from my mother. Please give it back. I'm asking nicely. Please?"

"I'm going to hang on to it just a little longer. A little insurance, you might say. In case you put the cops onto me! You know how it is," she said putting the necklace back into her pocket.

"If I was going to put the cops onto you, I would have done it already for breaking into my room. Now, please, give it back!"

"Just as I said, soon enough," she turned her back on us and walked away.

I was seething, "Let's get out of here, Tina. Before I kill someone!"

I placed my hand in the middle of Tina's back and gently guided her to move with me. We headed off in search of somewhere to sleep, my feet stomping the ground hard in anger.

Chapter Five: Forensic Freak Show

"Yes, Barbara. What is it?"

"I have John Myles here to see you, sir."

"Send him in."

No sooner had I said that I heard a knock on my door.

"Come in Myles... what can I do for you?" I asked as I finished off the sentence on one of my reports.

Myles was a good man. He had worked at the prison for the last 12 years and had always presented as a thorough professional. His resume was outstanding and he would make a great Warden one day. He stood six-foot-tall, of solid build and had slightly dark skin. His thick, black hair was always cut extremely short. He was a good guard to have on duty. From Mexican descent, his friendly and professional manner was always on display.

"Sorry to disturb you Warden but I just had to see you. I need to ask why I've been stood down. My record here is impeccable, sir. I love this job. I have taken no bribes, there has never been any funny business with any of the inmates, no drugs or anything. If I have done something wrong, sir, please tell me. I am happily married and you know we have our second child on the way. Times are tough and I need this job and I would never do anything stupid to jeopardise my position here, Warden," he said passionately.

"It's nothing you have done wrong, Myles. There has been an incident that I am not at liberty to talk about. Suffice to say, I've had to take hard measures and immediate action. Officer Hames vouched for you both and I believe her. I just had to do what I did. If you're ever in this position one day, you will understand. You don't make friends or keep any in this job. Listen, I'll put you in touch with a friend of mine who has a security business. He's always looking for good men. I'm sorry, Myles. I will explain everything further when I get a handle on this."

"Thank you Warden. I would be very grateful for the work."

"Is there anything else, Myles?"

"No that was all... and thank you again, Warden."

I nodded as he left and closed the door behind him. I slouched forward with my elbows on the desk, resting my head between my hands, trying to momentarily escape from my current reality. It was short-lived.

"I have the prison doctor here to see you Warden."

"Thanks, Barbara. Let her in," she entered the room quickly and couldn't speak fast enough.

"You won't believe what's just happened, Warden!" she sputtered out.

"Oh, I don't know Doc. Try me!"

"The two women in quarantine and Tyson in solitary just aborted."

"All of them? At the same time?" I said shocked.
"Yes Warden that's right. The guards found them all hysterical. They were screaming and in complete shock."

"Are they okay?"

"Considering what they just went through they are doing well!" explained the Doctor.

"What about Tyson?"
"She is not doing so good. She can't believe what just happened. How could she get pregnant after having her tubes tied and who did this to her? She's in quite a state Warden."

"Do you have it under control Doc?"

"I had them all sedated Warden. It was the only way I could get them to calm down."

"Good work Doc. You handled that well."
"There's something else Warden. I collected the fetuses. They... they-"

"Spit it out!" I snapped impatiently.
"They are extremely mutated Warden. I have never seen anything like this before."

"What the hell are you talking about? Where are they? Show me for God's sake."

We hastily made our way to the medical room. She unlocked the door to let us in. She opened the fridge door and pulled out a small box. With reservation, she slowly unwrapped the cloth, revealing an image that horrified me. I could not believe what I was looking at and began to heave and bolted to the washbasin to throw up.

I spent several minutes there to compose myself, washing my face and rinsing my mouth out with water.

"What in God's name were they Doc?"

The images had been etched into my memory bank forever. The arms and legs were puffy and swollen making the body look like a small piglet. The mouth was oversized with extruded swollen lips and large teeth could be seen at the top and bottom of its open mouth, separated by a large tongue that was poking out of its mouth. Instead of eyes, there were two pink fleshy sockets.

"I still feel nauseous. My stomach is churning... God! I mean those poor women! Even prisoners don't deserve this! I don't have to remind you Doc, that this stays in here. Have you ...ever come across this before?"

"Never! Warden. They weren't all like that though. One looked more human-like. Here, take a look at this one."

She led me to another small bundle and carefully unwrapped it. I could see what she meant. It was still deformed, yet you could make out the small human-like features. The obvious differences being its out-of-proportion head and its lack of reproductive organs.

"Jesus! What the fuck is going on here? Those women need to stay where they are. I don't want this getting around the prison. Do you hear me?"

"Absolutely."

"Who assisted you with the inmates when this happened?"

"That would have been Gomez and Pyke, Warden."

I reached for my portable office phone and called Barbara.

"Barbara, can you get Gomez and Pyke in my office immediately?"

"Paging them now Warden."

"Can you discreetly dispose of them, Doc? I don't want this place turned into some forensic freak show and I don't want the media getting a sniff of this. For the time being, we will lay low on this one. Are we clear?"

"Yes, Warden. Crystal," the doctor nodding her head in approval.

I made my way back to my office. No sooner had I walked into the room, I had Barbara letting me know Gomez and Pyke were outside my door.

"Send them in Barbara."

They sheepishly entered the room as if they had done something wrong. They removed their caps but kept their heads down avoiding eye contact. They were both clearly intimidated.

"Please take a seat ladies. Relax. You've done nothing wrong. Please, sit down."

They both reluctantly pulled a chair back from the other side of my large desk and sat down. I wandered around my office, fidgety, stalling, waiting for the right words to magically appear.

"I would like to commend you both for how well you handled that situation this morning. Officer Hames gave me a full report."

"Thank you, Warden," they replied quietly in unison.

"Ladies, I have been around prisons for most of my working life now and I've got to tell you I have never, ever seen anything like this before. What happened here today is not to leave this complex. Do you understand? Not a whisper, not a sniff or innuendo. I don't like using threats but I can assure you both, if one of the other inmates or guards hear about this, you will both be fired and sued for breaching your confidentiality contracts. Am I making myself clear, ladies?"

"Absolutely, Warden! Does that mean the inmates will remain where they are?" Pyke mumbled.

"If I heard you correctly Pyke, yes they will. I cannot have them spreading fear through the whole prison. Do you have any questions?"

Once again in unison and with a little more confidence, they replied, "No sir."

"Then you may go. Once again, great job out there today."

They stood up and politely pushed their chairs back. Putting their caps back on, they left the room.

That puts the 'inmates falling pregnant to male guards' scandal dead in the water! I thought to myself.

Who got in? How did they impregnate the inmates and how is it that the prisoners did not know they were pregnant? How does that happen? It just doesn't make any sense and why these women? Of all the women out there, prisoners! Really?

In truth, six months from now I won't really care. It will be someone else's problem. I'll be reading about it in a newspaper, not tearing out my hair. That'll suit me just fine. Those thoughts allowed me to be distracted and to daydream a little about my retirement.

I booked a world cruise some time ago, so I can sail away and leave all this behind. My health has taken a hit from the stress of running this place and these events are not helping at all.

I didn't plan on being alone either. The job also took its toll on my marriage. I never did find that work and life balance. I was so committed to this job, trying to resolve the never-ending drug problems going on in here. When I did try and go home early, there was a vicious assault on an inmate or a riot broke out necessitating my return. Then there were accusations of corrupt guards, that didn't help either and the department accusing me of being involved. None of this helped an already failing marriage!

So many nights with the very best of intentions, I would leave this hell hole in the hope of a romantic night out or just go home to a delicious home-cooked meal. Hell always seems to break loose, just at the wrong time.

It broke my heart to cancel our plans time and time again. I don't blame my wife for moving on. Too many broken promises. In truth she was always on her own and loneliness is a silent killer, giving the mind too much time to fertilise all kinds of diseased thinking. The more time you give it the more it will poison you.

Did I see it coming? Of course, I did! I am bemused when I ask some people that question and they say no. I watched the sparkle slowly leave my wife's eyes, replaced by sadness and emptiness. It didn't happen straight away, it never does. It's a slow painful death.

When you finally realise it and talk and even suggest counselling, you both know it's too late. You have already bled to death. That's what I find difficult to reconcile. I was the one who created all this and I could have been the one to turn it all around but I didn't. I kept choosing work.

So, here I sit contemplating years of missed opportunities – not delegating the problems over to someone else, allowing them to step up and allowing me to put my family first.

The really sad part is... for what? What did I gain? The more you give the system, the more it takes. What have I got now? An empty home and a body so riddled with stress, that I can't sit still for more than a few minutes. I'm surprised my body still functions.

Has it all been worth it? Absolutely not! I still miss my wife and I still love her. That's what hurts the most.

My wife couldn't have kids, so we adopted a little girl. That kid gave us so much joy, filled a huge gap in our lives. Then she hit those damn teenage years and became trouble. Her world fell apart when we told her the truth about her adoption and then so did ours.

We woke up one morning and she was gone. No trace at all. The Police stopped searching after two years. We never stopped looking. My wife never got over it. She loved that child so much; it was all she ever wanted. She had someone to love and nurture and that child loved her back tenfold.

Well, that's all gone now. It's all in the past. I sighed a cleansing breath.

However, I still have six months to go and a lot can happen in a prison in six months. I had an uneasy feeling about all the hideous events that had just occurred. I knew it wasn't over. In fact, I felt it was just the beginning.

The stabbings, the drugs, corrupt guards and riots are all, to a degree, controllable. Changes can be adopted and processes can be put in place to contain such events.

But this... I have no idea how it happened and nor did the inmates. I don't believe the male guards were responsible. Those things didn't appear to be human.

The overwhelming and frightening thing is, I have no way of knowing how to stop this from happening again. I will look like a fool if this gets out. A prison full of pregnant women! That'll be a story and a half for the media. I am already nervous about the upcoming results of the inmate's blood tests.

The next day passed with little incident which made my job bearable. However, it was still a prison and the tension was always simmering, ready to boil over at any moment.

There's always a pecking order in prison, to sustain a position of power and order between the inmates. To keep that balance in place there is always an underlying tension amongst inmates. Alliances are formed and boundaries are drawn. Inevitably the pressure reaches boiling point and if you stretch anything too far, it will snap.

I have seen it time and time again. The inmates get edgy days before and you know a coup is coming. Then, the well-planned coup takes place. For a few days, there's a little chaos and uncertainty, while the new leader steps into her role and flexes her muscles. No one knows what to expect. New alliances are formed, old ones broken and there is always collateral damage as the new leader asserts her authority. Examples of her power must be on show, along with what happens to those who don't want to fall in line. Some are more brutal than others. Some are more tactical. The dirty work is always carried out by her next in line, her closest circle. The Queen Bee never gets her hands dirty.

"Warden, the doctor is here. She has the blood results you requested."

"Thanks Barbara. Send her in."

She entered the room in a business-like manner. I was trying to read her body language to pick up on any signs of how my day was about to unfold. I have been anxiously waiting for these results. I am either going to go out quietly or wish I had never taken this job. All the sacrifices I have made for this job will count for nothing if I leave on a bad note or worse still, fired. That is an outcome I will not let happen. Not after all my hard work and service.

Without saying a word, she handed me a file. I opened it and began reading. My worst fears were quickly realised.

"What the fuck!"

"I have checked and double-checked, sir," she said in a professional manner.

"Are you telling me that nearly two-thirds of the women in this prison are pregnant? Christ, it can't be! These tests must be wrong. Someone's made a mistake. Can someone honestly tell me what the fuck is going on here?"

Chapter Six: Between a Rock and a Hard Place

"Sister Mary Ellen, a quiet word, if I may?" Mother Superior asked as she stood in the doorway of the infirmary.

"Mother Superior, yes, please come in," I replied.

"I've been giving a great deal of thought to this very delicate position you have placed us all in and there is only one conclusion."

I always felt so intimidated by her presence. My self-worth and belief in myself always took a battering whenever she was close to me.

"What would that be, Mother Superior?"

"Sometimes in life, my girl, one is placed between a rock and a very hard place. It seems either path does not have a pleasant outcome or offer a more favourable choice. You are damned if you do and damned if you don't. Are you following me sister?"

"Yes, I think so, Mother Superior."

I didn't like where this was going one little bit and my stomach was churning and I knew trouble was coming for me.

"Good. You see Sister, if you are to have this... thing... our convent will be the laughingstock of the world. I will be a scapegoat for the church and you will bring shame on all the other nuns who have done nothing wrong. It doesn't seem just. However, and it pains me to say this Sister, if you were to have a little 'accident', shall we say, no one will be the wiser. No one will find out. The whole sordid thing just goes away. No shame, no scandal, no humiliation, and no noise. And I would even consider letting you stay on, Sister."

"You're asking me to take a life Mother Superior? Break a commandment, the Lord's covenant?" I questioned.

"Don't be so dramatic Sister and don't you dare question my standing regarding God's word! Do you think he wanted nuns to run around having babies? Do you think you can come in here and start making your own rules?" she continued her tirade, "this isn't about the Lord's word? It's about you making a mockery of God's house. You have brought Satan inside his house. Surely you see that child?"

I'd had enough of her condescending talk and took a big breath then let it go.

"I have a question for you, Mother Superior. What if more nuns were to become pregnant? Are you going to start an abortion clinic in God's house?"

"You little slut! You foul-mouthed little harlot! How dare you?" Mother Superior said in an extremely hostile tone.

"When you squeeze oranges Mother Superior, you get orange juice. Isn't it surprising what comes out of people when they are squeezed? I am not at all surprised at the vile, vulgar and evil poison inside you. You have done well to conceal your true self all these years. It must have been difficult," I said summoning all my strength.

"Listen to me you little trollop, I want you packed up and gone by nightfall. I do not want one skerrick of evidence to show you ever laid foot on these sacred grounds. Do I make myself clear?" Mother Superior said forcefully.

"Oh, yes. Perfectly! I will gladly take this precious little life growing inside me and nurture it because this is God's will. I will not let your murderous hands get anywhere near it, you hypocritical butcher!" I screamed back.

"Who do you think you are, Mother Theresa? You wouldn't have any idea of God's will. He has placed that thing inside you to show others who you truly are. A cheap little whore, whose filthy ways have landed you in this position. You opened your legs! But that's not enough. You want to bring your shame into God's house."

"Get out, Satan! Just get out!" I cried as I picked up my holy water near the bedside table and threw it at her.

Mother Superior just stood there and stared back at me with a self-righteous smirk on her face.

"Perhaps you would like to perform an exorcism now, you little Harlot," as she laughed out loud and slithered out of my room, like the snake she is.

I burst into tears; her words burnt holes in my soul like a blowtorch. I was so shaken by the cruel barrage. She stripped me of any decency I was clinging to. It felt like she sucked my soul out and consumed it.

My stomach began to cramp and the pain grew worse. I tried to sit up, it felt very warm and wet around my hips. Concerned, I looked down and saw my bed covered in blood. The cramping was now unbearable. I was in so much pain I couldn't yell out... I lost consciousness.

I woke sometime later in the infirmary. I heard the comforting voice of Doctor Patel. Her soothing tone and gentle bedside manner were exactly what I needed.

"What happened, doctor?"

"You lost the baby, Sister. Do not despair. You've done nothing wrong. You must concern yourself with getting better."

"Where's my baby doctor? I would like to see it. Please, can I see it," I pleaded.

"Mother Superior took the baby away, Sister. She said she would deal with it, to save you worrying about it."

"Of course, she did. She is pure evil! I hate her so much; I wish she would die," I said with tears welling up in my eyes.

"You are clearly upset Sister; however they are horrible things to say."

"I'm not upset doctor. I'm bordering hysterical! Can you tell me anything doctor, anything at all?"

"You are putting me in a very uncomfortable place now, Sister. Mother Superior has sworn me to secrecy. She threatened me and told me not to say a word."

"See! She's evil! Mother Superior shouldn't be threatening us. doctor, something really bizarre is going on around here. Do you really think we wanted to get pregnant? I mean, Sister Francis is 50 years old. Do you have any idea how humiliated she must feel? Do you? And I know there is something wrong with my baby, doctor. I just know it." I questioned.

"As I have already said, I really can't say anything Sister. I am more concerned about the health and welfare of all of you at the moment," replied Doctor Patel.

"I get the feeling you are hiding something from me, Doctor. If there is anything you know about any of this, please tell me, I'm begging you."

"Sister, once again, I am not at liberty to talk freely about this. I'm sorry," she finished up and left awkwardly.

No sooner had she left Mother Superior marched back into the room. My moment of quiet and rest was short-lived.

"Ah, Jane. I see you're awake. It seems our little quandary is over. God has answered my prayers. He never lets me down. By the way, you have been stripped of all your religious rights and you are no longer a nun. I have already made all the necessary arrangements with the Archbishop. I was going to have you escorted from the grounds but it seems we have a lot of maids leaving at the moment, so I have a position in either the kitchen or the laundry for you. Both seem a lot more appropriate for your particular skill set. Wouldn't you agree?" she said smugly.

"I've just lost my baby. Do you not have any compassion at all?" I asked feeling defeated.

"That was no baby. It was an abomination, a mutant. You were given God's grace by having a miscarriage. If either of those roles are too complicated, you can always return to the streets," she said smugly.

I wasn't strong enough to retaliate. I was exhausted, sore and emotionally fragile. I desperately held back the tears in front of her, until she walked out.

I felt so alone again and in a dark place. I think Doctor Patel must have slipped in a sleeping pill with the last batch of pills as my eyes are becoming heavy.

I woke up the next day feeling physically better but still emotionally exhausted.

As much as it pained me, I decided to take the laundry position. I had been here for so long now; I feel I have lost touch with the outside world. I had no qualifications and, in a way, I have been institutionalised. The thought of leaving actually terrifies me. If I work in the laundry and live with the day staff, I may be able to avoid any contact with Mother Superior and I still loved the other nuns dearly. They were my family and I couldn't bear to leave them, not now.

As soon as I was strong enough to be back on my feet, I was moved to the day staff quarters. Mother Superior told me the rooms were for the nuns, not the day staff. I could not bear to be in a 100-metre radius of her anymore. Contact with her made me physically sick. Even the mere mention of her name made my stomach churn.

I soon picked up the swing of things and enjoyed my new role in the laundry, far more than I expected. I had the freedom to be who I was without anyone questioning my behaviour or thoughts.

I laughed freely with the ladies and slowly let go of Sister Mary Ellen and embraced who I have now become. My workmates were simple women, who didn't take life too seriously. They both had families and worked extremely hard in the laundry. They had a tremendous sense of humour which helped me recover and make the transition from that of a nun to a laundry worker.

I wasn't bitter, surprisingly enough. I loved my newfound freedom and while my workmates had me laughing every day with wicked stories of Mother Superior. I didn't add to them, laughing with them was reward enough.

It's been weeks since I've been banished, I had not sighted Mother Superior which was exactly how I wanted it. It gave me time to settle in and decide on my future. Running into her often would have forced my hand.

There was no reason to be brutalised by her anymore. I decided it wasn't good for my soul, if I still had one. I made a point of catching up with the other nuns when I returned linen to their rooms. It felt comforting to see them. I was extra careful to make sure Mother Superior never saw me when doing my rounds. They are still my family and I missed them a great deal.

Most nights I'm left alone to think about what happened. I had never properly considered the reality of being pregnant. I was so shocked and busy fending off accusations and injustices, that I had never allowed myself time to soak in the wonder of having something alive and growing within me. Be that as it may, I still have no idea of its origin.

Nuns just don't get pregnant! How do you tell others this wasn't your doing, when you don't even know how it happened yourself? Until now I never took the time to dwell on what could have been. To know I was going to be a mother and to give birth to another living thing. Then, to feel the loss. To feel the sadness of losing something, that had to be made from at least 50 percent of me. Not being able to grieve and not being able to say goodbye. That's why it's all such a shock. It's like it came and went while I wasn't home. When I did find out, I spent the whole time defending my innocence, shamed into feeling I'd done something evil. Now I feel my own shame for losing it. Was it God's will that I lost the baby? Had I done something wrong for this to happen? Would I be chosen again? I closed my eyes and drifted off to sleep.

I was up early the next morning and began my laundry rounds. As I did so, I always asked around for any information on how Sister Francis was doing. Was anyone else 'sick'? Or should I say the truth now – pregnant. Everyone kept their silence on the matter.

It had been a little over a month now and things had settled down. I was happy in the laundry. One thing was for sure, I knew somehow, that it was only a matter of time before more nuns would become pregnant and Mother Superior would struggle to control the situation. She managed to shut the last scandal down but what if there were numerous pregnancies? Then what? Perhaps we will have a convent full of women doing laundry while she prays alone for our wretched souls every day.

The next morning, I remember waking up having the strangest of dreams. I was taken to another place, maybe another planet and it felt like I was operated on. It was a medical procedure of some sort. These shadows moved around me as they delicately carried out their work. I didn't feel threatened or feel in danger. It felt so real, it was like I was awake but then I wasn't... I just can't remember exactly how they looked and appeared; maybe I wasn't meant to. I could not stop thinking about the dream. I felt very tired, drained and something felt different in me. Then it hit me. I was pregnant again. I intuitively knew beyond doubt I was pregnant. That was no ordinary dream.

I wasn't expecting anything to happen for at least a couple of weeks. However, this time I was going to be more aware. So, I paid extra attention to my body. My last pregnancy I would dismiss things such as stomach pains, thinking I must have eaten something that didn't agree with me, never thinking in a million years that I could have fallen pregnant. It was nearly two weeks to the day when I began noticing a sucking sensation in my uterus. I was right! Confirmation I was pregnant again. Am I the only one? Or will some of the other sisters be joining me?

Maybe I could start a mother's club, I laughed out loud. I am sure Mother Superior would throw her support behind that idea!

I will do my best to remain open to the thought that this is something completely out of my control and not to worry. It's the older nuns that I'm worried about. Their faith is undeniable but it may take a miracle for them to keep an open mind. Some will accept it but others may not get past their feelings of shame and humiliation, even if they do, they then face the gruelling showdown with Mother Superior.

I still have more questions than answers right now. Like will this pregnancy go full term this time. Will the birth be difficult? And what will the baby look like?

I so badly craved answers. The events taking place in this convent suggest something very odd is happening inside these walls and well beyond human comprehension. This I am certain.

It will be difficult to find out who else is pregnant here. I am not around the nuns all the time now. In any case, they will be doing their utmost to conceal their inexplicable curse, feeling like lepers carrying a contagious disease. I can't begin to imagine the dilemma most will be faced with, in having to accept their predicament. A pregnant nun.

There was no technology at the convent which meant I couldn't carry out any research. Mobile phones and computers were not allowed which made it impossible to gather information about not only my pregnancies but also any conspiracy theories.

I thought again about the possibility of this happening to others. Why would we be the only ones? Or are nuns the 'chosen ones'?

Sometimes, I think not knowing might be a good thing. I'm already sufficiently frightened.

More days passed without incident. The nuns walked the grounds praying while we carried out our duties. The gardeners tended the grounds. I was always alert, waiting for something out of the ordinary to happen.

I could feel the baby growing inside of me. I had, without doubt, surpassed the term of my last pregnancy. I could feel the baby moving inside of me already... I thought it was way too early to be experiencing that.

I can feel myself becoming increasingly anxious. Nothing was in my control and I knew it.

Chapter Seven: Friends, Foes and Terminations

As much as I have enjoyed Tina's company, the extra responsibility was weighing heavily on my shoulders. We needed a bed for a night or two, food, hot water and of course money. I didn't have enough money for both of us. The little I did have went on the bus fare. Still, I'm sure we can work it out.

As we walked around town sightseeing, I was looking out for places to crash for the night. An old warehouse, derelict house, anything vacant would do.

I noticed a couple of skip bins outside a large shopping center. We could come back when it's dark and check them out for food. These places are so wasteful with leftover food, so I'm sure we can survive on their throw outs.

"Oh, shit! No! Not now... not again!"

"What's the matter, Tina? What's wrong?"

"Oh fuck! It's happening again!"

"Tina! Stop! Look at me! What are you talking about?"

"I can feel them... they're fucking here!"

"Tina, who is here?"

"They've done it again. Fuck! I'm pregnant again!"

"Wait, what? How on earth could you know that?" I asked her.

Tina looked terrified, "I can feel something move inside me. It's the same as last time. It's only slight at first but it changes fast," Tina was getting agitated, "they are inside me!"

"Okay. It's okay, I'm here to help. You're not alone. Do you hear me? You're not alone this time Tina," I said.

I wrapped my arms around her tiny little body as she nestled into me and wept.

"That makes two of us. I forgot to tell you. I'm pregnant too!" I blurted out.

Tina pulled away surprised, "You're pregnant too? Why didn't you tell me?"

"I'm sorry, it just slipped my mind. I was feeling nauseous the other day and initially thought it was something I ate. Clearly, it wasn't. I had that dream again a few nights ago. I think I've been pregnant for a while now. Don't worry Tina, we are in this together. I'll look after you, okay?"

She took comfort and reassurance from my words and realised she wouldn't be going through this ordeal alone this time. I knew that meant the world to her right now.

"Sarah! What's going on? I just... don't understand. The first time it was like a bad dream, you know. I lost it, it's history. I just wanted to put it behind me but this time it's no accident and I don't want to go through this again. Of all the people on this earth, why us?" asked Tina.

"I'm not sure why us, Tina. I don't have any answers either. All I know is that we're in this together."

"I'm sorry, Sarah. I have no doubt that you'll get through this. You're strong, I'm not. I wish I was. It's so unfair and I really miss my Mum and my family," she was in tears again.

I had to keep an eye on Tina. She was vulnerable. I do not need to witness another suicide and I felt Tina could easily opt out the same way. It worried me. I have to remain calm, at least for Tina's sake.

"Come on! We still need to find somewhere to crash tonight. We'll come back here for our three-course meal later on," I said, pointing to the two large bins at the rear of the shopping complex.

When she saw where I was pointing, she laughed which broke the heavy mood, "Great! Fabulous! Can't wait. I love a surprise menu," she said, wiping her eyes.

We shared another laugh before heading off to find somewhere to sleep. After walking around for a while, we were no closer to finding a bed or meal and it was getting dark so we made our way back to the bins at the back of the shopping complex.

I jumped in and started handing Tina anything that looked okay to eat. We never knew where our next meal would come from and this bin would probably be emptied tomorrow.

As luck would have it, the bins behind the large shop were full of goodies, fruit that looked just fine – peaches, plums, and apples that only had a few tiny imperfections. We also found some items that had just past their expiration date – cakes, bread and even some ring pull cans of baked beans. Satisfied with our score, I jumped back out and we made our way to a quiet laneway to sit and feast. What we didn't eat we shoved into bags I'd found in the bin.

With our hunger satisfied and as it was quiet where we were, we decided to stay here for the night. It was a beautiful night, not cold at all.

We chatted away for hours about our plans and what we would do next, eventually falling asleep sitting against a wall, leaning into each other.

We were woken, just before sunrise, by a stray dog sniffing around our bags for food. We stood and stretched our aching bodies slowly. We both let out a huge yawn in unison and then giggled about it together.

"I'll give it some bread," I said excitedly, keen to make a new friend.

"What about the cake?" replied Tina.

"What about both?" I said, laughing out loud.

The dog had a good feed and then left.

"Sarah, I've been thinking and I've got an idea."

"Yeah... what is it?"

"Well, we didn't get pregnant by choice but I figure we can choose to get rid of it, right?"

I was really surprised by what Tina had said. It was early, I was still waking up and I certainly wasn't expecting that to come out of her mouth.

"Yeah... I guess so but is that what you really want? I mean could you go through with that. An abortion is pretty full-on Tina."

"Yeah, it would be but so is this. At least it would be all over and done with... finished! I'm sick of worrying about miscarrying again! Or worse still, will it go full term? I mean what the fuck is it, Sarah!" yelled Tina.

"Okay! If that's what you want, we'll see if we can find someone to help us."

"Can't we just do it ourselves? You know buy whatever it takes and just do it?"

"Don't you mean... me?"

"No, not necessarily but if we go to a clinic and some really weird thing comes out? We could be used as lab rats to find out how this happened."

"I hear you. I'm just not that comfortable with this. It's not me."

"Oh! I bet you have a really good impression of me right now?"

"No, I'm not judging. I completely understand. I'm just saying I couldn't do it. I'm not cut out for that."

From nowhere a voice yelled out, "She hasn't got the balls, Squeak! She's weak. She's a princess, a daddy's girl."

Scarface appeared out of nowhere.

"Well, if it isn't the freak show talking shit again! What's wrong? No money around here so you've come to steal from us?" I said sarcastically with attitude.

It was out of character for me to talk like that but she gets my shackles up instantly and I had to stand tall.

"So, the homeless have money hey?" Scarface turned to face Tina.

"If you want it done Squeak, come and see me. It'll cost yah though. No free dinners around here. I did it myself last time. It wasn't so bad. The first time is always the worst. It gets easier, you know."

I could see Tina thinking about it as Scarface continued.

"Oh, the look on your faces. Weren't you just whining about people judging you?" she said and then burst out laughing.

Tina just nodded. She didn't know what to say. I didn't think she'd go through with it but hey, sometimes people surprise you!

She turned to Tina again, "Let me know, Squeak."

She strutted off as she had just won an award. Long, confident strides, she knew exactly what she was doing and where she was going. Her body language was always so convincing. If she is pretending, she was damn good at it.

"She really scares me, Sarah, I mean REALLY SCARES ME!" Tina moved close and cuddled into me. I reassured her with a comforting embrace.

"Yeah! I know, she's intimidating, that's for sure. Come on. Let's go and check out this town a little more."

"Great idea. I need some distance from that whack job," said Tina.

"Tell me about it. I wonder what the story is with that scar. It looks like she pushed the wrong person too far one day."

We strolled through the streets window shopping and dreaming of what we would buy, if we had the money. There were beautiful clothes, gorgeous shoes, jewellery and of course, handbags. It was fun and torturous at the same time.

Each shop we visited, I asked about any casual work available. I guess my appearance wasn't doing me any favours. A hot shower, fresh clothes, and a little makeup would have gone a long way.

I checked out the notice boards on the off chance there was any cheap or free accommodation available. There wasn't a women's refuge center in this town. There were no jobs available either.

Having no money was becoming depressing. Every turn we took we had to rethink due to our lack of cash. The day was disappearing quickly and we were both tiring fast. Having endured a poor sleep last night, wasn't helping and I really wanted to sleep in a bed tonight, so we continued dragging our tired feet forward in the hope our luck would change.

"Hasn't anyone ever told you to lift your fuckin' feet when you walk?!"

I spun around to give a mouthful of abuse to whoever it was that just said that. As I turned, my expression turned to surprise.

"You've got to be shitting me. Red is that really you? What the hell are you doing here?"

"I could ask you the same," Red said smirking.

"I'm here looking for you!"

"What are you stalking me now?" Red said laughing, "I see you have a new travel companion?"

"Sorry! Tina, meet Red. Red this is Tina, a good friend of mine."

"Hey," Red said, looking at Tina and turned to me, "I'm guessing you're both starving, absolutely stuffed and need a shower?"

"Wow! You're psychic now?" we all laughed a little.

"Grab your things and follow me. I have the answer to all your prayers. I'm your saviour, don't yah know. I'm staying out on an orchard and the owners are looking for fruit pickers. Accommodation and a feed, in exchange for a good day's work. Oh, and all the fresh fruit you can eat."

"That's the best offer I've had in a long time. You don't have to twist my arm. I'm in," I said looking at Tina.

"Ah! Count me in too." Tina chipped in.

As we jumped into the back seat of the car, Red introduced us to Hans who was driving.

"Sarah, Tina, this is Hans. Hans is from Germany and doesn't speak very good English but he tries."

In perfect harmony and still on a high from our change of good fortune, we replied in cheery, loud voices, "Hello, Hans."

We looked into the rear vision mirror to see Hans nodding his head in approval and in a warm, foreign accent he replied, "Hullo."

We chatted away excitedly and loudly, exchanging our adventures to one another, without going into too much detail of our ordeals, especially in front of Hans. My legs were aching from so much walking and my feet were so grateful to be resting.

We drove for about 30 minutes out of town when I could feel the car slowing down. I broke away from the conversation to look out the window and saw a sign saying, 'Fresh Fruit Drive In'.

As we drove up the gravel driveway, we passed rows and rows of apple and stone fruit trees. We had never seen so many fruit trees in our lives. The sprinklers were on and we could smell the wet grass and damp ground below the trees. The car was now leaving behind a huge cloud of gravel dust as Hans sped towards the sheds in the distance.

We finally came to a cleared area. Hans slowed down, respecting the owner's rules and then parked the car in a large shed. As soon as we got out, we were overwhelmed by the fragrant smell of fresh fruit. I savoured the aroma of apricots, peaches, and plums.

Red introduced us to the orchard owners, a hard-working humble family who were equally thrilled for Red, to have found some much-needed help. Red assured the family that she would tell us what was expected and show us around.

Red led us to the worker's quarters. As soon as the doors opened, we could smell a home-made stew, bubbling away on the stove and some freshly baked bread filling the room with delicious aromas.

With the flick of a switch, we were in a completely different reality. The worker's quarters were old but clean. The room was full of history, showcased by hundreds of photos pinned to the walls of past workers, who had passed through all leaving a memory of when they were here. It was so homely I was almost waiting for Mum and Dad to enter the room at any second.

Red showed us to our room, which consisted of two single beds separated only by a small bedside table with an alarm clock on it. At the other end of the room, there was a tall cupboard for our clothes. We dropped our bags on the neatly made beds and rushed back into the kitchen to satisfy our grumbling stomachs. We ate so much that we couldn't move. It was then that I remembered I was now eating for two.

"I had forgotten how home-cooked food tasted. That was the best meal of my life." Tina's comments broke the silence as we finished our dinner.

"Yep! That's the reason I'm still here. I've been through rough times on the road and this place is going to be hard to leave," Red added.

"How long have you been here, Red?" I butted in.

"Since leaving Francesca's. That's a long time for me to stay in one place," Red then looked me squarely in the eye, "you know me!"

"Yeah on that note, why exactly did you bounce so quickly from Francesca's place?" curious, I asked her.

"I owed the wrong kind of people money and there were other things." Red seemed dismissive.

"Like getting pregnant with no idea how and then losing it anyway?"

Red looked at me with an annoyed expression on her face. I continued, "You're not alone Red. It's happened to us as well and there are others too. I tried to tell you at Francesca's but you left before I could speak to you."

"Yeah! As I said, I had to move fast, yah know?"

"By the way, a couple of cops came by asking for you. Was that another reason why you were in such a hurry?"

"Listen, Sarah. What's with the twenty questions? You know nothing about me and I'd rather keep it that way. Is that alright with you?" she said defensively.

"Sure... fine!" I said apologetically. "I didn't stop looking for you Red. I was really worried about you. I checked the hospital, doctors and asked all over town if anyone had seen you and I covered for you at Francesca's, hoping you would come back," her face softened at the thought of someone actually caring about her.

"So, the pregnancy thing you were banging on about. How many times have you been? you know?" asked Red, changing the subject.

"This is the second time for me," I said.

"How about you quiet one?"

"Oh! Ah, same," replied Tina quietly.

"Are you in some kind of trouble Red?" I asked.

"You could say that."

"You should have told me. I might have been able to help."

"Yeah well, sorry. You had enough on your plate... I could tell you were on the run."

"How have you been coping?" I asked.

"Coping? That's one way to describe it. I've been thinking I'm some sort of freak for the past two years. I've nearly gone insane with getting pregnant and miscarrying these 'THINGS'. Doing drugs was my only way of escaping from it. I couldn't deal with it any longer. I just didn't care anymore."

"But don't you see something weird is going on? I thought the same. Like, what the fuck is wrong with me? But then I met you and Tina. We're not alone. It's like we've been... selected. Don't ask me why I know it's a bit out there but I have a feeling this is supernatural. Do you believe in aliens, Red?"

"What the fuck are you talking about? Now you're scaring the shit out of me and that's not easy," said Red loudly.

"Well, what's your explanation then? Some invisible boy miraculously keeps popping babies in you. We didn't do this Red and it happened without our consent. Have you girls had the dreams? Have you also found marks on your bodies? Well, I have."

"Okay! Now you're scaring the shit out of me, Sarah," said Tina anxiously.

"I'm sorry but you know you can't pretend this isn't happening. I know how crazy it sounds but if either of you has a better explanation, I'm all ears!" I waited for a few seconds.

"No response." I continued as they both listened, "I hate to admit it because it scares the living shit out of me too but I can't think of any other explanation. I mean how else did it happen. And don't you find it strange we're all travelling in the same direction and yet none of us have mentioned a destination? I mean what are the chances of meeting you again Red. I have a feeling there are a lot more like us. We just haven't found each other yet!" I argued.

I looked at both of them waiting for an immediate reply.

"So, Sarah! I've passed out each time and to be honest, I've been too scared to even want to look. Have you seen it? The thingy? You know, the freak show?" Red asked.

"What are you talking about Red! You threw a towel over it and you were completely freaking out?" I replied.

"I have no idea what you are talking about. I hardly remember anything."

"Are you serious Red?! Nothing at all?!"

"I remember passing out on my bed, no idea how I got there, waking up and seeing the blood on my sheets and I just got up grabbed a bag, stuffed as much stuff into it as I could and bounced."

"That's it! That's all you remember?" thinking Red must be hiding something.

"Maybe I've done too many drugs?" Red said.

"Yeah... maybe you have," I said as I looked over at Tina. "Maybe we should drop it for now."

I didn't want to go into too many details. I could see Tina was getting very anxious.

"I can't believe we are having this conversation. We are talking about giving birth to alien babies like it's normal. I mean, you know like it happens every day... I don't think so," said Tina shaking her head.

I decided to push on with our discussion, "Look, as weird as this all is, I don't feel like we're in any danger, do you? If they wanted to hurt us, they would have done it already."

"Ah! Don't you think it's a bit early to be making that call?" argued Red, "I don't even remember being asked to be a baby incubator. Hello! Look at us now, again! Our lives have been turned upside down."

"Yes, I know it's been tough but there has to be a reason for all of this?"

"That doesn't give them the bloody right to just help themselves to our bodies, now does it?" said Red.

"Unless they have a really good reason and we just don't know it yet."

"I can't believe we're still talking about this," said Tina.

"Tina, I don't like it any more than you do but it's time we stopped burying our fucking heads in the sand and pretending this isn't happening," I yelled.

"No shit, Sherlock! Your powers of observation are razor sharp. I mean, wow!"

Sarcasm was Red's specialty. I wonder if she went to the same school of life as Scarface.

"Well, one thing's for sure. I believe we should all stay together and work this out as a group. We need each other for support. This could get really scary. At least we will have each other."
Tina doesn't say much but this did make a lot of sense.

"I agree Tina, well said. What about you, Red?"

"Yeah, okay, as long as you don't go all 'detective' on me Sherlock."

Red's sarcasm broke the serious tone and we all laughed. We felt safe here. We had shelter, food, work, and friends. It was the closest thing we had to home.

Chapter Eight: Beyond Comprehension

"You're the doctor. You tell me what's going on here?"

I was angry, fed up and still had no answers. I was at my wit's end. It was like some cosmic joke that I didn't understand.

"I have absolutely no idea how or why this is happening, Warden. I have never seen anything like this before. I know you want answers right now but unfortunately, I can't give you anything."

"Will the morning after pill work?"

"They are past that point Warden."

"Of course they bloody are. Well, we are going to have to abort every one of them and while we are at it, sterilise them at the same time! This is one way I can make sure this wouldn't happen again!"

"We wouldn't be allowed to do that without their permission Warden. It would violate their civil rights."

"Oh, is that so? I'm supposed to just sit back and watch this place turn into some sort of day-care centre? Not on my watch, doc. If you can't help me then get out! I need answers and someone who will work with me, not some prisoners' legal rights advocate."

"As you wish, Warden," shaking her head in disgust as she walked out.

I didn't like the way I spoke to her either, but at this point, I didn't care.

I could sense this was all coming down on me and no one else. I sat forward in my chair, elbows on the desk with my head in my hands in despair. This supernatural freak show was beyond bizarre and I didn't have the faintest idea how to tackle it.

My only hope was that they all miscarry, like Tyson and the others had. It was still possible. Perhaps the safest course of action for me then was to do nothing, stop trying to force an outcome in which I have no control over anyway. Let it play out and see where the cards fall. As much as I hated to admit it, the Doc was right. I couldn't force the women against their will. It was a reckless knee jerk reaction from a tired, baffled and grumpy old man.

I envisaged what would happen if the media got a sniff of this, my chest tightened and I found it hard to breathe. This was not doing my health any favours at all.

I was going over and over it again. I mean, I had taken every precaution possible and that included actions I probably shouldn't have taken. If the board found out, what would they do differently? Bring in some hotshot who would call in Ghostbusters? How would anyone else have prevented this? I was still analysing every minute detail and every possible outcome. I was mentally exhausted and emotionally spent. I decided to knock off early. I needed to get out of here.

On arriving home, I had a few strong whiskeys and ordered in some takeaway. Feeling absolutely shattered I went to bed early. I don't even remember my head hitting the pillow.

I felt surprisingly refreshed on my way into work the next morning. I took my own advice and let go of trying to control this situation. Unfamiliar territory for me, that's for sure, but this case needed a different approach.

I emailed the prison psychiatrist with the names of all the women who were pregnant, asking for any similarities between them. I didn't tell her they were pregnant.

I was curious as to why these women were pregnant and not the others. There had to be a link, something connecting them. Why these women? I have no choice but to keep an open mind on the 'why and how' questions.

I had all the pregnant prisoners' files on my desk in front of me. I decided to spend the rest of the day thoroughly reading through them one by one, looking for any thread of evidence that may shed some light on this situation. After a few hours had passed, all I ended up with was a migraine. Frustrated, I put all the files away and went home early again. A couple of whiskeys and some of last night's leftovers and I fell asleep in my chair again.

I came into work just like every other day, not knowing how it would unfold. In a prison, past experiences play on your mind. Suicides, murder, riots, drugs, anyone or even several of these things kept you guessing as you walked through the main entrance.

However, nothing prepared me for what I walked into this morning. It began as soon as I passed through those sliding doors. I made my way past the scanners and as I turned the corner to walk down the corridor to my office, I could hear the hysterical screams of terrified women.

My walk quickly turned into a run as I made my way to the cells where the screaming was coming from. I entered the cell block to find prisoners lying on the floor near pools of blood. Amongst the blood was these small fetuses still moving and gasping for air. There were dozens of them. Jesus, I couldn't move.

The women's screams were no doubt due to the shock of having miscarried. I too was in shock. They were screaming and staring in disbelief.

It was like a domino effect as one cell sent the next one off. The guards were just as horrified and clueless as to what to do or how to help, "Go get the doctor," I ordered.

Until she arrived, there wasn't a lot anyone could do.

I was about to ask the doctor to bring in some medical help but thought best of it. Keeping this confined was still my priority.

The deafening screams were cold and haunting and echoed throughout the concrete cells. It looked and sounded like a cold-blooded killer had just gone on a bloody rampage and these women were left in his aftermath. Fear and chaos were about to overtake the prison.

I walked past one cell after another and witnessed the same scene. Lots of blood, horrified women screaming and a fetus doing its best to survive. The only thing that differed between the women was the reaction from the mother. Some were in the corner trying to climb the wall in absolute hysteria. Others were curled up in a fetal position while some grabbed at the front cell bars screaming to be released.

Then almost surprisingly, I came across one prisoner holding and cuddling something wrapped up. Amongst all the screaming and chaos, this woman was calm and gently nurturing her... baby? I could not help but stop and observe. She wasn't screaming like the other inmates. I noticed that her baby looked more human than some of the others. It did appear to have long, pointed ears though and was very advanced for a newborn. I couldn't see much more of the body as she had wrapped it up in some of her clothes. The fetuses seemed to differ a great deal. Again, some were quite human-like but most were horribly deformed. I struggled to grasp the horror and fear the women were experiencing.

Not knowing they were pregnant was bad enough, but to give birth to a mutated thing that's been growing inside you is horrific. I'm speechless. I feel like I'm floating around in space. I wasn't going mad, this was happening. I am witnessing it first-hand.

I pushed forward. One of the few cells that had no signs of a miscarriage in it, still had a prisoner screaming to get out, to get away from the carnage.

I approached more cells, witnessing still more miscarriages, with women lying half-naked on beds, screaming in shock at this thing they weren't aware they were even carrying.

I kept walking, looking on helplessly. I tried to block out the noise, even covering my ears with my hands. It was impossible. I was nauseous and queasy and nearly heaved several times, after witnessing this bloodbath. I felt sorry for these women, even empathetic. It was a nightmare for them and all I could do was stand by helplessly, not being able to protect them.

"Get me the fuck out of here! You fucking screw! Now!" screamed an inmate grabbing the cell bars and yelling in my face as I got too close, bringing me back to reality from walking around in a daze. Other prisoners continued screaming profanities as I moved hastily past their cells.

In my peripheral vision, I could see the doctor and a nurse running towards me.

"Warden!" yelled the doctor! "why didn't you call me earlier? Warden! Can you hear me?"

"What? What did you say? I can't hear you."

"Warden! Are you alright?"

I was a little faint and light on my feet as I moved.

"Doc! I don't know what to do. Look at these things... these babies... they are too premature to survive and yet some of them are alive... tell me what to do?"

She gazed around to see for herself. I looked at her and saw the horrified look on her face.

"Fucking hell! The babies... they're all... they're..." she said walking closer to get a better look.

"I can't believe this is happening. I thought the first two were just some sort of mutation but I can't understand this at all," the doctor took a deep breath trying to compose herself.

"Fuck!... fucking hell! There's so much blood... where do we start?" the Doc asked, as if I knew.

"What did you say Doc, I can't hear you?" I was still trying to gain focus.

The Doc took charge and yelled into my ear, due to the deafening screams.

"Warden I need every available Officer you can call in immediately and I need to call in more nurses. We need to sedate all these women and clean up this horrendous mess. If we're lucky we might be finished by morning."

"No. I can't do that Doc. I can't let this out of this prison," I told her firmly.

"Warden, either you get me those guards and nurses or I'm walking out of here now. Got it? Or you can clean up this mess yourself!" she said defiantly.

"Okay... okay. On one condition, you make sure no one and I mean no one leaves this prison until I've spoken with them, do you hear me Doc?" I demanded.

The Doctor fired back, "I haven't got time for your demands Warden and these women need me. Perhaps it's time you stopped worrying about your bloody reputation and start worrying about your inmates," she walked off with one of the nurses, who was leaning in close doing her best to hear the doctor's instructions. She nodded her head in agreeance, as if to confirm she'd understood and then ran off to get extra nurses to help and the supplies that the doctor had asked for. A team of nurses and guards returned a short time later with trolleys of medical supplies, new clothes, mops, buckets, and cleaning equipment.

"Guards! This cell. Open this cell," ordered the doctor.

I nodded to Pyke to follow the orders. Pyke opened the cell door manually and entered, followed by the doctor and nurse. The other guard remained outside the cell with me. The prisoner was sitting on the floor rocking from side to side, half-naked and in shock, screaming profanities at everyone in the room.

The deceased thing was wrapped up and placed in a deep basket which fitted into another trolley, while the doctor sedated the prisoner. The female guards picked up her limp body and placed her on the bed. They stripped off her remaining bloodied clothes, quickly sponge washed her body and redressed her, covering her with a light blanket. The doctor, nurse, guards and I left to attend the next cell, leaving two other guards, who had just been called in to clean up the cell. No one would ever know what had just taken place inside this cell.

We continued checking one cell after the other, disposing of the deceased fetuses and sedating the prisoners, then cleaning the cell, methodically removing all traces of the birth.

It was a long, slow process that went well into the night. All the deceased fetuses were placed into the infirmary. The deafening screams that had bounced off the walls all day and into the night throughout the prison had now subsided. Like a raging fire, it was slowly extinguished as the medical crew moved closer to the final cell.

It was close to dawn when the exhausted staff had finally finished the clean-up.

Before the doctor left, I requested for her to meet me in the infirmary, to discuss the deaths. It was difficult to mourn at the time, as the screaming overpowered any emotion. The shock of initially seeing them and then trying to comprehend the atrocity of what was happening, didn't allow you to feel anything at the time.

I remember looking at the faces of the more human-looking babies as they tried to open their eyes and take in their new surroundings. But like fish out of water, their time was limited. They were simply too premature, as they struggled to breathe and adjust in their new environment.

I was shocked at how advanced some were though. The prisoners could have only been three or four weeks pregnant. It just didn't make sense.

The infirmary is now full of these tiny corpses and I have no idea what to do with them. Deep in thought with my dilemma, I watch on as the doctor unwraps another corpse to take a closer look.

This one looked almost human except for the long, elf-like pointy ears. The other noticeable difference was there were no male or female genitalia.

The doctor wrapped it up carefully and placed it back in the basket, then proceeded to unwrap another. She continued to look at each one. Making notes, collecting as much information as she could. The next one was completely different. Its body was much longer, while the arms and legs were short. Each foot only had three long toes. The hands had three long fingers and it too had no genitalia. Silently and amazed, we stared up and down in awe of this being, our minds being stretched wide open, trying to process what we were looking at. We were both filled with an overwhelming sadness for these little beings. It was like a mass suicide. Even Doc couldn't work out why this happened. Something went to all of this trouble for that outcome. It makes no sense.

"Doc, when do you think you'll be finished? The new shift begins in a few hours and I need all this sorted before that happens. I've decided to bury them here at the prison. I don't want anyone finding out what happened here tonight.

"Guards, when the doctors finished take all these trolleys and bury these things... these bodies, behind the maintenance shed. Are we clear?" I barked my orders.

"Yes Warden," they all replied in agreement.

"Then return to my office as soon as it's done, for a debrief. No one leaves this place today without talking to me first. Got it!"

"Yes Warden," they nodded and left to carry out their duties.

"Doc, great job under the circumstances here today. I apologise for being short-tempered. I wasn't coping too well and I sincerely appreciate your professionalism and how well you controlled the chaos."

"Thanks Warden. That was something I don't ever want to go through again," she said.

"You can say that again. Listen, can you make sure all the nurses and anyone else who attended tonight, report back to me before leaving. I can't let this get out Doc. This prison will turn into a forensic circus if it does and it's best to keep that from happening. Don't you think?"

"I'll make sure of it Warden. By the way, the women are highly sedated and will sleep for hours. I gave them all a big dose. They all needed it after what they just went through. It will be very quiet around here for quite some time."

I smiled at her and watched her leave. I was shattered and really wanted to follow close behind her and sink into my lounge chair, with a good strong drink in my hand but I had to give all the staff the 'none of this leaves the prison talk' before anyone left. God knows what I'll tell the prisoners but it's out now. Unless of course, they all have amnesia in the morning and don't remember a thing.

After giving the 'talk' to the last guards and nurses on duty, I grabbed my things and shuffled slowly out the door. My legs felt heavy and my feet didn't want to move. I stopped and took in the silence. Reflecting back to the screaming at the start of the day, it was so peaceful now. The silence was almost strange considering what had happened. Order has been restored for now but at what cost?

Chapter Nine: My Holy Grail

After getting out of the shower, I stood in front of the mirror and brushed my wet hair. It was beginning to get some length to it again, which I embraced. For practical reasons, I had been keeping it as short as possible. My hair was black and used to have a slight wave in it. As I continued to stare into the mirror, I could barely recognise who was looking back at me. My vow to abstain from vanity meant I hadn't looked for many years.

For so long now, I had denied my desires and my sexuality. I cut myself off from all my feelings and tried my best to transition into the personality that would most impress Mother Superior and our Lord.

Socially, I had always been a chameleon - taking on the personality traits of the people with whom I was spending time with and all the while desperately trying to be liked and accepted. I didn't honour my feelings, dismissed my thoughts and shunned my own authentic self for fear of being criticised, ridiculed or singled out. Terrified of being an outcast and exiled, I adopted the behaviours that would keep me safe and accepted.

Who had I allowed myself to become? A pathetic, empty shell who would allow herself to be moulded by anyone around her.

Even in this convent, I opted to become a saintly nun - pure and righteous - dedicated to carrying out God's work. I was subservient to the cruel and vicious Mother Superior.

Every day of my life had been spent worrying about what others thought of me.

I had suffered this 'disease' from childhood. Raised in an orphanage and farmed out to countless lonely, desperate women who couldn't have a child of their own. To make matters even worse, was being sent back to the orphanage, only to be told 'we weren't a match'. These rejections merely reinforced the belief that there was something wrong with me. I must be a reject - damaged goods. Otherwise, they would have kept me.

I finally found a home where I experienced love and acceptance. I made peace with my fractured and now very distorted personality. They were kind older people who really loved me and through their love and acceptance, my spirit began to heal.

He was kind and hard-working and his wife, unable to conceive, poured all her love into me. I was a bottomless pit for that love, I soaked it up like a sponge. She truly loved me unconditionally.

I stayed there until I was 17, when my demons resurfaced with a vengeance. My belief about rejection was then reinforced by boys, just because I didn't put out. The other girls at school confidently dated any boy of their choosing, yet I was never noticed and it was like I didn't even exist. So I began to throw myself at boys. I did anything to gain their attention and it worked, but for all the wrong reasons. They would call me 'easy' behind my back and only gave me their attention when they wanted something. Word spread fast and I soon became known to the girls as the school slut. I had always hated that word and I hated it even more when it was used to describe me. I juggled my self-criticism, which went from despising myself for who I had become to craving the desperate and horny boys who were lining up to have me. I couldn't stop. The sex gave me power and I was finally wanted. They would do and say anything to have me and I made them beg for it. I had control over them. It became my addiction and I couldn't stop. They held me, kissed me and it felt like they made love to me. I had never felt this wanted in my life. I didn't want it to stop.

My behaviour made news and my adoptive parents were summoned into school. The shame and suffering I brought to them was unbearable. I hated myself so much for the pain I caused them. The guilt was eating away at me like a cancer. I felt I was dying on the inside.

Like anything out of control, something had to give and I became pregnant, even though I was using protection.

Despite my adoptive mother promising to help look after the baby, I had too much inner conflict going on to stay. My guilt and shame and being pregnant around her when she couldn't have her own baby, was too much. I had to move on and so I ran away whilst pregnant - so alone and afraid, I just wanted to die. I was living on the streets and ending up giving birth in an alleyway, by myself. The baby was stillborn, so I wrapped it up in an old jumper and placed it in a dumpster. I didn't know what else to do. I have never felt that low in all my life.

That's when the nuns found me. They took me in and cared for me. After suffering through that pain, I had nothing left and I decided to surrender to God. Why not?

I was snapped out of my reminiscence by someone knocking loudly on a door next to my room.

After finishing getting dressed, I applied some makeup that Demi my workmate had kindly given to me to cheer me up. The blessing that has come from my fall from grace is that I am now embracing all those things I had to give up as a nun. Now, I loved my femininity and I was proud of who I was and who I had become. I had done nothing wrong and would not accept any guilt or wrongdoing for the position I was now in, despite the best efforts of Mother Superior to condemn me to hell. She was a cruel, critical and very judgemental person who had the power to crucify me with her looks and words. I promised myself I would not let her take me down. It was taking all the strength I had to stay positive and rise above it. Some days were very tough, having no family support and few friends with whom I could share my feelings.

I don't know how I became pregnant, I'm just so grateful for God's blessing. As much as I was thrown into a world of despair at the time, I now look back and realise that being pregnant was the best thing that could have happened to me. How would I have processed all of those feelings under the habit and cloak of religion? I was having all these natural, motherly feelings of love and nurturing and wanting to prepare my nest. Hormones were raging through my veins, filling me with a warm glow inside. If I remained a Nun, I had to bury those feelings - destroy them - like they didn't exist.

My life has changed in the blink of an eye. From feeling so low and depressed, to now looking forward to all that life has in store for me.

As the morning sun continued to shine through my window, lighting up my room and filling it with warmth, I began to embrace the idea of motherhood. My life had purpose now. It felt so right. Baby names would pop into my head, bringing a smile to my already beaming face, as I contemplated the potential name and sex of the baby. I smiled freely as I pondered these things in my dreamy state.

My head jolted back in fright as someone pounded ferociously at my door. I quickly opened the door. It was a shaken co-worker.

"Jane! Come quickly! It's Sister Rosemary. She has collapsed outside. Quick... quick!"

I ran outside to see what I could do to help. I could see some blood around her. My co-worker Demi stood there in shock, looking at Sister Rosemary who was unconscious.

I yelled at Demi, "Demi, can you go and get the doctor, please? I'll watch her while you're gone."

Trusting my instincts as soon as she left, I moved the habit and saw what looked like a premature baby. It was still alive and I wasn't prepared for that. To save her from immeasurable embarrassment and humiliation, I took the baby. It was covered in blood and doing its utmost to survive. I whisked it off to the laundry, which was nearby.

Using the towels from the laundry, I gently wiped the blood off the tiny body and then wrapped it up in more towels before placing it carefully in a cupboard, out of sight.

I ran back to Sister Rosemary. She was still out cold, which was a blessing.

The doctor eventually came rushing down the lawns with her medical bag in hand.

"It's Sister Rosemary Doctor. It looks the same as what happened to Sister Francis, I'm afraid."

"Thanks for helping Jane. I'll take it from here," as she started to check Sister Rosemary's vital signs.

"I've hidden it, for her sake. It's still alive. It's way more advanced than last time, doctor," I said.

"Doctor! doctor! Come quickly please," the doctor and I both looked behind to see Sister Celeste running towards us, screaming, "It's Sister Adele and she is bleeding badly and has fainted inside the church. Please come before Mother Superior finds her. Now, Doctor! Please hurry!"

"Jane, please stay with her. I've checked her over and she is stable. I'll be back as soon as I possibly can to check on her. I'm so sorry."

While Sister Rosemary was lying on the ground, I ran to the laundry to get some blankets for her. I also wanted to check on the baby I left in the cupboard. I watched on helplessly as the small baby which looked premature, struggled for survival.

Although it was very small, its features were fully formed. I noticed the baby had no genitals but that didn't seem to trouble me. Her energy felt feminine or maybe that was just my wishful thinking. If I was ever going to have a baby, I always fantasised about having a little girl.

"You are so beautiful, you know that? Just so beautiful," my eyes welled up and tears flowed freely as I watched her move helplessly in my arms as her eyes began to open slowly and begin to focus on everything in the room. Her eyes then turned to me, curiously watching me. Her eyes grew heavier and heavier and then eventually closed. They didn't open again. She was gone.

With that realisation I started to panic and feared for the little one growing inside me. I couldn't hold Sister Rosemary's little gift any longer and placed her gently under a pile of clean washing.

As I sat down, I realised I was starting to have a panic attack. I purposefully and with all my intention, slowed my breathing and calmed myself, somehow knowing that if I didn't, I had no chance of keeping my baby. I was walking a tightrope of realities. Stay calm and potentially keep the baby or lose control and lose the baby. I did everything in my power to keep it together. Long, slow, deep, breaths. One after another, again and again.

It worked. I went back to my room now that my panic attack had subsided. I wept as I began to mourn the loss of that little baby, wondering if staying here was my best option, as I was putting my own pregnancy under threat.

I have no idea where to go, where to stay or what to do about money. In my heart I know I'm only staying here out of fear. It's safe here but only to a certain extent. My needs are met but it's just not enough anymore. My problems felt so heavy and my eyes slowly began to close. I slept soundly on the couch, covered with my favourite throw.

I woke early the next morning, crystal clear in my thinking. The events that took place yesterday showed me there wasn't anything I could do for these nuns. I decided not to inform anyone of my plan. I believed it would only cause problems if I were to say goodbye to everyone. So, I packed a small carry bag with some fresh clothes and with a small amount of extra money I had borrowed from Demi, I was ready.

I waited until everyone attended morning church service and then absolutely terrified, I left the grounds for the first time in years.

I had somewhere in mind to go. It was a long shot but it's all I had right now. I made my way to the train station which wasn't too far from the convent. We could always hear the trains rumbling past in the distance, especially at night, that familiar clickety-clack as they roared along the railway tracks, past us.

I had been sheltered for so long in the convent, that even buying a train ticket felt like an ordeal. I had no idea how much living there had hindered my independence. I had spent years being told what to do and when to do it. I just hadn't realised how much until I left those walls. Perhaps that's why I stayed so long. I just wasn't being totally honest with myself. I didn't want to face up to other areas of my life. For me, it was the feeling of not belonging which had always been such a destructive and soul-destroying belief. It had caused me so much pain and loneliness. So, when the nuns accepted me, I felt like I belonged to a family again and jumped in. I found the structure of prayer and servitude helped me dissolve those feelings and they didn't have the same power over me anymore. At last, I had a weapon to fight those feelings, to silence them when they became overwhelming and I would continue to pray. We were all equal at the convent (apart from Mother Superior) and I would simply go about my day in a peaceful and calm manner. I loved how it made me feel.

After waiting an hour or so for my train to arrive, I finally boarded and timidly moved down the aisles looking out for a vacant seat. I felt vulnerable being outside the convent and of course being pregnant.

I chose to sit halfway down the carriage and took the window seat. It was going to be a long trip and that gave me plenty of time to contemplate.

I was returning home; I knew it would be challenging, so much would have changed. Would my old house still be there? Were my parents still alive? As I stared out the window watching landscapes blur past me, I had the realisation that not only did I leave my hometown pregnant, but that I would be returning home the same way. Would I tell them or keep it a secret for as long as I could? I wasn't showing yet and decided that maybe telling them wasn't the best way to reunite.

Perhaps I will keep it a secret a little longer. Deep in this thought, I was suddenly brought back to the present moment. The baby started moving inside me. There was strength behind its movement which was a little unnerving. Paranoid, I looked around to see if anyone was watching me. What if someone could tell that my baby was kicking? Was that a ridiculous thought? I felt so self-conscious. Not that I needed to worry, the people on this carriage were either reading, listening to music or staring out the window minding their own business.

My thoughts started spiralling and I had visions of having the baby right here on the train. After witnessing the nun's experiences, that's definitely not something I'd want to put these people through.

I could feel a panic attack coming on again and sucked in some long, slow deep breaths, struggling to maintain control and my equilibrium. The baby settled as I calmed myself with deep breathing and stared out the window. The repetitive sound of the clickety-clack of the train passing over the railway tracks soothed me. I wish I had brought something to read, to distract my mind from constantly forecasting how this will play out when I return.

Chapter Ten: The Wrong Place at The Wrong Time

We settled in so well at the orchard. The work was hard but rewarding and we laughed our way through each day. The food was delicious, our beds were warm and we were safe. It was good to have some normality in our lives after everything we had been through. I will never take food and shelter for granted ever again. I grew up never giving it a second thought. Now it's become the most important thing in my life.

Time passed and we began to think our lives were settled again. However, as the days were passing, so were our pregnancies. We could feel the babies growing and moving rapidly inside us.

It was very unsettling and of course we had so many unanswered questions. Would the fetus abort again? Or go full term? What will they look like and more importantly how are we going to look after them? The truth is that none of us knew. We kept working, doing our best to push it out of our minds. We had no control over it anyway and that hard-hitting fact didn't make it any easier.

After washing my face, I grabbed a towel and dried myself. As I looked in the mirror, it was showing someone I didn't recognise. I had changed so much since leaving home. I was looking at a strong, independent woman. Not a timid, naive teenager. When I think back to that day on the basketball court and remember myself then compared to who I am now, I can't believe I'm the same person. That timid girl no longer exists. I have completely outgrown her. My hair was now shoulder length and dark blonde. I hadn't been wearing my glasses for a while now as they had broken back at Francesca's and I couldn't afford to get them fixed, let alone buy another a pair. I hadn't noticed that I didn't need them anyway. Since becoming pregnant, my eyesight has improved, my skin has cleared up and my intuition has heightened. Are the babies changing us? I never really thought about it until now. I mean, their DNA is running through our veins.

What a crazy thought but strangely enough one that I've come to accept is possible. I don't think the others have. When I talk about how we got pregnant, it's like I'm the crazy one. It makes them feel uncomfortable so I must be conscious of what I'm going to say. I've always been one to embrace the truth, unlike the people around me putting blankets of denial over parts of their lives. They pretend that things aren't happening, or that their problems will simply disappear. Nowadays I'd rather hit it head on and move it out of my way so I can see a clear road ahead. Each to their own, I guess.

We started early in the orchard, it was cooler in the mornings and much more pleasant than picking fruit in the heat.

"Do you think you should be climbing that ladder in your state, Tina?" I questioned her concerned.

"Been doing it for ages now 'Mum', you just haven't noticed me," as she laughed at her comeback.

"Yeah, okay but I still don't think it's wise, Mum knows best!" I replied.

"I'll be fine. Go and do some work," she said. I told myself to stop worrying as I walked away. I hadn't gone far when I heard a scream and someone crying out in a lot of pain. I ran back to see what was wrong. Tina had fallen from the ladder and was on the ground. She looked at her shoulder, which seemed to be dislocated. It sent her into a fearful panic which then caused the inevitable. She miscarried again.

"Oh, my God! Someone help me! Quick!" screamed Tina.

"Red, help me get her up and to the car," I said, "you're going to be alright, Tina. I promise. Don't look! It will only make it worse, okay?" she nodded her head in agreement.

We managed to get her in the car, albeit slowly. She had lost a lot of blood by now and was in a lot of pain.

"Red, can you drive?" I asked, "I need to go back and get the baby."

"Forget that thing. That's what did this to her in the first place. Are you crazy?" Red angrily replied.

"Red, I need to get the baby. I'll be back in a sec."

I ran back to where she fell but the baby was gone. I know I saw the baby during all that commotion and it was breathing! What the hell? It was just here. No mistake or doubt in my mind whatsoever. Babies don't just vanish into thin air. I ran around the area searching frantically but I couldn't waste any more time. Tina was in pain, so I ran back to the idling car and jumped in and slammed my door shut.

"Glad you came to your senses," said Red sarcastically.

"What are you talking about?" I replied angrily. She was distracting my thoughts about what had happened to the baby.

"You left the baby behind. Good move," she said.

"Yeah, right," it was easier to agree than explain the disappearance in front of Tina.

"It's okay, Tina. Everything will be okay," I said, trying to reassure her.

After driving back from the orchard, Red pulled up at the packing shed to inform the owners of what had happened, minus a few details and that she was driving Tina to the hospital to get her shoulder looked at. They were extremely upset about what had happened and somehow felt responsible. We assured them it was okay and that it wasn't their fault, then quickly drove off to the hospital, much to Tina's relief. She was in a lot of pain and her face grimaced in agony.

On arrival at the hospital, the staff took her and guaranteed us that she was in good hands. Wanting some fresh air, we made our way outside.

The trauma had my baby kicking and moving about frantically. I turned from Red to compose myself. I slowed my breathing down with long, slow deep breaths. When I turned around, I could see Red was experiencing the same thing and appeared to be panicking. I placed my hands on her shoulders to get her attention.

"Red! Listen to me! I want you to take long, slow deep breaths, okay? We need to slow your breathing down. That's it loooong, slooowww, deeeeeeep breaths, that's the way. You're doing really well," I continued to help Red for another few minutes with her breathing, "keep going, looong, sloooowww... deep breaths. How do you feel now?" I said calmly.

"What the hell, that thing was going sick inside me?" Red said.

"You're pregnant again? Why didn't you tell us Red?" I said annoyed.

"I didn't know I was, until just then. Here we fucking go again. Fuck!"

"Apart from being pregnant, are you okay now?" I asked.

"Yeah I think so. I thought the last time I miscarried was going to be the last. It's been a while since it's happened again. Wishful thinking hey. Those fuckers aren't finished with me yet, hey?" Red said.

Suddenly, an ambulance screeched out from the hospital, lights flashing and sirens wailing, scaring the life out of both of us. I turned away from Red and watched it scream off into the distance.

As I turned back, I felt something warm splatter on my face. Red was violently coughing up blood.

"Red! Red! What the fuck?" I yelled, throwing my arms up in the air.

She dropped straight to the ground on her knees. Standing behind her was Scarface. She had a possessed evil look on her face as she shouted.

"That bitch had it coming for a long time now."

I knelt down to help Red. That's when I saw the tip of a long blade protruding through her stomach. Red was still coughing up blood and struggling to breathe.

"Oh my God! Red! Red I've got you... it's going to be okay... stay awake... look at me... stay with me Red... do you hear me? You stay with me damn it... Red listen to me!" I screamed. I felt helpless.

Blood was running freely down the front of her stomach and onto the pavement. She was still in shock, not knowing what had happened, just the realisation of the pain. As I looked down on the path, I spotted something moving about in the pool of blood, between Red's legs. I felt the anger rise within me. Clenching my fist hard, I sprung up and hit that bitch with all the strength I could summon. I couldn't have aimed better if I tried. Wham right in her throat! Bang on target! Shocked and stunned, she hit the ground hard, leaving her desperately trying to suck in air and holding her hands around her throat.

By now we had attracted an audience. Women were screaming. In the corner of my eye, I could see a stretcher being quickly pushed out the front doors of the hospital by two men.

I watched as Red was lifted onto the stretcher and quickly away.

Out of nowhere, a police car sped towards us then screamed to a halt where I was standing and two officers jumped out of the car.

Scarface was cuffed and dragged away and ushered into the back seat of their car. I had never felt so much anger and hatred towards someone in my life. I wanted to have another go at that bitch! I felt so vindicated when they arrested her.

Shocked onlookers were replaying events to one another exchanging stories of what they believed had happened as more Police arrived and the area was quickly taped off from the public.

"What the fuck, what are you doing?" I shouted as the two Officers then cuffed me, "I didn't do anything. It was that fucking bitch, not me... are you fucking crazy?" I swore angrily as they dragged me away.

"It was her... what's wrong with you? Are you out of your minds? It wasn't me!"

I continued to plead my case as I was also shoved into the back of the police car, right next to Scarface. I didn't say anything. I gave her a filthy look and turned to stare outside the window. The siren wailed as the Police car sped off to the station.

I had a sudden realisation; where was Red's baby? I remembered seeing it on the path before Red was taken into hospital. Amongst all that confusion and chaos, the baby had disappeared! Am I going mad?

Maybe someone took the baby when I punched Scarface and I missed it. My only concern was for Red. I hope she was going to make it.

"If she dies, you will too. I promise you, if it's the last thing I do," I told Scarface as I looked out the window, avoiding eye contact.

"I'm terrified, Pimples. Do I start shaking now? Was she your lover? Such a shame."

"I'll make sure that hideous scar goes right across your face before you take your last breath!" I said, furiously.

"Oh, officers! You-hoo! I do believe I'm being threatened back here. I may need some protection from Goldilocks. Help!" she laughed out loud. Her laughter got louder and louder as she stared at me.

The policeman in the passenger seat turned around to warn us, "These are serious charges. This is no laughing matter. I can assure you. You better hope that girl pulls through," he said sternly.

"I had nothing to do with her stabbing... I'm her friend," I said. "It was this crazy bitch! Please! I'm telling you the truth!"

"You have the girl's blood all over you and you were both at the scene. We are going to have to hold you for questioning," he replied.

"I can't do this... please... I'm pregnant! If I stress, I'll lose the baby. Please..."

"If you're pregnant, you will be looked after while we investigate this matter."

With all that was going on I could intuitively feel the baby was stressing. I calmed myself immediately with long, slow, deep breaths and gained my composure, which settled the baby once again.

"I knew you were trouble the first day I saw you. I just didn't know how much," I said angrily to Scarface.

"This never had anything to do with you Goldilocks. You were just in the wrong place at the wrong time."

"What did she ever do to you?"

"Now we're asking some better questions. It's a long story but I'll make it real short for you," she leaned over to whisper, "You see this scar? Compliments of that bitch! She did this. How would you like to look like this for the rest of your life? Watching people look away as soon as they saw you!" she said as she pointed to her face.

"What did Red have to do with that?"

She leant in close to me again and whispered, "Well, it goes like this. Our Red has a little drug problem. So, to pay for her habit, she starts dealing. Instead of starting small, Red decides she's going to get there really fast and straight into the big league," she stopped and looked me square in the eye then continued to whisper again, making sure the Officers could not hear.

"Are you keeping up Goldy? I had just finished unloading my last deal and was on the way to pay my supplier, when who should stick me and take all my money? It was dark and she was wearing a hoodie but I caught a glimpse of that star she had tattooed on her neck. She got away. Then my supplier came after me. They don't wanna hear how you lost it, they just want their money, at any cost."

I just stared at her, wondering if she was telling me the truth as she continued.

"They gave me time to get it back but I couldn't find Red and I couldn't get the money. They threatened me but I had nothing for them. They said if I didn't talk, they would do this to me," as she pointed to her scar, "as you can see, they weren't bluffing. I pissed myself as they slowly slit my mouth open. They were so high they didn't care. I could barely drink my food for months and now I get to wear this smile for the rest of my life. So, yeah! I had a debt to settle with that fucking bitch. I've been tracking her for months."

"That's why you were in my room going through my stuff, at the backpackers?" I asked, still unsure she was telling the truth.

"Yeah, I thought she was your roomie so I was looking for clues. She knew I was getting close and must have seen me. She somehow managed to skip town every time. I don't know how she knew."

"Why did you get into drugs in the first place?" I asked, curiously.

"None of your business."

"Were you actually trying to kill Red because of what those dealers did to you?"

"Payback is a bitch isn't it?" Scarface said smiling at me.

"Well, I'm pretty sure you succeeded there. What if you've killed her?"

"She won't die. The knife went through her stomach, not her heart."

"You better hope you're right. You know she was pregnant, right? She lost the baby because you stabbed her."

"Red pregnant? No fucking way!" she said laughing.

I couldn't respond. I wanted to shut her up... forever. I stared out the window contemplating the fallout from all of this. The timing couldn't be worse. I need a witness - someone who saw everything. That shouldn't be too hard. Surely.

Chapter Eleven: Gone but Not Forgotten

It was a long drive home and I made sure there was plenty of distance between the prison and me when I bought this house. It always gave me time to process the day's events but the last 24 hours of screaming women, desperate staff yelling out for help and terrified prisoners demanding to know what the hell was going on, continued to flash through my mind over and over again. I turned the radio on, up loud, to drown out the memories that still lingered in my consciousness. I flicked through the stations unhappy with the choices on offer until I found an opera singer pouring out her emotions to anyone who would listen. I was drawn in, lost in her sad story. It completely took my mind off the prison which was exactly what I wanted.

Upon arriving home, I poured a large whiskey and fell into my favourite chair and let out an almighty sigh. I was finally off my feet, sipping on my favourite scotch that slowly numbed my head and body. I pulled back the recliner lever as my feet were thrown into the air and my head went back at the same time. I closed my eyes, I was in heaven as I took in the peace of my empty home and before I knew it, I had drifted off to sleep.

With what seemed the shortest sleep in my life, I was woken abruptly by someone knocking on my door. At first, I thought I was dreaming but the incessant knocking continued until I consciously realised someone was at the door. I fought to wake up, my eyes squinting from the lights still on in the room. Gaining focus, I saw that I still had my whiskey glass in my hand with some whiskey still in it. What the hell I thought and then drank it.

"Okay, okay. I heard you. Hold your horses, alright!" I shouted angrily as I put the glass on the table beside me and grabbed the recliner lever and pushed it forward, bringing my feet back to the floor as I pushed myself out of the chair. Catching my reflection in the hallway mirror told the story, an unshaven, scruffy, tired old man. I looked back in protest, then threw my hands up in the air in defeat. I just didn't care anymore.

As the persistent knocking got louder so did my anger. I forcibly yanked the door open, nearly tearing it off its hinges, ready to serve an almighty backlash to the impatient, annoying knocker. I Struggled to focus as the bright morning sun shone in my face.

"Jane... is that you?" I thought I was seeing things.

"Hi Dad."

"Oh my God Jane! Is that really you? After all this time... what the hell are you doing here? I nearly didn't recognise you... you look so different," I threw my arms around her and hugged her.

"God it's good to see you again. I've missed you so much," I could feel her arms tightly around me in return.

"Oh Dad, it's so good to see you too. Where's Mum?" asked Jane.

"Ah she's gone honey, she left years ago. We were worried sick when you disappeared. We searched for you for years without a trace. We were never quite the same after you left and that's not your fault either... we were already drifting apart. God, I can't believe you're standing here. Come inside, I'll put the kettle on. We have a lot of catching up to do."

"That sounds wonderful, thanks Dad," Jane replied.

"I've got to say Jane, you look fantastic, you're glowing," I said excitedly as I closed the door behind her and ran to put the kettle on, so happy to have her back and hear all her news.

"I feel so bad Mum left. I'm sorry for both of you."

"It's done, Jane. We're okay... are you hungry? Can I make you something to eat?" I asked excitedly.

"Yes, please I'm starving."

"Poached eggs on toast?"

"Perfect. I could eat anything at the moment."

"So, where did you go? What happened to you?"

"Dad, I'm so sorry for the pain I caused you both but when I fell pregnant, I was so ashamed of myself and being around Mum who could never have a baby of her own, I had to leave. I moved from town to town and drifted from place to place, roaming the streets. Then I miscarried in an alleyway and staggered around until I passed out somewhere. That's when the nuns found me and took me in. I felt safe there and found peace in myself from prayer. I stayed, became a nun and lived there until recently."

I was listening as I cooked breakfast.

"Oh my God Jane. I don't know what to say other than Jesus you went through a lot," as I handed her a plate and cup of tea.

"Looks great Dad, thank you," she said as she began eating as soon as the plate was on the table.

"We might have to finish our catching up later honey, a lot went down at the prison last night. Sorry, I know I look like shit; I didn't get much sleep last night. I've just had the worst night imaginable. Something really bizarre has been going on at the prison. It looked like a blood bath last night. You can't repeat this to anyone!" I looked at Jane awaiting her answer, she nodded.

"You wanna hear something really weird? The women inside the prison have been falling pregnant for weeks now and I have no idea how. Crazy right?" I paused to make sure Jane was keeping up.

Then, last night they all aborted, just like that. One starts, then like dominoes they each abort, one after another. It's like they are in sync with one another. God, it was the worst living nightmare. There were dead babies everywhere."

"Oh my God," said Jane with her hand over her mouth, "it's happening here too?" she said trying to swallow her food.

"What do you mean it's happening here too?" I questioned.

"Dad, the same thing is happening at the convent, exactly the same thing. Nuns getting pregnant then miscarrying and at the convent of all places."

"Shit, you're pregnant, aren't you?" I questioned Jane.

She looked at me ashamed and nodded.

"I can't believe it's happened to you as well and you haven't lost it?"

"I can't believe you know about this Dad. I've been worried sick about how to bring myself to tell you. Dad, you know this baby may not be..."

"Human? Unfortunately, yes, I've had my suspicions after what I've seen at the prison. Aren't you scared of what you are carrying? What will be born?" I asked.

"I'm a little anxious but not scared. It's difficult to explain. I should be but I'm not. I don't feel threatened at all by them. I really believe they mean no harm. Despite the way this has all come about. I know it doesn't look good, being pregnant to... you know... something that may not be completely human. As hard as that is to say, it's the truth. Their energy is gentle and peaceful. If they were aggressive and hostile, I believe I would pick up on that," Jane said passionately.

"So, why do you think you are still pregnant when other women are aborting?" I asked.

"Good question. I've had a lot of time to think about this and it's only my opinion but I believe it's fear. If the women get too fearful or something major happens, it stresses them out and they abort. It has happened to me as well. This time, I've managed to breathe through the fear and not lose the baby. I'm not afraid of the birth or where it came from. I've seen them in my dreams, they appear as beautiful beings."

"Wow! That's out there," I said loudly, "so, are they a threat to us? Are they dangerous? I don't know enough yet. Last night was a massacre. You being here right now is so great but really spooky at the same time. The prisoners were heavily sedated and I have no idea what to tell the staff and the prisoners today. I've been doing my best to keep it from getting out to the media. Could you imagine if the press gets their hands on this? God help us all."

"Yes, I hear you, believe me, I know. Mother Superior has been doing the same. A convent with pregnant nuns? Now there's a story for you!" Jane smirked.

I tried to keep a straight face but I could not help but see the funny side. I began to smirk, then chuckle and then I just lost it and laughed out loud.

"Well, I'm glad you think it's a laughing matter," she continued staring at me trying to be serious.

My laughter was contagious and she soon joined in. We were both exhausted and overtired which made it seem even funnier. God! It felt good to laugh again. It had been a long time since I had laughed like that.

"So, you became a nun? Seriously? I always knew you were different and had to find your own path but a nun. No way!"

"Yeah, I know it's crazy, right? You're still at the prison after all these years?" she said sarcastically.

"As I said, after you left, we struggled and our relationship turned to shit and your mother left. I was devastated and the prison was all I knew. The damage was already done. It was too late for me to save the marriage. In her mind, she had already left years ago. After some time off, I went back. Only a few months to go now and I retire. We all have our different paths to follow. Human beings are such a complicated species."

"Now more importantly Jane... um, these babies... these... beings. What do they want? Why us? Why now?" I asked.

"Okay, once again this is only my opinion but I believe they need something from us and they need it now. I get the feeling they have been trying to do this for some time. I can remember sometimes the beings doing tests on me, while I was asleep. We keep losing the babies however they are not stopping. They need us desperately. I believe that time maybe running out for them. That's what I get from all this. It's hard to piece it all together. Even harder to explain."

"But why? Why breed with another species? Why humans?" I asked.

"Maybe... just maybe and it's only my thoughts, they cannot populate by themselves anymore. Maybe they are becoming extinct or their planet is in danger. Look at the state of our planet. Climate change, overpopulation, food shortages and war. Maybe they are in the same situation, somewhere else. I don't know. It's been challenging enough just to get through all this. I would love some answers too it would make it easier to understand, don't you think?"

"Damn right it would. I've been going out of my mind trying to understand this and make sense of it; I just can't get it out of my head. It doesn't go away and it's always on my mind. I don't know what to expect next," I said frustrated.

"This is not meant to go away, they need us. Don't blame yourself, Dad. This is really stretching all of us. You've done well to keep it together. A lesser man would not have coped at all. I'm proud of you, Dad," Jane said as she placed her hand on mine.

"Now, don't go getting all emotional on me now, okay? You know I've never been good like that," I replied placing my other hand on top of hers.

"Doesn't mean to say I can't tell you now, does it?" Jane said looking at me lovingly.

I was never good at receiving compliments or being loving and would always change the subject.

"I have to go to work now and see how the prisoners are doing this morning."

"Can I come with you?" Jane requested.

"Aren't you exhausted? Why don't you get some sleep?" I replied.

"I'm curious to find out what's happening at the prison and you know, see for myself. Can you wait five minutes, I just need a quick shower to freshen up a little?"

"Okay, you're on. I can do with some help on this."

After a hot shower and a good breakfast, Jane eagerly came with me into Benson Prison Facility. Curious onlookers were checking out who was with me. Everyone was quiet in light of what happened yesterday. I ushered Jane into my office and closed the door.

"This place hasn't changed much."

"No, it hasn't."

"You sure about that, Dad? I mean... pregnant prisoners!"

"That's not funny Jane," I said smirking back at her.

My office phone rang, "Yes, Barbara! What is it?"

"Warden, the prison psychologist left the papers you requested on your desk."

"Excellent, anything else?"

"No there's nothing to report, it's been quiet, so far."

"Thanks, Barbara."

I scrambled around on my desk and found the reports.

"Hopefully, this may shed some light on the subject. I became curious as to why this was happening to only some and not all the prisoners. So, I got the prison psych to profile the pregnant prisoners, hoping to find a common thread."

"That's a great idea Dad. Good thinking."

"It got me thinking that they were targeting specific women with particular personality traits. Here, take a look at these." I passed the papers to Jane and watched her eyes scan the profiles.

She began nodding, "Makes sense. Yep, I get it," Jane said to herself.

"All these women are strong, resilient types. They have all suffered a tremendous loss that would normally send a person insane or suicidal. They fight on, no matter what. Age, race or religion doesn't seem to make any difference," I said as Jane continued to read on.

"You're right. They all seem strong and resilient. These seem to be the traits they may be looking for. It's got me thinking about the nuns now, what would they be looking for in them. Their faith is their strongest virtue but when I think about it, it was those who were very compassionate who fell pregnant. There must be others out there surely. They appear to be targeting women with specific traits that must come through the DNA, the genes. I wonder who else is out there, alone and pregnant?

"Just out of curiosity, can I ask you a question,

Jane?" "Of course you can. Ask away," Jane replied.

"What do you think we should do here? Considering what's happened," I asked eagerly for her insights.

"Mmmm... well, they're getting pregnant no matter what you do Dad. How they are doing that, I have no idea. Maybe it's the same way for all of us. I feel these beings are superior to us and there are still so many unknowns here. I think you have handled this really well, considering the circumstances. You are completely in the dark here and no doubt you don't want any of this getting out to the media," said Jane.

"Don't worry, that's been my priority but where to from here? Tell the women the truth? Not that they're going to believe any of this anyway."

"I don't see you really have a choice in any of this. What can you do? By the way, I could be wrong on this but I think the pregnancies seem to be going longer. They appear to be adapting each time, despite our fears."

"Oh great! Gee, I'm so excited. Can I have a front-row seat now please?" I said sarcastically, then looked at Jane intently and I began shaking my head in disbelief.

"What is it, Dad?" Jane questioned as she looked back at me.

"I just realised... you're a pregnant nun."

"You have a real way with words Dad. I was always one for surprises! You should know that."

"That's true," as we broke out laughing again.

My phone rang again.

"Yes, Barbara. What is it?"

"I have Preston Ridges from Benson Police Station on line two for you Warden."

"Thanks, Barbara you can put him through."

"Preston, how are you? I haven't heard from you in ages. Is there something wrong?"

"Thanks for taking my call, Joe. As a matter of fact there is. I need to ask for a favour?"

"Yes, I'm listening."

"Two young girls have just been brought into the Station and we are absolutely chockers here at present. We intervened between two rival bikie gangs and all the cells are overflowing with big burly bikies. I can't put these girls in here and I believe one of them is pregnant. To make things worse all our computers are down with a bloody virus so I haven't been able to process them either."

"So what do you want me to do about it, Preston?"

"Could you hold them in a cell for a few days until I can clean up this mess down here?"

"You know this goes against all protocols Preston."

"I know but I have no other options, Joe, besides they look harmless enough."

"We are damn near capacity here too. Alright just for the weekend... you hear... don't say a bloody word to anyone or you'll have me to deal with!"

"Loud and clear Joe. I'll send them over now. Thanks again I owe you one."

"Yeah, yeah I've heard that before. You haven't paid for your last one yet. What are the charges?"

"Some girl was stabbed outside the hospital. It doesn't look good; the girl is critical. These girls were the only two found at the scene. One is claiming the other one did it and she is innocent. You know how it goes?"

"Sounds familiar. Okay send them over I'll be waiting for them."

Within the hour, the girls arrived at the Prison.

"The two girls from the Police Station are here and in the interview room Warden."

"Great! That's all we need. Thanks, Barbara. Can you contact Hames and have them processed and assigned a cell? I'll see them shortly in the interview room," I sighed and swept my hand over my head in frustration.

"Of course, Warden. Consider it done," Barbara replied.

"Can you believe it, if we aren't already going through enough here, I've got to babysit for the Police?" I said looking up at the ceiling in thought.

"Did I overhear your conversation correctly Dad? Something about two girls and one is pregnant."

"This can't be happening. Please don't tell me this is related. I don't think I can cope with any more of this."

"Even more odd...something is telling me I need to go with you. Dad... it's so weird," said Jane getting out of her chair.

"Okay! Let's go and see who's arrived. Could it possibly get any more bizarre around here?" I replied as I got out of my chair.

We made our way down the corridors and through several security sliding doors. After a long walk, we arrived at the interview room. There were two girls seated in the room with two guards standing with their backs against the walls.

We entered the room, ending the girls argument.

"This is Sarah O'Connor and Lux Shields Warden," stated Officer Pyke, stepping forward, then stepping back against the wall.

"I'm Warden Walsh, this is my daughter, Jane. Due to unforeseen circumstances, you will be staying here, instead of the Police Station. We will do our best to accommodate you for the time being. The reports state you are both to be held here, pending further investigations."

"I can't believe this is happening," Sarah interrupted.

"Ah, yes, Sarah, I believe you're pregnant," I said.

"That's right Warden and I had nothing to do with this at all. I swear. This bitch stabbed my friend in cold blood and that's the truth!" Sarah shouted.

"Well, no witnesses have come forward, which makes it difficult for you. Unless Lux changes her story, we have a stabbing with both you girls at the scene claiming innocence. Anyway, I'm not here to judge you. I'm here to keep you safe until your trial. Okay. Any questions?"

"Can I speak to a lawyer?" asked Lux.

"Yes, we can see to that," I replied.

"Can I have my own cell, please? I'm pregnant and need some space!" Sarah pleaded.

"That may be difficult but I'll see what I can do," I said as I closed the reports.

"So, you're pregnant?" Jane asked Sarah.

"Yes, that's right."

"This might seem like a silly question but do you know the father?" Jane asked.

"You wouldn't believe me in a thousand years, so let's skip the chit chat and mother's club meeting, okay?" Sarah responded, slightly agitated.

"Okay girls, these Officers will show you to your cells. They will be temporary. I need time to shift a few things around, so leave it with me Sarah," I said.

"Thank you, Warden," Sarah replied and then despondently followed the guard to her cell. Lux walked off tall and almost proud of herself. It looked like she had done this all before.

Once they were out of earshot I turned to Jane, "Well, what do you think, Jane?"

"They're an interesting couple, that's for sure. There is a story and a half there. I don't get a good feeling with Lux."

"I agree," I paused, "what about Sarah?" I asked as we headed back to my office.

"I know why I was drawn here, Dad. Sarah is also pregnant perhaps the same way I am and I think she knows a lot more than she is telling us too. I can feel it."

"Don't you think that's odd?"

"What is, Dad?"

"Well... if she is pregnant, you all seem to be ending up in here, including you."

"Good point... yeah! You're right. That is strange," said Jane.

"I've got an idea. I'll move Sarah into a single cell and maybe you could visit her and get her to open up a little."

"Dad, I need to talk to her now. I have so many questions and I'm pretty sure she has the answers. I have found someone in the same position as me. What are the odds that we share something so unique? I can't describe it and I can't wait. I don't know how long I have before I give birth. Or she, for that matter. I need to talk to her now, Dad. I can't risk her getting transferred back to the Station and there's another thing-"

"Yes, I'm listening," I butted in, getting impatient.

"When I got close to Sarah my baby started moving around like crazy. It's as if they were trying to communicate with one another. It felt really strange and I could tell Sarah felt it too and she was doing her best to hide it, I'm sure of it."

"Wow! It just gets better and better doesn't it?" I said shaking my head in disbelief.

I had listened intently to everything Jane had just said and maybe she was right. It could also help me if I kept Sarah here longer and Jane was somehow able to uncover some answers.

"Okay, I'll put her in the infirmary now for the night. She'll have peace and quiet and be safe away from the other inmates. I'll send a guard with you."

"Is that necessary, Dad," Jane asked.

"Ah yes, it is, Jane and I will. I can't let you roam this prison unattended," I picked up my phone and called Barbara, "send Pyke into my office please Barbara."

"Yes Warden," Barbara replied.

"You have to be extremely careful Jane and don't get too close. You don't know that girl at all and she could well be lying. If you don't take this seriously, I will come in there with you. Pyke will have to remain outside at all times," I said protectively.

"I've got it, Dad," Jane said, with a big grin on her face, picking up on his protectiveness.

I ordered Pyke to take Jane down to see Sarah. As she walked into the infirmary, Sarah had just been escorted back from the shower block and was drying her hair. Pyke gave Sarah clean prison clothes and remained in the corridor, outside the infirmary, as ordered.

"Sarah! Can we talk?"

"Do I have a choice?" Sarah replied with attitude.

"Hey, I'm not the enemy here Sarah. We're both pregnant and still have our babies and when all the... oh, never mind," I said, mindful to keep calm.

"Fine... whatever!"

"Look, I was assuming you're in the same boat as me and-"

"What boat would that be?" Sarah interrupted.

"I'm too scared to say now. It's so bizarre and I don't want to freak you out any more than you already are."

"Sorry, I'm a little bit pissed off with being behind bars for something I didn't do! So, what are you trying to say?" Sarah said taking charge.

"Well, I'm not sure how to say this so I'll just come out with it. As weird as it might sound, I'm pregnant and I didn't have sex and... I have this strange feeling you are also... the same way. Pregnant that is, without having sex either?" I said, hoping I had not made a mistake by telling her.

"Yep, that's right. Pregnant to aliens. Is that what you're trying to ask me?" said Sarah.

"You're kinda blasé about it. Like it's no big deal."

"Really? You know me that well already, hey? I've just accepted it, that's all. It's out of our control anyway, don't you think?" said Sarah.

"True, but everyone else I know who is going through this is really freaking out?"

"Yeah! I know. But I'm not everybody else, am I?" Sarah said confidently.

"Do you think there are others out there in our position," I paused for a bit, "it is as though we've been drawn to this prison for a reason. Coincidence? I mean really what are the odds, Sarah?"

Sarah listened to everything I said and didn't bat an eyelid but now appeared less defensive.

"Before I go any further, I need that favour I spoke about earlier," she interrupted. "I have two friends in the Benson hospital, Red and Tina, I need to know if they are alright. Tina relies on me. I need you to let her know where I am and what's happened before she starts to freak out. She's a timid little thing. I've been looking out for her, you know, like a big sister and of course my friend Red, I need to know she's going to pull through after that bitch stabbed her."

"I'll call the hospital myself; you have my word. That's really sweet how you look out for Tina. Believe it or not, I used to be a nun."

Sarah was gob-smacked, her bottom jaw dropped.

"You can go ahead and laugh! That's fine. Anyway, in the convent nuns were falling pregnant, the same as us, then all miscarried. I became pregnant again and decided to leave. It's my guess the other nuns maybe pregnant again. I've been doing my best to piece this all together, Sarah. As you can imagine, the convent kept it quiet for obvious reasons and Dad, the Warden, has had prisoners going through exactly the same thing here with all of them miscarrying the other night. He said it was a blood bath, a real nightmare and he's doing his best to keep it all under wraps. I can't find any answers and until now have only been able to second guess everything," I said.

Sarah was looking at me intently.

"Can you help me, Sarah?" I asked kindly.

"I did wonder if others were going through this. At first, I was petrified but now I'm okay with it. There is a group of us and we kinda just met and stayed together and have gone through similar things."

"Okay Sarah, here's a question for you. What do you think you all have in common? I mean, is there something unique about you and your friends?"

"Yeah! Funny, I've thought about this a lot too, why us and why would they pick us? As far as I could tell we're all virgins, young, innocent and open-minded," replied Sarah who was now opening up.

"Anything else spring to mind, anything at all?" I asked.

"Yes, there is. The girls I've spoken to, appear to be highly intelligent as well. What about the nuns?" queried Sarah.

"Well, I guess if I had to pinpoint it, I'd say we all have a strong faith and are highly compassionate. I took a peek at Dad's reports on the prisoners and it appears they are strong and resilient and their will is unbreakable, the ones chosen that is," I pointed out.

"Wait! There you have it! These have to be the characteristics they are searching for, surely," Sarah paused, "can I ask you something, Jane? Have you been scared at any time?" Sarah asked.

"I was scared at first but I don't feel threatened by them anymore. I can only go by what I feel, like intuitively. I've kept an open mind and that's why I believe I'm still pregnant. I can now calm myself when I get overwhelmed and I do not allow my fears to override me." I paused, "I've Gotta say, Sarah, are you sure it's not strength as the reason they chose you? You have been through so much and for someone so young!"

"Yeah! Well I had to grow up... and fast. Getting pregnant at 15 is not exactly the news your parents want to hear, especially devout Christians!" replied Sarah.

"Yeah, but if there'd been a boy involved, at least that would have made some sense, right?" I asked.

"No, not really, they didn't understand. They didn't believe I was still a virgin. Red, Tina and the other girls all went through the same thing, running away was our only option."

"I know, it must have been really hard for all of you." I was finding myself in awe of Sarah. She is so strong I wish I had her strength.

"Intuitively, how do you feel about these beings?" I asked.

"Well, we don't know, do we. I can only go by how I feel with one inside me. But you know what? We've been lied to all our lives, even the government's take on UFOs and aliens is a pack of lies. The governments have brainwashed us into what they want us to believe.

I remember being told about the native American Indians and how they were portrayed as savages, then I learned about their side of the story. I know who I'd believe. I really feel these beings need our help desperately, as much as we need theirs," Sarah said passionately.

"I know it sounds kooky and weird right but I've had dreams about it. I didn't want to believe it for ages, now I do. I just know I'm going to be part of something phenomenal. If it goes wrong and I'm wrong, so be it. I'll take my chances," Sarah said with conviction.

"Wow! I knew you were different as soon as I met you. You would make a great leader." I said.

"I'm just following my hunches and like you, I didn't really have a choice. I've just got on with it and had to grow up really fast. Sink or swim, you know? I realised I was chosen after my initial fears subsided. Instead of rebelling and denying, I embraced it. I was honoured by it and accepted it as my destiny. Where's all this going? I have no idea but I'm up for the challenge and I'm willing to see it through to the end," Sarah spoke with real conviction.

"What if none of the others get pregnant again? It's just us?" I said.

"That has crossed my mind. Oh, and I almost forgot something, a bizarre thing happened when Tina and Red aborted last time. Their babies were either taken or they simply disappeared. Both times I was right there and it's as if the babies vanished into thin air. I have a theory they are running out of time and because they were more advanced this time, they were able to take them and keep them alive. How's that for a theory?" said Sarah.

We spent the next hour discussing the baby's disappearance, our dreams, our journey, and experiences but most of all why we are here. Sarah was so insightful and inspirational and a real leader. I understand why she was chosen.

"Can I come back and see you again Sarah?" I asked.

"Sure, I'd like that," Sarah nodded her head. "I feel we will come together again, soon," as I left the room, she went back to brushing her hair. I was led back to Dad's office by my chaperone, Pyke.

"Hey Janie, you okay? asked Dad, "how did it go with Sarah? Did she give you any answers?"

"Actually, she did. She's amazing Dad and only 16!" I replied.

"Really! What did she say?"

"She believes the other girls and herself were chosen because they are highly intelligent, open-minded and virgins. She believes these beings are purposefully breeding a new bloodline selecting women with very particular traits. So, it's sort of a bit of us and a bit of them."

"What like a hybrid?" Dad asked.

"Yes, exactly!"

"Listen, Jane, sorry to change the subject but I have a favour to ask. The women will be waking from their induced slumber, angry and wanting answers. I cannot hide what's going on here any longer. In truth, I didn't know. I have been in the dark here the whole time until you arrived. I cannot keep this a secret any longer and I need to come clean with them, especially now you have some answers. To be honest with you, I'm very anxious. These women are not going to understand, nor will they believe what I'm about to tell them. Can you help me?"

"Dad, there's only one person who can tell them and it has to be Sarah. There is something about her. I know they'll listen to her. Plus, she has been through it." I said strongly.

"She's just a teenager. You're a woman. They'll listen to you." Dad argued back.

"No Dad. You're wrong. You're missing the point. When she talks, she talks with passion and purpose. She is your spokesperson; they'll listen to her, I promise you. If they don't, I will try but not before Sarah."

"Not much of a choice. Do you think she will do it? I can't say I'm totally comfortable with this so please make sure you are close by if this goes south, I may call on you if this doesn't go down well."

I immediately went with Dad to ask Sarah. She was lying down with her head looking up to the ceiling, deep in thought, no doubt processing everything that had been taking place.

"Hi Sarah, how are you feeling?" Dad asked.

"I've been better," Sarah said quietly.

"Jane and I have been talking and there is something I'd like to ask you."

"Yeah, I'm listening Warden."

"Okay probably best if I just come out with it. Sarah, I'd like you to tell the women here all you know. I have done my best to control this situation but I'm struggling with the whole alien thing, to be honest. In fact, I'm still trying to come to terms with our female prisoners getting pregnant and yet there are no males around. Who's going to believe me? So, I've been keeping them in isolation and away from the general population, for as long as possible. The other night however there were dead babies everywhere. We did what we could and sedated the women, for their peace of mind. They are now starting to stir and I'm assuming they will be angry and wanting answers. They deserve the truth and Jane believes you are the right person to tell them. We both feel they will listen to you. Will you help us please?"

We both stared at her patiently, waiting for her response as she listened intently. She stood up and walked away, turning her back on us. After a long silence, she turned around and demanded.

"I'll do it on one condition. That I'm allowed to go to the hospital to see my friends."

"I promised you I would call them Sarah I just haven't had the chance yet!" I butted in.

"It's okay, Jane. I believe you but I'd rather see them for myself. As soon as the talk is finished, you'll take me to the hospital so I can see them. Deal?" asked Sarah.

"You've got a deal and I will make all the arrangements. However, you will be escorted there and back," Dad said firmly.

"Okay then," Sarah nodded in agreement.

On Dad's orders, an announcement was then made over the speakers requesting all inmates to assemble in the main hall to listen to the Warden's message.

As the room filled with prisoners, the tension could be felt with loud and angry tones of frustration and rebellion in the air. The women wanted to know the truth about the macabre series of events that had been taking place in the prison over the past weeks.

Dad tried to speak over the heckling. Then he grabbed the microphone and demanded the prisoners to quieten down. The room slowly went quiet.

"You have all been patient and understanding about what's been going on here over the last weeks. I urge you to keep an open mind to what you are about to hear."

The room erupted in angry outbursts of women yelling abuse and demanding the truth.

"No more lies!" one shouted.

"How did we get pregnant?" demanded an inmate.

"Keep your screws away from us. We're being raped," they continued with their rants.

"They weren't babies. They were mutants," screamed another.

"Tell us the truth you bastard," yelled another from inside the crowd of prisoners.

Dad tried desperately to calm them down. "Okay, okay! That's enough! I know you're angry and I don't blame you but I need you to be quiet now so I can explain it to you."

But it was no use. The angry outpouring drowned out anything Dad tried to say. He threw his hands in the air in defeat and stepped aside. Prisoners became even angrier with shouts and abuse coming from every direction. The prisoners began waving their hands in the air chanting, "Kill the screws! Kill the screws!" It was loud and it was ugly. It was about to erupt in a full-blown riot as the guards were on alert, getting edgy and reaching for their tasers.

Then, bravely, Sarah walked out in front of all of them and she just stood there, staring at them. Showing no fear, she waited patiently until the noise quietened.

One prisoner whispered to the next to quieten down and so on until the room was quiet. She continued to wait until some random heckling in the room had ceased and there was absolute silence. She didn't seem intimidated by them or her surroundings.

Then she spoke.

"My name is Sarah O'Connor. I know you are angry and you want answers. I don't blame you, so do I. The same thing has happened to me."

The room was so silent, you could hear a pin drop. Sarah had their full attention and they were tuned into her voice. Sarah continued to talk, as she walked up and down in front of them.

"This is my story, I hope it helps you in some way. I was first impregnated at 15. I didn't even know what sex was. So no, I hadn't slept with any boys, I was still a virgin. I miscarried on a school sport's day in front of a packed gymnasium. I lost a lot of blood and passed out. I woke up in a hospital with no idea what was going on. My parents were ashamed of me, the nurses didn't believe me, no one would, I didn't know what else to do so I left home at 15."

Apart from the odd murmur here and there, the prisoners remained silent.

"Well, you're all grown women, perhaps you could tell me how it felt when you miscarried and you didn't even know you were pregnant in the first place. I was 15 when this happened, I should have been enjoying my teens."

Sarah paused, maybe to make sure they were all listening, "I know how bizarre this sounds. I know at least three other girls, my age, this has happened to. So you are not alone and I believe there may be others. I know some of you are beside yourselves worrying and question constantly why this is happening. It's hell scary... right?"

Sarah still had their full attention and she continued to do her best to explain what was happening.

"The same thing is happening to others, outside these walls, it's not just happening to you. The guards in here are not drugging and raping you. I mean, if I was you, that would be the most logical explanation, right?"

"How do we know it isn't the screws? How else could this have happened? It's gotta be the fuckin' screws!" yelled an angry inmate, which incited the others to vent their anger and the room became loud again with inmates shouting their injustices.

"That's enough... shut up and let her finish or I'll throw the bloody lot of you in solitary," Dad shouted, as the loud yelling began to slowly subside. Sarah waited patiently until the room went quiet.

"The Warden didn't know how or why this was happening. He has done his best to contain this and stop the media from getting involved. Otherwise, you would all be lab rats in some research facility by now, while the FBI carries out tests on you to find out all they can and why this is happening."

That comment tipped them over the edge and the room broke out again in loud angry outbursts. Sarah waited for them to calm down, so she could finish what she wanted to say but then eventually decided against it and turned her back on them and walked away as Pyke led her back to the infirmary.

"That's all we have to say at this time. Guards send all prisoners back to their duties," Dad yelled into the microphone to end the angry chants and outbursts.

Dad and I made our way back to the infirmary, to check in on Sarah.

"I'm impressed, Jane said you were good. That must have been very difficult for you to stand up in front of that hostile crowd. You nearly got through to them. Maybe you can talk to them again in a few days, they may need some time to get their heads around this," Dad explained.

"I'm happy to do that but I'd like to go to the hospital now," Sarah asked.

"You don't waste any time, do you?"

"I don't have time to waste and my friends need me."

"You delivered and so will I. I take it you want to go right now?"

"Yes, I would."

"Can I trust you won't do anything stupid? I'm sorry but I still have to cuff you, Sarah."

"No. I don't want any trouble either, Warden."

"So, I have your word?" Dad said firmly.

"You have my word Warden and as long as you trust your guards, you have nothing to worry about, do you?"

"In a perfect world no but we don't live in a perfect world, do we, Sarah?"

"No, we don't Warden. That's why I'm still inside a prison for being in the wrong place at the wrong time. Pregnant and waiting for justice to prevail. I'll see you when I return, Warden."

"I'll have the guards escort you there shortly. I need to make the necessary arrangements at the hospital. The guards will wait outside the room and then bring you straight back. Are we clear?"

"Crystal."

"Jane has asked to go with you. She would like to meet your friends and be there to support you as well. Are you okay with that?"

"Whatever," said Sarah impatiently.

We were escorted through the front doors of the hospital with a guard either side of us, which was not a good look. I watched people's faces imagining the worst possible scenarios. They side-stepped around us or turned their heads in fear, thinking Sarah may lunge at them at any second.

Sarah's bright orange overalls, handcuffs, and now clearly protruding stomach didn't help our cause.

Standing at the front desk I could feel all eyes were on us. After the desk nurse nervously gave us the room number, we made our way to Red's room. To our surprise, Tina was at her bedside, her arm was in a sling supporting her shoulder. Red was not conscious. She lay there lifeless with tubes in her nose and throat and drips in her arm, heavily drugged.

Tina lunged from her chair when she saw Sarah.

"Oh, Sarah! It's so good to see you. Where have you been? I've been looking everywhere for you, asking everyone if they have seen you. You vanished without a trace," she said excitedly without taking a breath, "why are there prison guards with you and why are you in cuffs, Sarah? What's happened?" Tina asked upset.

"It's a long story, Tina, I'll explain later, I don't have a lot of time," Sarah said as she managed to lift her arms over Tina's head and give her a warm hug.

"Are you okay, Tina? Where are you staying?"

"Yes, Sarah but what about you? I don't understand!"

"Tina listen to me. I'll be okay I promise you. There's been a mistake and I'm just waiting to be released. False charges... trust me, it's fine."

"Okay... well when I was released from ER after they put my shoulder put back in, I walked outside right into the middle of that chaos... with what had happened to Red. They let me stay by her bedside as her friend and family. I was playing hide and seek with the nurses."

"So, what's the update with Red, then? Is she going to be okay?" Sarah asked Tina.

"No one knows yet, Sarah. They said there were complications in surgery. Now it's a waiting game to see how she pulls through," said Tina as she touched Red's arm.

I looked over at Sarah and could see she had become distracted in her thoughts and worried about something.

"What is it, Sarah? I don't like that look on your face. What's wrong?" Tina queried.

"Red is my one and only witness. Scarface was the one who did this to Red but the cops nabbed both of us and we're being held at Benson Prison until the hearing."

"Oh, shit, Sarah! But it wasn't you! What are you going to do?" said Tina.

"Do you want to try telling them that?" said Sarah.

Sarah looked at Red, staring at her lifeless body and wondering if they would ever talk again. She leant in closer and whispered into her ear, "You need to pull through this, Red, stop being such a pussy. Anything for attention, hey... please get through this Red and come and find me when you do," then she kissed her forehead.

Sarah turned to say goodbye to Tina and took her hands,

"You need to be strong for both of you. Take care of yourself Tina and Red, okay? And don't do anything stupid you hear me... I'll try and keep in touch but you know where to find me, okay?"

Tina hugged Sarah and cried, "Don't go... please! I'll tell them it wasn't you... please don't leave me."

The guards guided us out as Sarah raised her cuffed hands in despair to Tina as we walked down the corridor. My mind suddenly opened up to the possibility of Sarah escaping,

"Don't do it, Sarah, it will make you a fugitive on the run and it will be seen as admitting guilt," I said concerned.

"Aren't we the psychic one now?" said Sarah who looked at me, then turned around and continued walking.

We returned to Benson without incident. Dad was pleasantly surprised. I believe he expected Sarah to try something as well. I don't think anyone likes being held captive but it's safe here for Sarah and people know what's going on here. If she gave birth in the hospital, the staff would not know what they were in for. The prison can at least keep her safe and deliver her baby when the time came.

Chapter Twelve: Prison Blues

"Barbara, can you send for Hames? I need to see her right away."

"Onto it, Warden. Paging now."

I was pacing up and down my office like a caged lion, I hate feeling helpless. I like to attack, set things in place and be prepared. Not wait around like a sitting duck.

Barbara knocked on my door and said, "Hames is here to see you, sir."

"Send her in Barbara and hold all calls and I don't want to see any visitors today," I ordered.

"You sent for me Warden?" Hames said quietly as she entered my office.

"Yes, Hames. Come and sit down."

"I'm fine standing Warden, thanks," she politely replied.

"Here is the list of all the women who did not get pregnant. I want them moved to C block. I know that's a big ask and will take some organising but I need it done now. Do you hear me?"

"Warden, that'll create a lot of unnecessary tension and trouble amongst the prisoners. I would really advise against this."

"I don't remember asking for your opinion, Hames. If you can't follow an order, perhaps I can get Pyke back in here, who is good at following instructions."

"Just trying to make your life easier, Warden."

"Noted, now get to it."

I knew this would cause friction but I didn't want a repeat of the chaos last time. It was unfathomable. If it divides the prison in two, so be it. I am confident we could be better prepared this way. Plus, the others don't need to hear the screaming and all that terrifying commotion.

There was another knock on my door and I picked up my phone immediately.

"What part of 'I didn't want to see anyone else today' didn't you understand Barbara!" and then slammed down the phone down on my desk.

"Someone's woken up grumpy this morning," Jane said tentatively as she entered my office.

"Oh, I'm so sorry honey I should have checked to see who it was. Grumpy is an understatement. What are you doing here? I thought you were going to rest today?" I asked.

"I can't rest even if I wanted to. Dad I'd like to talk to Sarah again if that's okay with you?" Jane replied.

"Yes of course. Guards tell me she looks down today, a visit by you would be good for her. I'll send Pyke to go with you."

"That won't be necessary Dad, honest."

"Jane, that's the only way you will be seeing her. No buts about it, okay?" I demanded.

"Okay grumpy pants," she said as she smiled and left my office.

I grabbed my phone to inform Barbara.

"Barbara send Pyke to go with Jane immediately... please," I said in an apologetic tone.

I waited for Pyke to arrive outside Dad's office. Then we made our way down to see Sarah.

"Well this looks like a private party, or can anyone join in?" I said on approaching Sarah and seeing her despondent look.

"Have you come to join Miss Happy?" Sarah responded in a sarcastic voice.

"This is not like you. Is there anything I can do to help? You know a problem shared is a problem halved."

"Thanks for caring but no, I don't think so. I've been on the run and unsettled for so long now I haven't really had a chance to take all this in. I didn't think it could get any worse than this. Here I am stuck in a prison while a good friend is fighting for her life. I can't even be there to support her and let's not forget I'm becoming a mother to an alien baby soon of which I have no idea how I'm going to cope with that," yelled Sarah who immediately began to calm herself.

"Well, I'm not sharing a cell but I still feel like a prisoner. I do understand what it feels like to lose friends and being a mother soon which is also scaring the shit out of me. I mean this is my clumsy way of saying you're not alone in this. But I get it, it's easy to say this from the other side of a cell," I said doing my best to reassure her, though I wasn't sure it was helping.

"It's funny, isn't it? Some people choose their paths in life and some have it chosen for them," Sarah said staring at the ceiling.

"I think this is the part where I'm supposed to say something really profound, isn't it? Especially being an ex-nun. Guess what, I don't have anything," I said throwing my arms up in the air.

We both had a laugh which broke the sombre mood. After the laughter subsided, I continued.

"I believe some people never grow in a lifetime, Sarah. This experience has stretched you, tested you and through all those challenges, look who you have become! You don't grow if you are not challenged. How you respond to life's challenges defines you as a person. You can either shrink and wither away or rise stronger and wiser. Becoming someone capable of handling anything as you prepare to face your next challenge. Did you know Dad asked me to speak to those women, Sarah? I didn't decline as such. I just told him there was someone far better to deliver the message: you, Sarah. You were so busy in the moment; you didn't even see how brilliant you were. The inmates were hanging onto every word you said. They respected you and listened to you. What you did yesterday was nothing short of amazing. You took on a group of angry, hardened prisoners. I guarantee you, they would have heckled and destroyed anyone less than you." I said passionately.

"Thank you, Jane. I needed that"

We hugged each other in a supportive embrace.

"I have no idea what to expect either Sarah, with the birth and afterwards. Just remember I'm here for you, no matter what?" I said warmly.

"That's the best thing I've heard in a long time. You may see strength; I'm still scared shitless!"

"Well, at least we have each other," I reassured Sarah.

"Have you seen anyone give birth to these babies? I really want to know what I'm in for," I asked.

Sarah replied, "I've seen a few to know they can be scary. Some babies were hideous but were premature. I think the more advanced they become, the more human they could look. Perhaps they can change from one species to another or the fetus is fighting within itself, like am I human or alien?"

Looking concerned Sarah continued, "I still have trouble believing all this, even though it's happening. I've always believed in UFOs and have sort of felt there had to be other life forms out there but now I'm pregnant to an alien. Do I sound like a freak? A real wacko? Because if I heard anyone else speak these words, I would kinda make some distance between them and me, fast!"

I chuckled. "Yep, we can't blame any of those women or girls for reacting the way they did," I said, "it takes a massive stretch of the imagination to even allow yourself to feel comfortable with this. I wish we could talk to them, meet them... to understand them and make sense of all this."

"Be careful what you wish for, Jane."

"Well, wouldn't you like some answers, Sarah?" I asked.

"Right now, what I want is to get out of this prison. That would be a good start."

"I can only imagine," I said sympathetically.

"Listen, Jane. As I said before, I'm going with the flow with all this. There's so much more I need to understand. I feel these beings are friendly and I meant every word I said to those women back there. Make no mistake though, if I'm wrong and these aliens aren't friendly, I'm not going to run away," Sarah said defiantly.

Sarah continued, "If I have gone through all this to be betrayed by something that puts my life or my friend's lives in danger, I will fight them. Sorry, Jane, I don't mean to scare you. Just being totally upfront with you and forewarning you, in case it happens. I like to put all my cards on the table."

"Well, I certainly wasn't expecting that. Let's hope they are friendly." I said feeling a bit startled.

Sarah put her hands to her mouth and gasped.

"What is it, Sarah?"

"Oh my God, of course! It makes sense... a prison... a convent. They're choosing somewhere safe to have these young ones. You can't just walk into a prison or a convent. Both these institutions would safeguard themselves from this information getting out to the public.

They are so clever to have drawn us all here. This is no coincidence. They have planned all this. I'm sure of it."

Sarah continued, "I'm intuitively picking up thoughts from the baby. They're developing and growing extremely fast. It won't be nine months... it's going to be more like... ten weeks."

"You're kidding! That is exactly what I'm picking up too!" I said and then blessed myself with the sign of the cross, "I don't think I'm ready."

"You'll be fine. Believe in yourself, Jane. Can I ask you a personal question?"

"Something tells me you're going to anyway. I can feel something deep coming on."

"Why did you become a nun? I mean... I know that's a personal question but you're young... didn't you want a career and family?" asked Sarah.

"You're asking me to go somewhere I don't like," I replied sharply.

"Yeah! I get it, sorry. It's okay. Don't worry about it. Just forget I asked," Sarah apologised.

"No, actually that's not fair. You have been more than upfront with me. I'm just a very private person that's all and the less people know about you the better, I always say."

I paused and took a deep breath. "Where do I start? Okay, do you know what it's like to be invisible? Like when you're in a room and no one knows you're there? Like you don't even exist in their eyes. You feel so small, worthless, like a piece of dust that could be blown out of the room by a puff of wind and no one would be the wiser you were ever there. I grew up in an orphanage and bounced from one foster home to another. Even when I hit puberty, I was never even noticed by one boy. It left me feeling like damaged goods until I decided to do something about it."

"What? Don't keep me in suspense," demanded Sarah.

"I became the school slut, that's what I did and had every boy in that class lining up to get his rocks off."

"You little harlot! No way! Not innocent little Jane," Sarah said surprised.

"I loved the attention. It felt so good to be wanted and I couldn't stop. It became an addiction. I would stay out all night, never even telling my parents where I was. I put them through hell. Like all wrecks, I had to crash somewhere. That's when I got pregnant with a boy, imagine that? My parents aged twenty years in that small amount of time. You can imagine they were crushed from my behaviour and Mum would avoid people just to protect herself from the cruel whispers. After destroying everything I ever cared about and ending up pregnant, I didn't have a clue what to do. I couldn't live with the guilt of killing something that was my fault, so I did a runner and ended up giving birth to a stillborn in some lonely alleyway, near the convent. Luckily, I was found by the nuns. They gave me medical attention and allowed me to stay. So began my new life, undoing all my sins and wrong-doings by being of service to God and others."

Sarah looked spellbound, "Shit that's quite a story... I never would have guessed that."

"Yeah, sure is. I left home pregnant and came home the same way. What a legend," I said sarcastically.

"So, what happened to your parents?" asked Sarah.

"Well, you know Dad, he's a good man. He always tried hard to fix things and make life better for Mum but she only ever wanted a child of her own. Apparently, after I left, they slowly became distant. Dad buried himself in work and continued to work longer and longer hours, never switching off. He became married to his job. It happened slowly, he never even noticed or maybe he did. Mum lost everything she ever wanted and blamed herself. They were so lost in their pain. Now.... life in the convent, that's another story, I'll save that for another time," I said adding a bit of a spark to liven up our talk.

"You call me a hero, come on, you had a really difficult childhood. You're too hard on yourself Jane."

"Well, you see Sarah, I was a really rough rock and years of prayer and asking for forgiveness, the rough edges were slowly polished. I finally grew up and took responsibility for all my actions and made peace with my childhood."

"Okay, now it's your turn, I want to know how you became Sarah O'Connor."

"There's not a lot to tell, I can assure you," Sarah said smiling.

"Come on, I'd love to know more about you, that's all."

"I've never spoken about this to anyone. No one has ever really given a shit to ask."

"Okay, here I am asking," Jane said.

"Shit, where do I start. Okay, well I grew up in the shadow of my sister who was bullied for so long at school she took her own life..."

I gasped and instinctively put my hand on my mouth, "Oh Fuck! I mean shit, I'm so sorry Sarah I had no idea. That must have been horrible!"

"Guess who found her hanging from the garage ceiling cold and blue?"

"Oh my god, Sarah. I don't know what to say!" as I still had my mouth covered in shock.

"So, then I get to watch my parents self-destruct for years, while my sister's bullies turn their attention onto me," Sarah's voice began to break a little.

"I'm sorry, Sarah. I didn't mean to upset you," I said apologising.

"Upset me? How can you possibly upset me, Jane? I've learnt to overcome those feelings."

"Perhaps all your struggles in life were preparing you for what was coming?" I asked.

"I've heard our lives are perfectly scripted. Look, I don't want to make a big thing about it, okay? You asked and I've told you enough. I really don't want to go into any more details. I accept it, you know. I'm not after sympathy, making excuses or anything. Just doing my best to get on with it, okay?" Sarah had become defensive.

"Okay, I hear you. God forbid you would ever seek help or confide in someone," I said sarcastically.

"I can hear daddy calling, Jane. Best you go!"

"So that's where we are leaving it? I share everything with you and you just give me a little? Someone starts getting close to you and you shut them out," I was a little annoyed.

"Why are you turning this into something that it's not? Can't you just respect my choices?" Sarah replied.

"Yes... yes, of course, I can. It's just that... I'll shut up now. I've got to go," I got up and walked out of the cell. I put my hand up to wave goodbye as Pyke led me back to Dad's office.

Chapter Thirteen: Freedom at a Cost

Questions swirled around and around in my head. There was no letting up and being cooped up in here wasn't helping. I was worried about Tina and Red. Time has come to a standstill in here. My anger towards Scarface began to seethe inside me once again. Jane's words, 'maybe you're exactly where you ought to be right now,' kept repeating in my head. I wanted my freedom back. I hated not being in control of my destiny, waiting for it to unfold.

The baby's movements were getting stronger every day. Some days my stomach felt like a punching bag, as this baby grew equally restless and wanted out.

Talking to Jane did get me thinking of my parents. I often wondered how they were going. What they were doing and if they were okay. It would be so easy to lose it right now. That's why I didn't want to revisit my past, in my last conversation with Jane. I was way too vulnerable and I needed to stay strong and focussed.

One thing that has become crystal clear to me is the longer I have been pregnant the more perceptive I have become. I can hear them talking to me, like little whispers in my head and I've been getting the same message for a while now. I now understood it was time to get out of prison, as soon as possible. No sooner had I got that message; the Warden entered my cell. He had a very concerned look on his face. I immediately felt uneasy.

"What is it, Warden?" I asked.

He looked at me and turned away before letting out a huge sigh, "Sarah, I'm sorry, I have some bad news to tell you."

"What's wrong? Tell me!" I pleaded loudly.

He turned back to make eye contact with me and the look on his face spoke volumes.

"Oh my God! It's Red, isn't it? Please no!" I immediately placed my arms around my stomach, to protect my baby, "please God, no!"

"I've just received a call from the hospital. The wound was more severe than first thought and there were complications with the surgery. It's not looking good Sarah," explained the Warden sympathetically.

I could not believe this was happening. I really thought Red was going to pull through.

"Again, I'm so sorry Sarah... is there anything I can do for you? Put you in touch with anyone? Anything, Sarah, just tell me and I'll do my best to help."

"Anything, Warden?" I said sobbing.

"For you, Sarah? Yes. I know you have been wrongfully caught up in all this and you have helped me tremendously. So, yes. Name it."

"I need to see Red. She needs me."

"You realise this is a difficult decision for me."

"Yes, I know but I didn't let you down last time," I said.

I had created a dilemma for the Warden. If I didn't return, he would be in deep trouble and he knew it. He also knew I had more of a reason now to make a run for it.

"Okay, Sarah. I owe you that much and you kept your word last time, so I'm trusting you will keep it again this time. Same rules as last time, you will be under strict supervision. You know the drill."

"Yes, I do and thank you, Warden. She's a good friend and I need to be by her side."

"I understand. Just remember our deal, that's all I ask," said the Warden firmly.

"I do have one more favour, if I may. I don't want to go in my prison clothes this time. It's not a good look and I haven't been charged yet. Can I put my clothes on?" I asked.

"You know how to push your luck, O'Connor. Alright, you can go in your clothes but don't do anything stupid. I've had enough trouble to last me an eternity!"

This was my opportunity. I needed to find a way to lose the guards at the hospital. My mind was focussed on an escape plan but first I had to see the girls. I just hope Red can hang on until I get there.

The Warden was true to his word and acted quickly. I quickly got changed into my clothes.

We arrived at the hospital and the guards opened the doors to the back of the van where I sat alone busily scheming.

"Okay, O'Connor, out! Don't try anything stupid. The Warden assured us you wouldn't give us any trouble and has authorised us to remove your cuffs only when you see your friend. We will be on you like a second skin O'Connor."

"Got it," I snapped.

We walked through the hospital front doors and down the corridors. We knew where to go. I was scouring opportunities – left, right and centre, whilst being careful not to attract attention to myself.

We entered Red's room and as promised my cuffs were removed. I couldn't see Tina. I made my way over to Red, under the watchful eye of the guard. She looked so beautiful and peaceful. I reached for her hand under the sheet. My eyes welled up and I whispered,

"You didn't deserve this Red. You always told me you were gonna go out on your terms. Your way. This wasn't the way it was supposed to go. What am I gonna do without my rebel, hey Red? Damn it Red I need you; we all need you," I cried softly.

I kissed her forehead and continued to stare at her while stroking her red hair as tears were running down my cheeks blurring my vision. Memories flowed through my mind of our time together. As I gazed at her in silence, I could hear a loud commotion in the background followed by a gunshot.

"Pyke! Go and see what's going on out there. I'll stay here with her."

Pyke acknowledged and then left the room. Another shot was fired. People were screaming. Panic was rife.

"Stay here, O'Connor. Don't leave this room. You got it?" ordered the guard.

As he shouted those words at me, he cocked his gun and then carefully poked his head around the doorway. He held his gun in the air at arm's length and cautiously left the room and made his way down the corridor. It was chaos, now is the time. I gave Red a big kiss and quickly made my way to the outside window and managed to open it. I could see it led to a garden area and then to the streets. As I climbed out the window, I looked back to hear the sound of Red's heart monitor flatlining, "Goodbye Red," I whispered and then dropped to the path below and walked briskly away trying not to look suspicious.

I couldn't believe my luck. It's as if someone had just planned the whole thing. I didn't care. I was free and I wasn't going back to prison. I needed to get away from this area fast, so I made my way down some side streets searching for an unlocked car. I knew this was wishful thinking but hell, I was desperate.

I continued looking into each car walking as fast as I could. I ran across the road to check out the cars on the other side. In an instant, I turned, my shocked eyes were staring at the windscreen of a small truck, closing in on me. I could hear the screeching of its tyres as the driver slammed on his brakes with all his might. It hit me and I flew up onto the bonnet. As I lay face down on the bonnet, the noise of the screeching tyres was reverberating in my ears. I could smell burnt rubber as I slowly opened my eyes to see the blurred image of a startled old man, staring straight back at me through his windscreen. He jumped out of the truck to see if I was okay. He was a large man, wearing overalls and had a huge grey beard. He looked like a farmer.

"What the hell were you thinking girly? You came from nowhere! Are you okay?" asked the driver.

"I think so, I'm sorry," I replied, short of breath and holding my pounding head.

"Were you running from something?"

"No... no. Nothing like that. I just didn't see you. Sorry if I scared you. Um, where are you going, if you don't mind me asking?" I said, rubbing my sore head.

"Hell, I'm just heading back to my farm north of here. Just came in for supplies."

"Great... you're heading north of here?" my head was sore but I couldn't stop smiling.

"I couldn't bother you for a ride, could I?"

"I better get you to a hospital first and get you checked out. You may be concussed or something," said the driver concerned.

"No, I'm fine. Honest! I'm kinda in a hurry to see my family. My sister's having a baby and I promised I would make it home to see her in time, for the birth.... you know?"

"Are you sure, girly? Well, I guess that's the least I can do for nearly running you down like that. You scared the wits out of me. Damn it girl, if it didn't take another 20 years off my life," he said.

"I'm so sorry. I have had a really rough day and-"

"Are you pregnant, girly?" he butted in, staring at my stomach, "the baby could be hurt."

"It's fine. We're both fine, I promise you. It's still moving. I just hit my bum and my head. Oh, there it goes! It just kicked again," I said doing my best to distract him.

"You seem kinda young to be having a baby. Are you sure you're okay?" he said seeming very concerned.

"No... no! I mean, you're right, I'm young but not in any trouble. It was an accident, a happy accident if there's such a thing. I'm on my way home to tell Mum and my sister the good news. Surprise them both."

"Oh, what's her name? I might know the family. Small towns up where I come from."

"Do you mind if I don't? We both know how fast word gets around these small towns and I don't want to spoil my surprise."

"True. Well, I wouldn't want to be the reason for spoiling your surprise now, would I? You just don't look that familiar that's all and I know most of the folk up there. Lived there all my life, yah know?"

"I'm sorry. What's your name?" I quickly asked, attempting to change the subject.

"Jebediah Harris. Lived in these parts all my life. Folks just call me Jed."

"Jed, I have had an awful day on top of getting run over," I said with a smirk, "if you could give me a ride north, I'd very much appreciate it. I've got a really bad headache and would just love to sit quietly for a while. Would that be okay with you?" I asked holding my head.

"So, what am I going to call you girly?" he said

"I'm Sarah. I left these parts a long time ago, that's why you probably won't recognise me."

"Well then girly, I'm glad to meet you and I'm more than happy to give you a ride. I have a long trip ahead of me so hop in and let's get going. Godda warn yah, I'm a bit of a chatterbox, so my wife is always telling me."

"You wouldn't happen to have any headache tablets, Jed?" I asked. My head was throbbing.

"As a matter of fact, I do. There should be some in the glove box compartment and there should be a bottle of water at your feet. Always keep 'em handy, don't like headaches."

I scrambled through his glove box and found them. As we drove off, I was relieved to be heading out of town and away from the prison. I knew the Warden will be pissed at me but I'm not to blame for all of this anyway. God, it feels good to be free again.

I could not get out of Benson fast enough and as we finally passed the 'Thank you for visiting Benson' sign, I could feel the headache tablets start to kick in. True to his word, Jed did not stop talking and began telling me his whole life story. He loved the company. As much as I wanted to tell him to shut up, I was grateful for the ride and chose to just stare out the window watching the scenery blur past my heavy eyes. I could feel the heaviness and stress begin to lift off my shoulders with every mile we drove.

My mind began to calm, ever so slightly. The reality of losing my friend Red meant I now have no witness and I'm officially a fugitive, is starting to sink in. I'm screwed.

Way to go, Sarah! I have no money again, nowhere to stay again and about to give birth, but the upside is I'm free and out of the prison.

Between the drone of Jed's engine and his slow, monotonous chatter, my eyelids became too heavy to stay open any longer. They finally surrendered and the cogs in my mind slowly, slowly stopped turning. Jed may be a chatterbox but I feel safe with him and that is precious to me right now. My head was nestled against the passenger window and feeling safe, I asked Jed if he minded if I took a little nap.

"You go right ahead girly; I probably tend to talk too mu...."

I was asleep.

What seemed like minutes later, my head knocked against the window, waking me. I wasn't sure where I was or how long I had been asleep.

"You're quite a sleeper," laughed Jed, "I don't think you moved once. I got you something to eat and drink when I pulled up for gasoline. Thought you might be hungry. Young girl in your condition should be looking after herself."

"Thanks, Jed. That's very sweet of you Jed," I said as I realised I had slept for a few hours.

"That's okay. Listen, Sarah, I keep to myself pretty much. Don't go inviting trouble into my life. Don't need the drama... not like some folks I know, but while you were sleeping, I caught the news on the radio. Seems the police are looking for a missing girl, fitting your description. There was a shoot-out in the local hospital back in Benson, two prison guards and a security guard at the hospital were killed by some crazed gunman, wanting revenge for his wife dying or something. Didn't say what the girl had done or what she was wanted for, just that she had gone missing while under guard at the hospital. I'm not going to ask any more questions but I have a whiff as strong as a bloodhound that something doesn't smell quite right about your story. So, here's what I'm going to do."

We were driving into a new town and Jed pulled into a 24-hour petrol station.

"I'm going to let you out here. I won't tell the police. They can do their own job. You don't look like a bad girl to me but something is on the nose here and I don't invite trouble into my life. So, I'm going to wish you all the best. I'm sorry I can't be of any more help," as he looked forward, to the road ahead.

"That's okay Jed, I understand. I really do appreciate all your help; you've been very kind to me. I'm truly thankful," I touched his arm and smiled warmly at him.

I grabbed the food and drink he bought me and then climbed out of his small truck and closed the door.

"Bye, Jed. Thanks again."

"You're most welcome Sarah and good luck," said Jed as he held his hand up and drove away.

Even though he was out of sight now, I could still hear the loud muffler from his truck. Like everyone else in my life, he was gone as waves of despair descended on me, once more.

Chapter Fourteen: When Dreams Become Reality

I was far enough away from Benson and safe enough to stay put for a while. As I walked towards the small town my attention was drawn to a track which disappeared into dense scrub. My logical mind was telling me to keep walking and head into town to find a room before it got too late in the day. I listened to my head and started walking when my baby became agitated and wouldn't settle. Then it felt as if someone then had their hand on my back and gently turned me around and guided me towards the opening of the track. I felt conflicted, still unsure what to do, when my feet literally started moving me towards this track. It looked like an old track that hadn't been used in a long time. The narrow track led out of town and I followed it, not sure why. It veered left towards some dense area of trees and then headed right, crossing a small creek which was still flowing.

At first, I was intrigued where I was being guided but the further I walked, the more concerned I became. I ducked under a low -lying branch and when I came up, I walked a few more metres before entering a small clearing which was the end of the track. Great. The path had stopped in the middle of nowhere. It's as if you couldn't get in or out. I questioned my intuition for the first time.

I looked around in despair and fell to my knees. I was exhausted, angry and I had nothing left.

I was alone and my lip began to quiver and my face began to twitch as tears began to roll down my cheeks. I was so tired of bracing up my inner strength, protecting myself from this emotional avalanche. My walls came crashing down. My last line of defence had finally been eroded away. I was spent. No one was here to witness the strong Sarah lose it and lose it, I did.

The soft cries turned into sobbing and then loud heaving; I was powerless to stop the flow. Months of pent up emotions and pretending to keep it altogether came pouring out and I simply didn't care anymore. My stomach ached as I purged the deep-seated emotions I had buried for so long.

When the crying finally subsided, I had unconsciously curled up in the foetal position, which epitomised my current state. As I lay there in the silence, I realised how pathetic and powerless I must have looked. I stood up in defiance, angry and demanding answers, to whoever would listen.

"I'm done with this!" I yelled at the top of my voice. "I know you can hear me. I know you're out there somewhere. Find someone else to do your dirty work. I'm over it! You hear me? I've lost everything I love and for what? For fucking nothing. I want this thing out of me. I don't care anymore. I'm not who you think I am... I'm finished! Fuck you! Do, you hear me? Fuck you!" I continued screaming.

"Fuckkkkkkk... Fuckkkkkkkk!" I screamed louder and louder. The venting released some rage but not my frustration. I yelled out again hoping to purge more anger. "Fuckkkkkkkk! Arrrrrgggggghhhhh!" I screamed so loud my voice broke.

I laid on the ground kicking the dirt, doing my best to release as much frustration as possible. I wasn't consciously thinking about it, I was doing it instinctively.

I laid there in the silence. I was exhausted from my outburst but was feeling free and unburdened. It felt fantastic. The silence was also healing and I had created a void from my releasing, a void that now had to be filled.

I felt like I had been broken down, bit by bit, my resistance weakened, my boundaries exposed and now ready to receive or open up to anything. Like a wild horse ready for the rope and saddle, after hours of thrashing about and refusing to yield, here I lay.

I'm done and I'm not running any more. This ends now.

Suddenly I was startled by a voice coming from behind me. It was a tone of voice I had never heard before, different, very soft and gentle.

"Sarah have no fear, you will not be harmed. It is not our intention. We are always watching over you and have been for some time now. You are safe here. It is safe for me to visit you here. We guided you to this destination in the hope of speaking with you."

I was listening intently. At first, I thought my mind was playing tricks on me as I continued to listen, entranced by his voice.

I slowly sat up, keeping my back to the voice for two reasons. Firstly, all the answers I wanted were right behind me and yet I couldn't turn around, I was frozen with anticipation.

If I'm right... no, it can't be and it's impossible. It doesn't happen. It's not true. I'm tired, delirious and would believe anything right now. Therefore... just ignore it. It will go away soon and this will be all over.

He continued to speak softly, "Sarah, we can feel your emotions through the hybrid as we are connected to the hybrid baby. We have been feeling your pain and suffering for some time now. We were unable to intervene with your friend, Red, for this we are truly sorry and wished there was another way. We do our utmost to keep our surrogates safe. We did not foresee this happening. Human beings can be very cruel and unpredictable."

"You know about Red? We are your surrogates? Why are you doing this to us? Leave us alone and go back to wherever it is you came from," I said looking straight ahead.

"That is becoming more difficult as time goes by. Our civilisation is almost extinct and we need human help. We are almost out of time as a species however you have given us hope Sarah, a chance to survive. Our theory has been proven successful, thanks to you Sarah."

With my back still to the voice I retorted angrily, "Like we had a say in this? You have been using us as your own little baby makers."

"Yes, to you it would appear to be so. Please, I am unable to continue this discussion at this time."

The suspense was killing me and I had to look. I had to turn around. He felt familiar to me.

"Okay I'm turning around now? Slowly turning around," I told him calmly.

"If you wish. Please do not be startled. This is beyond the comprehension of most human beings," he replied.

I made sure I was very slow in turning around, so as not to startle him and because I was shit scared. My body was trembling and my heart was pounding. There was a familiar feeling with the energy of this encounter.

I continued to turn around, inch by inch, ever so slowly, with my eyes closed. When I knew I was facing him and full of trepidation, I opened my eyes and saw him. I saw those familiar eyes.

"It's you! The one appearing in my dreams." They were always vague but his eyes were so distinctive. Here he is, standing right in front of me. He was so beautiful and the fact he looked so human was unexpected. It threw me off guard a little. There was a pristine aura surrounding him and only gentle, loving energy permeated from him.

I knew I was safe with him. His presence was captivating and I couldn't stop staring. His hair was blonde, parted in the middle and flowed down past his shoulders. His body looked like it was covered in a silver-bluish lycra-looking material. He was tall, so very tall and of course those eyes, the eyes in my dreams were such a piercing blue colour, but they were soft and warm and they invited me into his soul. I could feel his love and compassion beaming out of those eyes, straight into me. He then moved closer to me, I could feel myself blushing uncontrollably.

"Why do you look at me like that?" I asked flustered.

"Is this too close for you?" he asked softly.

God I can't feel my heart, "Ah, I don't know... I'm not sure. Ah, um, yes, a bit too close."

He took a step back, "Sarah, it is me. I have visited you many times before in your dreams. Do you remember?" he asked.

"Yeah... I think so. You seem so normal, human like. Yet, are you from... up there?" I said, pointing to the sky.

"Yes! That is correct. My name is Lexus. I'm so pleased to finally meet you, Sarah, in this way. I have waited for this day for such a long time."

He stepped closer to me. He had gained my trust a little more and he knew it.

"Me too... I think," I blushed again, "my name is Sarah. Wait! Did you say that already? Did I say that already?" I stuttered, as I stared back into his eyes.

"You must have many questions Sarah. I will do my best to answer as many as I can for you," he said.

I stood there staring in silence, tongue tied.

"You do have questions, don't you?" he said, stepping even closer again. I could nearly touch him now.

"Ahh... yes. You could say that," I felt ridiculously giddy.

His energy was so pure – he emanated love. I could feel he had no hatred or evil within him and he filled my entire body with his incredible love and energy. I felt completely connected to everything and so alive, it was a fantastic feeling. His eyes sparkled and the colour changed from blue to gold occasionally. He was hypnotic.

"This connection does not happen often. Your species has demonstrated great hostility towards other beings and we have suffered many times on previous visits. We avoid appearing like this, but it is safe here, for now," he continued speaking while I continued staring.

"As you can see Sarah, we are much like you. The truth is our civilisation is almost extinct and humans are our only source of hope. Your species is the closest living beings to ours and yes, you are not alone, despite what you have been told by your people. Am I going too fast?"

"Ahh, maybe... just back up a little! So, are you really from up there somewhere? How many of your kind are left?" I asked still flustered.

"Yes, I am from the planet, Luve. We are Luveians. There are less than 20 of us left and we are no longer able to reproduce. Hence, we seek your help. We have been undertaking tissue samples for some time now, desperately trying to make this work. Our research and trialling were succeeding. Humans were able to conceive with our DNA. However, the fetuses did not survive."

"Hang on a minute! You never asked our permission for this! And we had no say in these experiments! Do you have any idea how many girls have suffered from all of this down here?"

"Actually, you have given permission on another level. You agreed to this contract before you incarnated this lifetime, to help us with this cause."

"Woah! Okay, hang on a minute there!" I said throwing my hand up as a stop signal, "what do you mean agreed to contracts?"

"Every soul comes in with a contract in each lifetime, to carry out unfinished or unfulfilled work from previous lifetimes, or to learn new lessons. You never remember this when you are born."

"We do? I did? We don't?"

"All the chosen women, including you Sarah, not able to conceive in past lifetimes were so desperate to have a child this time, agreed to the contract."

I took in a long breath, ready to speak, "Now I have so many questions-"

"Sarah I cannot stay long in this dimension. Please, let me finish. Until now, all the unions have continued to fail, then we finally had a breakthrough when you managed to keep your hybrid. Then Jane succeeded, which gave us great hope. We hold tremendous faith and expectation in you. We now understand how humans are affected by fear especially when it spikes to high levels.

It's similar to an electric shock to the fetus and it's this knowledge we believe you have learnt and why your baby continues to grow. The fear in your species keeps your vibration low, while ours is very high, causing the complications you have come to experience. Your frequency must remain high Sarah. You hold the key to our survival. We can finally see our future."

I continued to stare in silence. This was a lot to take in.

"My time here is coming to an end Sarah. You know the birth of your hybrid is very soon and although you may not see us, you will feel our energy and know we are with you. You can't always see us, but know we are here. Never fear for we will not abandon you. The hybrid babies will also help your species. In time, you will see my words are true. I wanted to tell you all this in the beginning but it was not possible. My light is fading, I must go now. You are strong Sarah and your hybrid child will be called Isabella Trixit. Bellatrix, if you like and over time she will have the ability to change many things, in time you will know this to be true. I will try my best to visit again. Goodbye for now, Sarah."

"Wait... wait... please! Hold on this is important. Some of the fetuses were mutated. It really scared us. How do I know my baby won't be like that?"

"Sarah, due to the intensity and destructive nature of human fear, combined with our sensitivity, the fetuses are mutating under stress. It has always been a concern to us. We are truly sorry however we are desperately fighting for our survival and need you to understand."

"You kissed me. I felt it. Was I dreaming or did that happen?"

"I have been visiting you for many lifetimes Sarah and it is only in this lifetime you have been able to see me, first in your dream state and now in the new consciousness. Most humans do not remember our night visits; they are not consciously awake yet. I have been watching over you for so long and I have come to know you well, that I have developed strong feelings for you. We are discouraged from having feelings for humans however I've been unable to stop these feelings from happening. I must go now. My light is fading fast and I've already stayed too long."

I was doing my best to take in as much information as possible, in my awe-struck giddy state, staring in adoration of this being as he communicated. Before I knew it, he had disappeared. I stood there with my jaw open and still nodding even after he had gone.

"So that's it? After all that, you just disappear on me. Come back and talk to me! I've got more questions," I shouted, spinning around in circles frantically looking for him but he was gone. I stared up at the sky wondering. I stepped forward only to trip over a rock and nearly fell face-first into some scrub. Welcome back to your life Sarah. So now that I am not star-struck; questions are coming to me faster than my brain can cope. Memo to self: 'Write down all your questions for next alien visit.' Of course, no need to flip out just yet. I mean I only spoke to an alien. He did tell me my baby's name is to be Isabella Trixous... Bella Trixy or maybe Bella Bella... Bellatrix! That's it. Bellatrix. That's a common name, not! She will fit in easily. Bellatrix O'Connor it is. Yeah, I can see it now. You know the one, the alien hybrid thingy! She can disappear and is half alien but apart from that, she is just like you and me! So, please everyone give her a big warm welcome and let's not forget our visit home, "Mum, Dad! This is Bellatrix. She is your alien granddaughter! She is the reason I had to run away, just what you always wanted hey Mum?"

Okay, places I can never return: home, prison, Benson and avoid all cameras, if possible. How hard could it be, walking around the neighbourhood with an alien baby?

All I could hear in my head, over and over again was 'you're not ready for this.' I know I'm not but I couldn't stop thinking about him. The way he looked at me, the way it made me feel. He was so present and the tone in his voice was so... so... sexy. God can you hear yourself Sarah? He's an alien. You live on different planets, Hello! But I couldn't stop these feelings and was already missing him. I could have stared and talked to him for hours, days. When I was near him, I felt so alive, I could feel the attraction, the connection. I have never felt like that before.

"No... oh God! Please not now... oh no! Oh FUCK! Not now!" I screamed. I felt a warm sensation run down my legs. You have got to be shitting me! Did Lexus say I'd be giving birth soon? Like now soon?

Reality check! I'm going to be all alone for this! No mum, no nurse and no friends. My breathing was faster and I could feel my heart was pounding so hard. I mindfully regained my composure and slowed my breathing down.

"Get your shit together Sarah, think." I could see a gigantic old tree nearby which caught my attention, I made my way over to it. It was very tall, the trunk as wide as a small car and its roots looked like long fingers high above the ground, anchoring the tree into the ground. I sat between two large roots with my back against the trunk. I could now feel the contractions starting and I began to pant in rhythm to calm myself.

"Shit this is really happening!"

Instinctively I pulled my jeans off then my underwear. This was happening fast; I could feel it.

"Mummmmm! I'm scared. I need you right now. Please give me the strength to do this Mum," I said, hoping I could gain the extra strength I needed.

The contractions began getting stronger and closer together. I continued panting to a rhythm to help me cope on all levels. An hour or so had passed, which seemed like days and I hadn't progressed anymore. I placed my hands on my stomach to feel the baby's heartbeat, which was very strong and fast. Something was wrong, I could sense it. The baby wanted to get out but couldn't.

"Lexus, pleeeaase! help me. Something is wrong I can feel it. I need you, please be here. Someone, anyone, please help me!" My eyes welled up. I was trying to control my fear and my anxiety.

The contractions were strong and now close together. I was in a lot of pain and scared for the baby. Sweat ran freely down my face and I knew the baby was in serious trouble. I began to cry in frustration. I didn't know what to do to or how to help the baby. I became lightheaded and dizzy, my vision became blurred, as I then heard a whisper which surrounded me.

"Do not be afraid child we are here to help you."

I passed out but then woke in a dream state. I was floating high above myself having an out of body experience. I watched on from above and witnessed what looked like several Luveians by my side, reassuring me and helping deliver my baby. I was in a peaceful state, much like my dreams as I watched the miracle unfold before my eyes. They were enveloped in a circle of beautiful bright light. One had their hands on my stomach, another had their hands on my heart sending what looked like healing energy to the baby and myself. After a short time, Isabella appeared. They held her and took care of every little detail. I watched on blissfully as they wrapped her in a garment and placed her snuggly in my arms. I could see myself grinning from ear to ear and then peacefully drifted off to sleep.

I woke from my dream state on a rickety bed in what looked like an old abandoned shack. I slowly gained focus as I gathered my senses.

Where am I? How did I get here? I gazed around the room, it was quiet and felt safe. I struggled to remember anything. The last thing I recall was trying to give birth. My attention was broken by Isabella who lay next to me, wrapped in a garment which appeared to look like Lycra, it felt warm and soft.

I gazed down at my little miracle; my heart melted. I was overflowing with pride and joy. My heart was bursting with love, I could feel myself glowing. She looked so adorable and to my relief very human. She looked like a very small version of Lexus, the beautiful being that just visited me. Her golden curly hair had a sheen to it and I was surprised how much hair she had.

I unwrapped her and began to softly touch all her beautiful features from her face to her arms, down her tummy and legs. I was also hoping and praying not to find anything odd or wrong like all the other babies I had witnessed. She appeared to have no reproductive organs, still she looked perfect to me in every way. I felt so proud and protective at the same time.

"You are just beautiful Isabella... Bellatrix. I can't even imagine what's in store for you. I do know you are destined for big things, or so I've been told. Just to think, out of all those babies, you were the only one so far to survive. We must be okay. What do you think?" I whispered to her.

Her eyes opened slowly, then gained focus as she looked straight at me. I knew she recognised me. Instinctively she began to move quite strongly as she smiled at me and then nestled into me. I was overcome with emotion and tears once again rolled down my cheeks and onto Bellatrix. I was smiling and crying at the same time. I was mesmerised and I couldn't take my eyes off her. I felt so different now, so grown up.

I now felt something has shifted, transpired in me. It was like a switch had been flicked when she was born. Questions were rolling through my mind with no one to ask for answers. I knew I would have to tackle it as I go, or perhaps I wasn't supposed to know yet.

Instinctively she nuzzled into my chest with some help from me. After making my breast available she latched on. This explains my sore breasts of late. Another question answered: they do breast feed. She suckled as I watched, cradling her in a loving embrace. She was tiny but looked so much older than a newborn. From what I had seen, babies were helpless and fragile for months. I continued staring at her in adoration as she suckled on my breast. I'm a mother. I have a daughter now. It seemed so crazy thinking those words.

I looked around the shack as Isabella fed. Hopefully we were placed here because it is safe and no one would bother us. Isabella went to sleep so I placed her on the bed. I took the opportunity to look through the shack. It wasn't perfect, but it was home for now. I found an old broom in a cupboard and swept a huge pile of leaves outside, as I swept, I accidentally tripped on a loose floorboard which revealed a hidden stash of beans and other various tinned foods. Maybe it was someone's idea of an emergency shelter. It was a fabulous windfall and I was so grateful. Hungry and exhausted I did not fancy the thought of searching for food right now as I needed rest and to be with Isabella.

With Isabella still asleep and the shack still in sight, I made my way down to a creek not far away. I needed to wash myself, as best as I could. The feel of cold fresh water on my skin was so refreshing. I ran back to the shack and returned to the creek with an old saucepan to fill for water. I was as quick as possible. I didn't want to be seen, nor leave Isabella too long on her own.

On returning, Isabella was still asleep, my timing was perfect. I pondered my next move. Stay here for as long as I can or go home? Should I return to Benson and turn myself in? Maybe someone has come forward as a witness who can testify it was Scarface and I'm no longer an accessory to murder. Upon reflection, I felt the best option was to stay put and let my next move present itself.

Thinking about Benson reminded me of the unfinished business with Scarface. There has always been something about her that has bothered me, even before what she did to Red. Whenever she shows up, trouble is right behind her. But there is also a vibe about her, something odd I can't explain. She is beyond cold and unfriendly and I get this bad feeling she has killed before. She showed no remorse after killing Red.

I know Red was a troublemaker but she didn't deserve to die at the hands of that bitch. I would love to get revenge for her. While I was contemplating Red's fate, I began to hear voices. They were faint at first. Then they began to get louder, as they approached the shack. They were men's voices, maybe two or three and they sounded drunk, slurring their words. They caught me unaware and it was too late to leave without being seen. It was early afternoon so I couldn't use the dark of night to escape. I was trapped inside and becoming worried. I quickly hid Isabella who was still asleep in the bottom of an old cupboard. Think, Sarah Think! Their voices now sounded close. Shit!... shit... shit! They are here.

It was too late and I was caught off guard and couldn't find anything to defend myself with. The door burst open under force and hit the wall as I did my best to hide by the side of the cupboard, close to Isabella.

I could just make out two men, who seemed drunk, unshaven and dirty with scruffy clothes.

"Looks like someone's cleaned our pig pen, Lou," slurred one of them.

"I reckon you're right, Skinny."

Skinny was thin with greasy long grey hair and wore a faded torn old blue singlet that stretched partially over his protruding belly and old jeans which failed to cover his dirty feet.

The other was fat and sleazy, balding on top, leaving a rim of hair around his ears and back of his head which was also long and greying. His fat belly proudly pushed out from his t-shirt and it fell down over his baggy track pants, that looked two sizes too big for him. The sight of them repulsed me.

Although I was a good five metres or so away, I could smell the alcohol on their breath. I pushed up against the side of the cupboard trying to appear less visible. I even took small, shallow breaths, doing everything I possibly could to avoid being noticed. Instinctively, my thoughts were of protecting Isabella, who was also in danger.

The men continued to stagger around, slugging away at their bottle hidden in a brown paper bag. They passed it back and forth after each had guzzled several mouthfuls.

Drunk or not, it was only a matter of time before they would spot me; the shack was only one big open room. At one end was the old rickety table and chairs next to the bed and at the other end of the room stood a tall cupboard, next to a fireplace, where I hid pretending to be invisible.

"Well, well, Lookie here," said Skinny laughing as he continued, "look what I just found, Lou, Goldilocks! So, you're the one whose been cleaning up our country chalet, eh?" slurred Skinny, bursting out in drunken laughter.

"Why you sure are a pretty little thing. I'll bet you cause a whole lot of pain to the boys, don't cha?" said Lou.

I chose not to speak at all. They repulsed me so much and I knew if I said something, I'd regret it and I didn't want to put Isabella in any more danger than she already was.

"What's wrong, Goldy? The cat got your tongue... meooww" mimicked Skinny still laughing.

"Oohh! Fancy seeing you all the way out here on your lonesome. Now, how the hell did I get so lucky Skinny? This has gotta be my lucky day."

"Don't forget me, Lou! You know our rule... we always share our pussy!" as he licked his lips.

"Where you hiding that tongue, Goldy? Open up your mouth and show me, yah hear?"

I ignored them with a defiant look on my face, failing to hide my repulsed facial expression.

"Oohh! I'll bet you're a feisty little thing, aren't cha? Yeah! I just know it! Wadda yah think, Lou?"

By now I had moved slowly around and in front of the cupboard and Isabella.

"It's a pity there's no one around to help yah or hear yah scream, ain't it, sugar?" slurred Lou.

Something had changed in me. I was in danger, but not afraid.

"You sure are a brave little thing. I've seen girls piss themselves by now and you haven't even flinched. Who are yah? Where yah from, little lady?" asked Lou struggling to pronounce his words.

Skinny swayed up to me and got right in my face, "You heard the man. Where yah from, Goldy? Yah know it's not polite to keep a man waiting," his putrid breath pushed at my face and upon seeing his decaying teeth, I dry retched.

"Yar really starting to piss me off now," said Lou, "I think it's time you learnt a little lesson. When someone speaks to you it's polite to answer 'em darlin', yar hear me?"

Then my luck ran out, Isabella began to make noises.

"What was that? What cha hiding in there? Step aside Goldy," Skinny pushed me aside and opened the rickety old door.

"Well! What do we have here? It's a little baby," Lou mimicked a small child's voice.

"Now we know she puts out, hey Lou. Got proof of that now, don't we?" chuckled Skinny.

"Yeah, we do. I'll bet you don't wanna see her get hurt, hey pretty? Now we might get some answers Skinny."

Lou reached down and picked up Isabella, much to my disgust. "Well, you're a pretty little thing, just like your Mum," his foul-smelling breath polluting her face.

"Now we have Mummy's attention, don't we sugar? Yes, we do. I'd hate to see anything happen to a cute little thing like you, wouldn't we Skinny?"

"Damn right Lou! Damn right! I need another drink Lou."

I was powerless and hoping for a miracle, all I could do was look on. I knew if I said anything, I would get us both into more trouble, my silence was already getting under their skin.

It was unbearable watching this cowardly scumbag hold Isabella... I wish I had a gun.

"Time for you to get undressed Goldy. I'm gettin kinda horny and this baby is getting heavy," ordered Lou.

I could tell Skinny was getting angry at my lack of cooperation and he made his way over to me again twitchy and hyper.

"We're getting tired of you not listening to us Goldy. Now, either you take off those rags or I'll do it for yah? Do yah hear me bitch?" shouted Skinny.

"I've never seen you get all worked up like that before Skinny... strip her!" demanded Lou.

His hands were shaking and I'm not sure if that was from being an alcoholic or if he was scared of stripping me. He reached out and grabbed my top and tore it violently from my body. I held my ground and stared at him defiantly.

"Now that's what I'm talking about Skinny, some action. Look at those little titties. Now ain't that a pretty picture? Well, don't stop boy... get her bra off. You slow or something!"

Lou put Isabella down on the bed and began to undo his pants, trying to untie the cord to his sweatpants from under folds of belly fat.

"Hang on a minute, Lou! I'm going first this time! You promised, remember?" argued Skinny.

Standing still half naked, exposed and awaiting my fate, I remembered what Lexus had said: Know we are here do not be afraid.

I closed my eyes and in my mind called out to Lexus: *Lexus! Please help us! We're in danger and we need you now. Please help us. Please!*

"Ohh, look, Lou. She has even closed her eyes. She must be looking forward to it as much as us!" he laughed out loud.

"Yeah, I do believe you're right Skinny. Well I'll be damned. This is one crazy bitch."

I sensed Skinny was still close and heard him undoing his belt. The stench from his body odour and the mix of decaying teeth and alcohol was putrid.

"How did we get so lucky today, Lou? Tell me that," snorted Skinny.

I was about to puke all over him when suddenly I felt something spatter my face, as I heard a sickening thud and the sound of glass smashing. I opened my eyes. Lou had cracked Skinny over the head with his empty bottle and I was covered in Skinny's blood.

"Never did like sharing much yah know and Skinny can be such a dickhead at times, you know what I'm saying? Oops! I hope I didn't wake the baby cos you still have some work to do," Lou said laughing as he turned around to check.

"Where did that baby go? Are you messing with me, girlie?" said Lou angrily.

I was frantically looking around the room giving no thought to the rapist in front of me.

The room suddenly turned super bright, blinding me for several seconds before it faded, revealing Lexus standing there. He was here.

"You took your time. We were in danger! Isabella could have been hurt," I was short and unapologetic.

He touched Lou on the temple who immediately went into a daze and then just walked out and kept going, marching like a zombie into the wilderness.

"Where is she... what have you done with her?" I demanded.

"Know she is safe Sarah. We were watching over both of you. I understand your anger but we have much to discuss and I have little time on this plane as I told you last time. This incident was not an accident Sarah. We needed a demonstration, something to confirm the hybrid's ability. Isabella succeeded. The hybrid baby removed the earth-based fear from you. You now have the knowledge and experience to keep the hybrids full term. It is up to you Sarah; we need your help to guide the others. We now ask that you go back to the prison and tell the other selected women."

"Wait a minute! I was nearly raped, just to prove a point. I don't believe this!" I stood there furious, shaking my head in disbelief.

"We have upset you greatly and we are extremely sorry for hurting you this way."

"So you tell me!"

"Sarah, we know it was a harsh lesson but we don't have a lot of time and we thought if we could show you how important this is then-"

"Like being raped by a couple of low-life losers while your baby is in danger you mean?" I snapped back.

"Sarah it has always been about fear. We evolved from fear a long time ago. It controls humans and despite every attempt for better outcomes, your planet is still firmly gripped and seeded in fear. As I told you before the hybrids must survive for both our species. You will need them."

"I thought we were helping your species?" I asked confused.

"There is an evil alien species desperate to inhabit Earth. They need Earth as their planet has limited time left and their resources are nearly exhausted. They know earth can provide everything they need and they are coming to take it. Make no mistake, they will take Earth, effortlessly! You won't even know it's happening. They do not want the hybrids to survive. If humans have no fear, these aliens will not succeed. They have been watching for a long time now, waiting to see if we were successful with the hybridisation. They hacked our intelligence base and found our research data. They must also hybridise with your species to ensure their survival on earth. We believe there may be a connection between them and the killing of the hybrids. They are very intelligent and an advanced race and if they have succeeded in creating one hybrid, they will escalate their programme immediately."

"Time is critical here, Sarah. For all of us."

"You said if the humans have no fear, they will fail. I don't understand how that will change things for them?" I asked.

"As you know, the fear in humans will abort our hybrids. Ironically it is fear that feeds this species. They need fear as it provides the fetus with the energy to grow. Fear is an energy and

they have learnt how to harvest it. Can you now see why we are
warning you what's at stake? Fear in the human race will enable
their species to thrive on Earth and take over. The pregnancy is quick
and they will outnumber humans within months."

"Earth is their next target. We know your friends have suffered
but you will experience suffering like you have never known before, if
these aliens spawn with your race. You must make the others aware.
And hopefully, if you don't run out of time, save your planet."

"Fuck! You should have told me all this earlier. Save all this
time."

"It's taken us this long to get you to trust us. To just talk to us.
You have an open mind, Sarah. How many earthlings do you think
would talk to me?"

"Not many. Okay, probably none! Arrgghh! I don't believe this
is happening."

"You weren't ready Sarah. You now know just how important it
is when you to go back and tell the others. You must open their
minds, Sarah and prepare them for change. At the very least, open
the door for new possibilities in this universe."

"And if I don't?"

"Well, you end up like us, exhausting every effort to find a path
for survival. We never believed it possible at the time. We were
thriving and our population was vast, like earth now. Then they
came. They visited our planet to discuss universal peace treaties.
Unbeknown to us they had depleted nearly all their resources and
were desperate to take our planet. They put a substance in our water
which made us sterile over time. We had no idea, until it was too late.
Fortunately, we had been storing genetic material for future research
in incubators, which they didn't know about. Your people were our
only hope and when it was placed in humans it was miraculously
activated and the union was successful. We weren't sure it was ever
going to work. It was a longshot. The reason I'm telling you all this
Sarah is they have ways of taking over Earth you would never have
thought of. They will not invade in the crude manner your
government will expect. There will be no violence. They are far more
advanced. They wiped us out, without any bloodshed. You will not
see the end coming, just as we didn't."

He paused, "You know whose been killing our hybrids?" Lexus
asked.

"Actually, I do." I just knew it. My intuition was so strong.
There was no doubt. It was Scarface.

"Then, you know I speak the truth. She has been sabotaging the successful hybrid pregnancies, such as your friend, Red and others you are not aware of."

"Yes! I know that now too."

"I know this is a tremendous burden and we understand your dilemma as you understand ours. You have succeeded Sarah to be the only human so far to have a hybrid reach full term. My time here is now over, Sarah."

"Damn it! You always do this. You come in when I'm completely overwhelmed and help me as you do, then go when I have millions of questions."

"I am sorry. I wish I could stay. I must tell you one more thing before I go. You may have noticed your telepathic abilities have greatly increased since the birth. You can now reach us whenever you need. Use this gift Sarah, you have inherited this with having a hybrid."

"I'm glad there are some..." I replied smirking.

"There will be many more gifts that will become apparent in time."

"There you go again with when the time is right. Is the time ever right with you?" I questioned.

"Please do not be offended. We can only give you a small amount of information at a time. If we download you with too much too soon, it will overwhelm you and you will not retain it."

"Yeah, point taken! My head hurts now," I agreed as I looked into those eyes.

"Please don't go, Lexus. I feel so safe with you. Take us with you," my heart yearned to go with him, wherever that was.

"You have much to do here, in so little time Sarah. I must go now, it is time. Remember to use the gifts we have bestowed upon you. Watch Isabella, she will teach you," he waved at me, then the room filled with blinding bright light, once more and he was gone.

I always felt incredible around him. All my senses were heightened as I was drawn into him like a powerful magnet. The love that emanated from him was surreal and I just melted into it. Nothing mattered when I was next to him, nothing. I felt so empty when he left.

"Lexus! Please come back," I pleaded, "I love you!" I shouted, looking up to the sky.

In all that chaos, I realised I was still standing there half naked. After laughing at myself, I went to the cupboard and found a flannel shirt amongst some clothes and tried it on. It was a little too big but I didn't have a lot of choice, so I put it on. I picked up Isabella and hugged her tightly. I was amazed at the love generated from these beings. I have been angry and full of despair and yet after being in his presence for only a few moments, these feelings dissolved. Incredible, to experience such extremes in an instant. I was truly grateful to have those negative feelings disappear so quickly.

I looked into Isabella's eyes and spoke to her.

"Well it seems like our next move has just been decided for us. It's back to prison we go, Isabella."

This will be interesting. My intuition tells me we will be safe regardless of what happens but after what Lexus just said, I'm worried about Jane.

I would have liked to stay here a bit longer as Bella is growing at an extraordinary rate already and with the future so uncertain, this time is invaluable for us to bond and learn. That could have gone horribly wrong and we were both in great danger. I value every minute now with this incredible being, my baby, my hybrid.

Isabella distracted me and I found myself looking down at Skinny, still lying on the floor. Great! What do I do with him? I can't drag him out and I'm certainly not digging a grave for that piece of shit.

As I stood there looking at his sorry arse, I kicked him in the side, to see if he was still alive and to my shock he moved and his eyes opened. He sat up dazed, still adjusting his eyes to the light. His facial expression reflected his mind trying to piece together what had just happened.

He began rubbing his head, which made the wound bleed again. He tried to make it to his feet, bracing himself against the small table, swaying from side to side trying to find his balance.

Instinctively I grabbed the broken bottle and lunged at him with a threatening look on my face.

"Now, get out of here before I cut you, you low-life scum. Get out! Your mate has already gone. He got it far worse than you, so count yourself lucky, scumbag," I shouted at him.

The look on his face was priceless, as I watched him stagger away still dazed. He looked back several times trying to piece together what had just happened, all the while still rubbing his head, as if by rubbing it, he would miraculously remember what had happened. I was struggling to keep a straight face as he finally disappeared out of sight.

I was thankful I didn't have to deal with him. I honestly thought he was dead but glad in a sense he wasn't. The last thing I wanted was to be looking at his sorry, skinny arse all night on the floor; a cruel reminder of the possibility of being raped. Every girl's worst fear, which I should have been paralysed by. I was angry and repulsed but not fearful. It got me thinking about what Lexus said about the other species, using our fear to feed their energy and the violent and destructive outcomes from that energy source. I now fully understand the gravity of this situation and what Lexus was trying to tell me.

As I nursed and fed Isabella, I began to think about what I need to say when I meet the other women and how to get them to rally behind me. But it's not just about the Luveians anymore, it's about all of us. We must be prepared to fight back, or we will lose everything. Now I will fight for them. I will fight for Isabella, my family and my friends. Maybe all this time on my own has prepared me for this very purpose. If it is true, if I am a leader, then it is time. I must stand up and lead. It feels right. I am ready for whatever I need to do.

"I am here for you!" I shouted as I looked up at the sky.

Chapter Fifteen: Surprise and Sabotage

"Jane, take a look at this, it's incredible. Who would have thought?"

"What is it, Dad?" I said looking at his puzzled face.

"I have just received a copy of the birth certificate for the young girl killed outside Benson hospital, you know, Sarah's friend Red."

"Why would you need Red's birth certificate?" I asked.

"Her mother is an inmate here. Can you believe it?"

"What!" I said stunned.

"True. It knocked me over when the detectives told me. Tyson is one of the toughest women I have ever known. She's been in here for years. Strong, resilient, nothing stops her or gets in her way, safe to say, I wouldn't want to get on her wrong side and I hold the key."

"I wonder if Red knew. So why is she inside, Dad? What did she do?"

"She was initially charged with drug possession, given a suspended sentence and was on probation. The story has it she was drugged and raped repeatedly by her parole Officer. She made allegations to the authorities but who would listen to an addict. Destroyed and angry, she hunted him down and killed him herself. That was a long time ago."

"That's horrible, that poor woman. Are you going to tell her? You have to tell her she has the right to know!"

"Yeah probably, although sometimes I think it's better to let sleeping dogs lie. Listen, Jane, the guards have told me the girl they call Scarface, has been asking to see you."

"Oh, really? What for?" I replied in a curious voice.

"She heard you've been counselling some of the inmates and she's been making noises about seeing you."

"Is It okay if I pop in and see her, she's in solitary, right?"

Curiosity got the better of me and I asked dad to make the arrangements with the guards as soon as possible.

"Yes and you be careful, I don't trust that girl. She's in solitary for a reason and I insist that guards are with you at all times. You hear me?" he said firmly.

"Yes, Warden. Loud and clear!" I said mimicking one of the guards. I was escorted to solitary by the guards. I always felt important when I had my own bodyguard.

Scarface was waiting for me, both hands on the bars in front of her as if holding on in a desperate attempt for help. Her head was sandwiched between the bars and she had a sorrowful look on her face. My eyes were instantly drawn to the ugly scar that stretched from her top lip to high on her cheekbone. With her jet-black hair pulled back tight in a ponytail, her eyes looked sad but empty and mean. Seriously mean! Like a dog that casually walks up to you with its head down and at the moment you think of patting it, it bites you! She couldn't hide that look.

"You asked to see me?" I said.

"Yeah, that's right," she said in a depressed voice.

"How can I help you?" I asked.

"You Jane?" she said sharply.

"Yes," I replied just as sharply.

"I heard you've done some good work with some of the inmates here and I'm not doing so well. I thought it would be good for me to talk about it with someone like you, you know?"

"So, what do you want to talk about," I questioned.

"It's kinda hard to talk about. I'm not as hardnosed as the crims that are in here. I mean, I didn't do anything wrong. It was all circumstantial evidence and I am being framed for it."

"Listen! I'm sorry but I can't actually help you in a legal sense, just how to cope in here."

"No, no! You see, that's just it. I'm not coping. It's what the others think about me, the horrible things they say and the hateful messages I get. It's taking a toll on me and I'm... hurtin you know?"

"Okay, as much as I sympathise with you, there's not a lot I can do about what other inmates say. I'm not sure how you expect me to help you." I felt sorry for her.

"So, you're just the same as all the other scumbags in here. One of them goody-two-shoes who goes around pretending to give a shit, when what you really are is a fraud. The worst kind ever," she said with a bit of venom.

"You finished? Guards! That's it, I'm done here, let's go," I demanded.

"No... no! Please don't go! Please, Jane, I didn't mean it. This place is getting to me. I didn't mean those things I said. Honest I didn't," her face had softened and she looked desperate.

Her hands slipped down the bars as she slowly slumped to the floor. She was on her knees and her hands were still holding onto the bars, her face now staring at the cold, sterile cell floor. She began sobbing, pitifully.

I couldn't help it, my heart opened and I moved closer to her, bringing strong intervention from the guard. As she raised her arm to block me from getting any closer.

"Miss Walsh, that's far enough! We have strict orders not to let you get too close," said one of the guards who stepped forward quickly.

"It's okay," I placed my hands on her arm and slowly pushed it down, "I know what I'm doing."

"Please, mam! I repeat, we have strict orders from the Warden and we are not to let you get any closer under any circumstances."

Scarface was now crying uncontrollably.

"That girl needs me," I demanded, "the Warden is not in charge of me and if you don't let me pass, I will file a full complaint against you. Have I made myself perfectly clear?" commanding her to move out of my way.

"But... but... mam we have-" the guard stuttered.

"That's enough! You can stay right there and watch me if it makes you feel better," as I pointed to the far end of the cell and now made my way slowly to where Scarface was still kneeling, sobbing.

I bent down slowly and put my arm through the bars to comfort her, to stroke her jet-black hair. I was always a softie when it came to someone upset and crying. I melted and dropped my guard.

"It's okay," I said softly, "I'm here now, talk to me. I'm sorry for being abrupt earlier. It's been difficult here lately, for all of us... please stop crying. It's going to be okay," I tried to reassure her.

"Stand up and let's put all this behind us. What do you say?" as I offered her my hand for support.

We slowly stood up as I continued to stroke her hair. Her crying began to subside.

Then, everything slowed down to nothing more than a blur, as if I was instantly teleported into a dream state, outside of my body watching from above.

I watched her grab my hand from her head and pull me tight up against the bars pulling a knife from her overalls, she shoved it with furious force into my belly, my womb, my baby.

She did it again and again in a frenzied attack.

My blood sprayed up against the bars of the cell. I watched on as the guard, who was blindsided by me, rushed to grab me as I fell to the floor in shock, desperately holding my stomach, pressing against the gaping wounds, trying to stop the profuse bleeding.

The other guard reached for her baton and then smashed it over the head of Scarface, sending her unconscious and reeling back onto the floor. I heard the guards yelling for the doctor. The other guard had her hands on my stomach doing her best to stop the bleeding, as they waited for the doctor and a stretcher. The doctor soon arrived and I watched on, as they rolled me onto the stretcher and took me to the infirmary.

I knew instantly my baby was dead.

I'm looking at the guards and, in my mind talking to them but they can't hear me.

Please let me be, just let me be. Let me go. Please take me now, Lord. I ask forgiveness for all my failings and sins. I am ready to go... I am yours.

I watched Dad burst into the medical room as the medical staff did their best to slow the bleeding while waiting for the ambulance to arrive. I caught a glimpse of my baby as they picked her up and wrapped her in towels. She looked beautiful, as I had always imagined. She looked very human, from what I could see. Dad was breaking down.

"Damn it, Jane! Why didn't you listen to me?" he cried, "don't leave honey... hang in there... I... I love you, Janie," he said as tears ran freely down his face. He was leaning against the wall as he watched my life force trickle away with every drop of blood. "She will pay for what she has done! I promise you, Janie. I promise you!" he angrily shouted.

With sirens wailing the ambulance arrived and I witnessed my body being whisked out on a trolley out of the prison. The distraught guards watching on despondently, Dad trying his best to keep it together and the ambulance drivers, prison doctors and nurses frantically working together, shouting out instructions to each other as the trolley was pushed frantically into the waiting ambulance. Within seconds, I am placed in the ambulance and the doors are closed behind me. With sirens and flashing lights, the ambulance sped off to the hospital leaving Dad with his head in his hands crying, trying to hide his outpouring of emotions.

It's ok Dad... I love you.

The greatest tragedy is that I was savagely separated from my baby, my joy. I was so close to giving birth, so close to being a mum. No time to mourn, to grieve, to say goodbye.

Chapter Sixteen: First look at a Thraxion

"Warden! The prisoner is conscious now," said a quietly-spoken and remorseful Pyke.

"I'll be there shortly. Get me Tyson in here now!" I ordered.

"Yes sir."

Within minutes, there was a knock on my door.

"Yes?" I snapped abruptly.

"I have Tyson here, Warden."

"Send her in Pyke."

Tyson shuffled in. She wasn't in chains, it was just the way she walked, as though she had all the time in the world. The fact is she did and she wouldn't be getting out of here for quite a long time, not that Tyson seemed interested in getting out anyway. These walls were home now and she always had that 'What have I done now?' look on her face.

"Sup Warden! You wanna see me? It's gotta be important. This is the second time in weeks. You got a crush on me or what Warden... I've actually been keeping out of trouble for a change, so I know it ain't about me," she said very casually.

"I'm not in the mood Tyson... look, I'm not sure how to tell you this but I have some bad news. I just had a couple of detectives see me regarding the death of that young girl killed over at the hospital recently. It seems she was your daughter." I paused to allow her to absorb the information," I'm sorry, Tyson... truly. If there is anything, we can do just please let me know, okay?"

Tyson stood there, stunned. She would have been utterly shocked but tried desperately not to let it show. I had never seen her vulnerable, shed a tear or display any kind of weakness in all the time I had known her but then again that's how they survived within these walls.

Her face started to glisten under the lights as a few tears streamed from her eyes and rolled down her cheeks. She continued to stand in silence as she came to terms with what she had just been told. I could see her processing it all. Any chance of seeing the daughter she had given away, a long painful time ago was gone. Tyson didn't question me; she knew Red was hers and now she was gone.

After a long silence, she spoke, "That bitch who stabbed her, the ugly mutt, she's the one in solitary, right? The same bitch who just stabbed your daughter?"

"Yes," I replied.

"I need to ask you something Warden and I reckon you want me to ask..."

"Go on," I knew she would click on to what we both wanted but we still had to play the game.

"There is something you can do for me, Warden."

"What is it?" I asked.

"Release that bitch from solitary into the General Area... for both of us."

Bingo! There it was.

"Consider it done."

"Thank you and hey... I'm really sorry about your daughter... I hope she pulls through."

I nodded accepting her sincerity which was more of a shock than what she was about to do.

"Pyke! Take Tyson back to her block and make immediate arrangements for Lux Shields to be released into the general population. Put her in a cell near Tyson."

I glanced at Tyson as she left with Pyke, her face displaying a look of satisfaction, knowing she was going to deliver justice for both our daughters.

I was going to the hospital to be by Jane's side. It was also best if I wasn't here at the prison.

***

"How's your head? Still hurtin' I hope?" Pyke said mockingly.

"What's it to you cocksucker?" replied Shields.

"Okay, on your feet Shields, you're being upgraded."

"Upgraded! What are you talking about?"

"Just grab your things," Pyke ordered.

Scarface grabbed her belongings and was escorted along the corridor.

"So where are we going? I don't like the feel of this."

"You'll find out soon enough," Pyke said.

As they got closer to the general area block, Scarface stopped and began pushing backward; her feet pushing hard into the floor, trying to back up, as Pyke pushed her forward.

"Wait! Wait! What the fuck. I can't go in there! You can't put me in there! I'm not safe here!" Pyke wrestled with Scarface pushing her forward.

"Well look who we have here! If it ain't our own little prom queen. Welcome to cell block P... for pain!" I said as I helped Pyke push Scarface into the cell.

"What's she doing out here?" shouted Scarface. "I want to see the Warden... now! Cocksucker!" Scarface screamed at Pyke, as she tried to move backwards.

"You mean the Warden whose daughter you just stabbed and killed her unborn child? Well, this cocksucker guard just happens to be carrying out my orders," said Pyke.

Scarface was looking around frantically, her eyes darting from side to side.

I moved into the cell door with Scarface and Pyke. Within seconds Scarface was surrounded by my gang. I hadn't told them everything, I didn't need to, I was top dog on this block and they would do anything for me. Literally, anything!

"You look a little nervous, princess! What's wrong? You remember that young girl you stabbed at the hospital? Remember bitch? Let me refresh your memory... she was young, pretty and had red hair. You know the one."

Scarface was on alert as I continued.

"You see, you took something from me that was truly precious, she was my daughter... Red," I said slowly with malice.

"I swear... I never knew she was your daughter. I swear," interrupted Scarface, defiantly.

"That may be so, bitch, but you fucken knew Jane had a baby and I heard she's not doing too good. So, it seems we have a score to settle. You and me!" I raised my voice, "showtime, girls! Grab the ugly mutt!"

They grabbed her arms and dropped Scarface to the floor.

"Give me the bolt cutters, Campbell. See these, bitch... courtesy of the Warden. Hold her hands on the floor... that's it... now stand on them," I demanded as I began to sing one of my favourite songs, "now, this little piggy went to market."

I then closed the cutters around Scarface's little finger with force, severing the finger above the knuckle. Blood spurted all over Scarface as she let out spine-chilling screams of pain, which carried down the corridors, stirring all the inmates into a frenzy.

One of the gang licked at her blood on the floor and arched her back and stretched her head as high as she could and howled like a wolf, making the rest of the gang laugh.

I continued with her torture, "And this little piggy had roast beef, while this little piggy had none," as I clipped another finger which fell to the floor. I systematically removed all of Scarface's fingers from both her hands. Scarface had fainted. I slapped her face hard several times as another prisoner threw water on her face. She came around and with painful pleads whispered, "no more... I'll do anything you want... I'm begging you... please no more."

"Not this time bitch!" I shouted, "now take her fucking shoes off!"

I went through it all again, only toes this time. The floor was a bloodbath, with the fingers and now toes of Scarface scattered around her as she lied there in excruciating pain. The gang was hysterical while the guards watched on from outside the cell block gates. Warden made sure all the cameras had been turned off as I went about inflicting more excruciating torture on my victim, extracting as much pain out of Scarface as I possibly could.

"Grab the rope, Hennessey!" I shouted.

"Sure thing, Boss," replied Hennessy.

The rope was quickly placed around Scarface's neck, the other end tied to a large overhead beam.

Scarface began laughing which got louder and louder, "You have no fucking idea who you are messing with bitches!" as she continued laughing again, "they're going to come for each and every one of you bitches and there's nowhere to hide."

She continued laughing, despite the pain.

"Get the chair, Campbell. Let's put this bitch out of her misery!" I ordered ignoring Scarface's threats.

The girls forced her to stand up on a chair.

"What the fuck was that?" shouted one of the girls.

"Did everyone just see that? What the fuck! There she goes again... this shit ain't human... what the hell is she? I'm outta of here."

Glimpses of some kind of Reptilian body was flashing in front of our eyes, revealing dark scales.

"What's wrong with you weak pussies? Do I have to do everything myself?" I yelled angrily.

The images stopped for a while and an eerie silence came over the room as we stared at Scarface in anticipation, waiting for more glimpses of who or what she really was. My gang was now divided as most of them had retreated in fear, back to their cells. Only my most loyal girls remained. They looked on in disbelief. Who exactly were we about to execute and were Scarface's threats real... are there going to be consequences for our actions? Fuck it I thought.

"Time to dance, Prom Queen! Come on show us your quickstep bitch," I said laughing loudly.

I kicked the chair out from Scarface's feet as her blood-drenched body swung around, she desperately clawed at the noose around her neck without her fingerless hands as blood gushed from the amputations. After tense seconds passed, her body began to shake violently as she gasped for breaths. Everyone was mesmerised as they watched her clinging on to the last seconds of her life. The sounds of gurgling and choking noises were gut-wrenching as the rope twisted and stretched. Her legs stopped kicking frantically and her bloodied hands now fell to her sides, as precious seconds past. Her legs stopped kicking. The rope stopped swaying and she hung motionless staring at us with a revengeful look on her face. Some of the gang began to hide their faces in fear, the others had already run away, believing that she was truly evil and would come back for revenge. They weren't going to wait around.

"You can come back for me, yah bitch! I'll be waiting. I'm not afraid of you. Now, die you piece of shit... die!" I yelled. "You can get her down now, you pussies," I ordered. As they untied the rope, her body dropped to the floor with a thud, surrounded by dismembered toes and fingers in a pool of blood. There was a different atmosphere in the room now. Scarface's taunts had clearly rattled most of the gang. "She is all yours," I said to the guards. I circled the body.

"This is for you Red" and spat on Scarface as I left to go back to my cell.

Chapter Seventeen: The Impossible Pitch

I was pacing back and forth like a caged animal in the waiting room at the hospital, praying for Jane to pull through. She was still in theatre. Having her return home was the greatest thing that has happened in a long time. I am so proud of the woman she has grown in to. I was reminiscing when she was younger and how much joy she brought into our lives back then. She had a good heart and would always oblige when someone asked for help, offering her heartfelt love and support. I lost her once and all that sadness and despair was resurfacing. I could not bear the thought of going through it all again.

Every time a doctor appeared in the waiting room, I rushed up and confronted them anxiously, only to find that Jane wasn't their patient. Hours passed until one doctor finally told me that it would be quite some time before I could expect any news. The doctor insisted it would be in my best interest to go home and they would call me with any updates. Exhausted and frustrated, I agreed but decided work was the best place to be.

From the moment I arrived back at the prison, I sensed dark energy, something I had never experienced in all my time here. The energy is haunting, eerie and it's chilling my blood.

As I walked to my office, I passed Pyke. She just looked at me with no expression. A reference to me that the job was done... good!

I passed Barbara at her desk, who immediately asked about Jane's condition. I could only tell her to hold my calls. I closed the door to my office and sat at my desk. I was about to call Pyke in for a rundown of what happened when the phone rang.

"Yes, Barbara! I thought I said no calls?"

"It's the hospital Warden, line 3."

"Okay thanks, put them through."

I picked up the phone, dreading any bad news, "Yes, speaking, yes... yes... oh my God, that's wonderful news. That's such a huge relief, thank you so much for calling."

I was so relieved upon hearing the news that Jane had survived the surgery and was now conscious and recovering. She was covered in so much blood the last time I saw her; I'll never forget that image. I was so scared she wasn't going to make it. She will be inconsolable when she finds out she lost the baby. Her baby meant the world to her and there's only one person I know who could help her right now but she's not here and I had no idea how to find her.

Jane needs Sarah and I knew it. She left this place running from it and who could blame her? She was just in the wrong place at the wrong time. Anyway, I can't see her coming back here any time soon.

The phone rang again.

"Yes, Barbara! What is it this time?" I snapped.

"You have two visitors wanting to see you, Warden."

"I thought I told you I wasn't seeing anyone today! What part of that didn't you understand?"

"Sending them through now Warden," Barbara replied, ignoring my outburst.

"What?" I yelled back but Barbara had already hung up.

The door opened slowly, as I sat there annoyed at Barbara's refusal to follow my orders. I was about to explode in anger when a smile spread across my face instead and my heart beamed with delight at the sight of the two who were now in my office. It was the best surprise!

"Oh, you've got to be kidding! I was just thinking about you," I got out of my chair to greet her.

"What are you doing here, Sarah?" I asked joyfully.

There was something special about this girl.

"Well, you see Warden," as she smiled, "I just can't stay away from this place. I miss it so much," she said, letting out a rare laugh.

I moved closer and bent down, slowly looking at the little girl by her side and asked, "And who is this little one?"

"This is my daughter Isabella," said Sarah proudly.

"What!... really? But the last time I saw you which wasn't that long ago, you were only..." I questioned, surprised to see Sarah with an infant.

"Yes, I know Warden. Pregnant. Ahh they grow fast."

"Fast! That's... incredible!" I smiled at Isabella, who then turned and hid between Sarah's legs.

"Good luck with that, Warden. She is extremely shy."

"That's okay. It's so good to see you're okay Sarah, actually both of you. So much has happened here."

"Where's Jane? I thought she might be here. I was hoping to see her," Sarah asked, concerned.

"Oh God, Sarah. Have a seat," I said sadly, pulling out a chair for her to sit on.

"This doesn't sound good," Sarah replied as she sat down with Isabella, still clinging to her legs.

"Jane just lost her baby..." I said with my voice breaking.

"Lost the baby!" Sarah gasped, "oh my God... I'm so sorry. Poor Jane."

I took a pause. I could feel my eyes welling up, "There was an incident here. Shields set Jane up. It was just an excuse to get close to Jane. I shouldn't have let her do it. It didn't feel right but you know Jane, she could never say no to helping someone in need. Long story short, she stabbed my girl. Her baby was killed and Jane is in hospital. She's just come out of surgery," I took a cleansing breath.

"Oh shit! Is Jane okay?" Sarah asked.

"I've just heard that she's now stable and conscious, thank Christ. I thought I was going to lose her."

"Damn her! They've done it again," Sarah said angrily.

"What do you mean they've done it again? I don't understand Sarah, what's going on?" I asked.

"Sorry Warden, I got distracted. So much has happened since I've been gone. What's been happening here at the prison is also happening at the convent. It's just the tip of the iceberg. I now understand that this predicament has far-reaching consequences for us all and to make matters worse...we don't have a lot of time!" Sarah said. I knew instantly she was deadly serious by her tone.

"I don't think I can take much more of this. My ticker won't take it!"

"You know the end of the world movies where only a few people are left to save the world and time is not on their side. Well, we're right smack bang in the middle of one of those movies...except it's not a movie. It's real and its unfolding right in front of our eyes."

"Did you hear me say my ticker isn't good. I don't think I can take any more news like this Sarah, honestly."

"I understand Warden but I need you to listen. It's in everyone's interest that I explain exactly what's going on, once and for all. Can you assemble all the prisoners together, as soon as possible?"

"What! Now! Don't you want to see Jane first?" I asked.

"It's that urgent Warden. I'll have to see Jane as soon as I'm finished here."

"Okay, if you think that's best. I'll make the necessary arrangements and get all the inmates together. Do you want to leave Isabella with Barbara?"

"Would that be okay with Barbara? I will bring her out and show the women but not just yet. I need to talk with them first without the distraction."

Sarah picked up Isabella and spoke, "Isabella, you must stay with Barbara for a little while. I'll come and get you shortly, I promise."

Barbara had a way with children which made Sarah's request easier. She distracted her easily and Isabella seemed happy enough to go with her.

"Thank you, Barbara. I'll call for her shortly."

"Okay, Warden, let's do this?" said Sarah, inspired and motivated.

We walked into the main hall where the guards had gathered all the inmates. The mood seemed grim and there was little talk amongst the women, probably second-guessing why they had been summoned here, once again.

As we got closer, the prisoners began to catch a glimpse of Sarah and I could see their walls go up instantly. Their body language was very shut off and they didn't want to be here. Sarah sensing the situation, decided to start immediately.

"Ladies, the last time I spoke with you I was pregnant. Today, I am proud to show you someone very special. I'd like you to meet her but first I would like to share with you some new information that I have recently learnt about the pregnancies we have all endured."

The prisoners began to chatter amongst themselves and the noise in the room grew loud quickly.

"To begin, the reason we all fell pregnant in the first place, is we were chosen or selected by an intelligent race of beings called Luveains who are on the verge of extinction, to carry their young and..." she didn't finish the sentence when the heckling began.

"Bullshit!" shouted a prisoner.

"No way," yelled another as comments began flying around the room.

"That's impossible! Bullshit."

The outbursts continued, so Sarah waited, allowing them to say their piece and for the room to go quiet again before she continued.

"Please! Let me talk. I know... impossible, right? About as impossible as having a sexless pregnancy in prison. Or that impossible when the aborted fetuses were only weeks old but way more advanced than a human fetus. Ladies, in case you haven't already noticed, there is nothing normal about what's been going on around here. I beg you all to keep an open mind with what I'm about to tell you. This isn't normal, none of it and that's because it isn't."

"You're telling us aliens are responsible for this? Are you fuckin' kidding? What the fuck are you talking about?" an inmate shouted.

"You're full of shit!" they continued to shout. Sarah paused and waited for the noise to subside before she continued. I could see her frustration but she persisted.

"Okay, the simple reason is, you are miscarrying when your body experiences high levels of fear. This causes the fetus to mutate and abort, which is what you have seen and experienced. They are not evil or monsters. Although, even I can see why you would think that by looking at the fetuses. Trust me; it is our fear that is the cause of these mutations. In effect, we are responsible for the miscarriages."

The room erupted again with loud angry protests. Again, Sarah let it go for a while, then intervened and then shouted, "LADIES, PLEASE LET ME FINISH!" she commanded.

The room slowly went quiet and Sarah continued.

"Please open your minds. I know how much of this is a stretch to believe but it's true... I am telling you the truth."

"So why are you here and what do you want from us?" shouted an inmate.

"They need willing surrogates to help them survive. I'm asking you to help them?" Sarah replied.

The inmate closest to Sarah shouted so all could hear, "Now, why would we go through all that again? We all know how it ends. A pile of blood and guts on the floor! No thanks!"

This unfortunately raised similar feelings amongst all the inmates and the angry outbursts continued to fill the room once more.

"I saw my baby and it was evil. I will never go through that again!" yelled one inmate.

"We owe them nothin'!" shouted another.

"How can we stop them doing this to us? We want it to stop!" as they continued to vent their frustrations at Sarah.

Sarah interrupted, "Okay, you're pissed... I get it... I was too. Now, if you let me, I'll do my best to answer you," as she took a pause.

"Why didn't they just ask us?" shouted an inmate.

"If it were that simple, don't you think they would have!" Sarah fired back.

"You said you had someone special here today... show us, get on with it!"

Sarah looked across at where I was standing and waved at Barbara and I to bring Isabella out, "If you had managed your fears and gone full term, you would have given birth to a healthy hybrid baby."

As Barbara and I walked Isabella out in front of the prisoners, Isabella shook loose of Barbara and ran to Sarah, grabbing onto her jeans tightly. She was shy and tried to hide behind Sarah's legs. Sarah bent down and wrestled with Isabella, who resisted being picked up. I was close enough to hear Sarah whisper into her ear.

"Isabella, it's okay. We need to do this. I need to show these women. They won't harm you. I'm right here with you, okay? We need to do this for your people, Bellatrix. You know this and it's time, Please!"

Sarah's words saw Isabella loosen her grip and Sarah gently lifted her up and let her sit on her shoulders for all to see. She sat there with her little legs wrapped tightly around Sarah's head, her little hands holding tightly on to Sarah's. Isabella was softening the inmates and I watched as their body language changed and their hearts opened up to this little girl.

"Ladies, this is my daughter Isabella. She is a hybrid being, meaning she is half human and half... half... alien."

I saw the inmates looking at one another as the room remained silent. Sarah continued to speak.

"Now, to be honest, I'm still struggling with all of this and if it wasn't for Isabella, I would probably think it was all a weird dream or something. The truth is, she is the best thing that has ever happened to me and you all have the same opportunity in front of you."

The prisoners were arguing and shaking their heads. There's your answer Sarah, I thought to myself. She still persisted, passionate about getting her message out.

"We were all carefully selected as surrogates by the Luveians. We all have traits that give these beautiful hybrids the best chance of survival, as long as we can control our fear. The Luveians have promised to help us and you'll receive gifts as you carry the hybrid, which you will understand over time."

The inmates became very disgruntled with Sarah's last comments.

"How about my last gift!" yelled an inmate.

"If you call those mutations gifts... they can keep them," as more yelling broke out. Their noisy protesting now made it difficult for Sarah to continue. I could see Isabella was becoming frightened by the angry exchange and Sarah gently pulled her down into her arms as she buried her face in Sarah's chest and wrapped her arms around her, squeezing tightly.

Sarah turned around to see me with my arms folded and shaking my head. The noise in the room was now deafening. I walked over to her and said,

"You're wasting your time. You're not going to change their minds. They're bloody criminals. They don't have open minds! Who are we kidding?" I said angrily.

"It takes time, Warden," Sarah tried to reassure me, "it's a tough ask. Would you give up your body for an alien? They need time to process what I've already told them before they can take in any more information but I think it may just be too much for them."

I escorted Sarah and Isabella back to my office. The silence was blissful after leaving the disgruntled inmates. We sat down at my desk and both looked at Isabella.

"That didn't go well," Sarah said.

"No, it didn't and that was the second attempt," I said.

"I always knew it would take time Warden. I have to go slowly with them. I'll give it one more go and then it's out of my hands."

"Do you have time for that?" I replied.

"Not really. By the way, I almost forgot. What happened to that bitch Scarface after she… sorry Warden?" Sarah said, remorsefully.

"That's okay, Sarah. I understand I know you care deeply for Jane," I replied.

"I imagine what happened didn't go down well with the inmates. They knew Jane was pregnant."

"Yes, they knew and no it didn't end well for Shields. Turns out Red was actually one of the inmate's daughters, Tyson."

"What? Red's mother was one of the inmates! No way!" Sarah's eyes opened wide in surprise

"It's true, I received confirmation from a couple of detectives who investigated the murder. We were all totally shocked, none more so than Tyson. When Shields killed… killed… my Jane's baby," I paused for a while to gather myself. I found it hard to swallow with the lump I had in my throat. I turned away from Sarah as I continued,

"I shouldn't be telling you this but Tyson pleaded with me to transfer Shields from solitary to the general population and you know what? I didn't hesitate for a second. They tortured her and then lynched her. Was I sorry for my decision? Not at all. Will I get in to trouble if anyone finds out? Absolutely. Care factor? Zero. That bitch or 'thing' got what she deserved," I said, feeling a sense of satisfaction.

"Jesus! That's horrible Warden."

"There's more. As they were hanging her the inmates reckon they saw flashes of what looked like scales on her body, like some sort of reptilian-looking animal. Do you know anything about this, Sarah?" I asked.

"Actually, I do. The Luveians warned me," she replied.

"What? Oh come on, Sarah! Now you've spoken to them. I'm really trying to get a grip on all this but that is too much," I said shaking my head.

"I can't get you to believe me and yet you want them to listen to me, to come on board? How is that going to work?" Sarah said looking at me with raised eyebrows.

I rolled my eyes back and gave a smirk.

"I know, I get it, well the basics anyway. It's bloody hard! That's all," I sighed.

"Look, Warden. I'm not here to convert you. Either you believe or you don't and I get it, it's okay. If it wasn't for Isabella, I probably wouldn't believe either but think about it seriously! They can impregnate us but can't communicate with us? Really?" Sarah said with more conviction.

"Well, when you say it like that. I know you think I don't believe you but I'm still struggling with it. I know what's happened but there's still this part of me that goes, there has to be another explanation."

"Don't worry Warden, listen, I'll come back tomorrow but right now I would really like to see Jane."

"Okay, I'll take you." I said as I grabbed my car keys.

"I'd rather go alone Warden, if you don't mind? Just Isabella and I, if that's okay?"

I couldn't hide my disappointment; however, I did understand and it was probably best for Sarah to see Jane without me.

"I nearly forgot Sarah, I can officially allow you to leave the prison without a guard," I said, handing her documents from my desk drawer with a huge grin.

"The District Attorney dropped all charges against you. The knife came back from forensics and they found Shields prints all over it. You're a free woman Sarah. It's over!" I said.

I was surprised by Sarah's cool demeanour, she didn't seem to be taken back by the good news at all.

"You knew about this, didn't you? It's that intuition thing."

"Maybe," Sarah said, smiling.

"Well I'm happy for you Sarah. Really happy... now go, I've got work to do," I said trying not to get emotional, "can you give Jane a hug for me and tell her I'll be there very soon?" I asked.

Then I crouched down in front of Isabella, "It was very nice to meet you, Isabella."

The Warden waved us goodbye with a huge smile on his face as we made our way quickly out of the prison. This time a free woman. It did feel liberating. I hailed a taxi and headed straight to the hospital. I knew returning was going to be difficult, seeing where Red was stabbed and later died. Isabella cuddled into me. She sensed my emotions. It all came flashing back to me as the Taxi driver dropped us off at the front entrance. Staying strong, I picked up Isabella and quickly walked inside. After getting directions from the nurse at reception, we made our way to the ward and found Jane's room. We entered quietly. Jane was sleeping. It was a private room. We walked in and I sat on the edge of the bed and quietly placed Isabella on my lap, who was looking intently around the room, observing everything.

As I sat there looking at Jane, I pondered and now realised what Lexus meant when he said, 'You won't know how unprepared you are until you try.' If I could not convince the Warden, an intelligent, educated man, what hope did I have with a prison full of cons! Maybe the Warden was right. Who was I kidding? I could feel pressure weighing down on my shoulders.

My moment of silence ended as the door was pushed open.

"Miss Walsh... cup of tea?" asked one of the kitchen staff, pulling a trolley.

Startled, Jane woke up.

"Tea? Cup of tea, Miss Walsh?" she repeated.

Jane shook her head with her usual polite manners, "No thanks." Her face then lit up when she saw Isabella and me sitting next to her.

"Does anyone ever sleep around here with all these interruptions and visitors? Jeeesus!" I said, smiling warmly at Jane.

We both laughed.

"What on earth are you doing here, Sarah? I thought I'd never see you again... oh my God! And who is this little girl by your side? She is so gorgeous," she said as she reached out and touched my hand.

"Jane, this is Isabella, she is my daughter," I replied proudly, "can you believe it, Jane? She has grown so quickly."

"Sarah! She is just so beautiful. I can't believe it. I'm so happy for you," she said sincerely.

In typical Jane fashion, she pushed all her emotions aside.

"Thank you, Jane. You're always so kind to me," I said as I reached out and took her hand.

"I am so sorry, Jane. I wish I could have been there with you; maybe it wouldn't have happened."

"I felt I was so close, only hours away from giving birth. It was horrible, Sarah!"

I decided to let Jane know what happened to Scarface.

"It's crazy Jane, the inmates found out what she did to you and your baby and killed her," I gave Jane a moment for that to sink in. "And it turns out that Red's birth mother is an inmate at the prison."

"Really, Sarah. The inmates killed her," Jane replied, shocked.

"Scarface was on a mission to kill the hybrid babies and the surrogates too if need be."

"Sorry Sarah, I don't follow. What do you mean?"

"Sorry! I know I'm going too fast. There's just so much to tell you."

I placed Isabella on the chair and helped Jane to sit up. I poured her a cup of water and then picked up Isabella, who was now smiling at Jane as I placed her back on my lap. I went into depth about what happened at the prison, which had Jane totally shocked, with her hand over her mouth in disbelief. I then told her my encounter with Lexus.

"I have spoken with them Jane, well actually him, Lexus. They have been responsible for our pregnancies. I tried telling your Dad but it was too much for him to get his head around. I've also tried telling the inmates, but quite frankly, I'm up against it. I'm not sure even I believe what I'm saying sometimes," I said frustrated.

"I believe you Sarah," Jane said, touching my arm to reassure me, "it's funny, I dreamt you had the baby and were coming back to rally all the women together but then I woke up."

"Well, that makes one believer!" I said, smiling softly.

"Come on, help me get out of here. I'm going back with you," said Jane as she pulled the sheet back and sat on the side of the bed.

"Are you kidding. Is that's wise, Jane? Shouldn't you rest, surely you need time for the wounds to heal."

"Rest, does it look like I'm getting any rest in here? Anyway, my wounds have all healed. Here, take a look."

Jane pulled up her gown to reveal very faint scars.

"This is where she stabbed me. The doctors can't believe how quickly they have healed. It must have been the healing powers from carrying a hybrid. Besides, they are only keeping me in for rest and further observation, not sure why, I actually feel ok, considering. Besides, I need to go with you Sarah. You need help with the inmates and my father!"

"Just so long as you tell the Warden exactly what you dreamt. Deal?"

"Deal! I'll get dressed and gather my things together. God, I've missed you Sarah O'Connor. Let's get out of here; we have a lot to do."

"Is this the new and assertive Jane Walsh? I like it!" I said as I placed Isabella on the floor so I could help Jane pack.

"Maybe," we both laughed as she went to the bathroom to change and I packed up her things.

Not taking no for an answer, Jane signed all her release forms with the doctor and then we hailed a taxi to return to the prison. We jumped in the back seat and buckled Isabella in between us. The Taxi driver turned the radio on, a little too loudly but that didn't bother me as it allowed us to talk without him listening. As we drove off, I noticed Isabella was holding Jane's hand and I intuitively sensed she was somehow communicating with her. Jane looked at me and said, "They want me to try again, don't they?"

"I believe so, Jane," I said, smiling, "they are beautiful beings in need of our help. I have to convince as many women as possible to help but no one wants to go through it all again and to be honest, I can't say I blame them." I said, gazing out the window at the passing traffic. We had a moment's silence and then Jane asked,

"Did you really speak with them Sarah? Seriously?"

"As clear as I'm speaking with you right now. In fact, I spoke with him... Lexus. He is truly gorgeous, Jane. His eyes just pull you in and his energy... wow. Oh, my God! Listen to me gushing. It's just they have so much love you can feel it and he's so hot!" I couldn't believe I just said that.

"Are you kidding? So, you have actually met and talked to a HOT alien?" she said which made us both laugh.

"I have never been more serious in my life Jane but it's not all about him. It's about them and saving their race. He is just... well, a bonus you could say," I looked at Jane biting my lip.

"Oh, my God! I have goose bumps all over me. Do you think I will ever meet him? I mean them?"

"Don't know, that's a good question. He appears just when you least expect it. Sorry to change the subject Jane but just letting you know, I need to go back to talk to the women again. I don't think I'm explaining myself very well and they really did struggle with what I said to them. I can't say I blame them. I'm not giving up, so I have to give it another go. We need as many women as possible."

"Good luck with that Sarah. I mean, how do you ask prisoners to become pregnant to aliens nicely? Really!" said Jane.

"Well, I haven't been able to do it yet. I can't believe I'm even doing this sometimes. It's just that I really do believe what Lexus told me. By the way, I was going to ask you if you could take me to the convent? I have to speak to the women there as well.

"I'm happy to take you there but if you thought the inmates were a challenge, I better teach you how to pray. You're going to need all the help you can possibly get," said Jane seriously.

"Amen to that, sister!" I said, throwing one arm up in the air, as Isabella watched on inquisitively.

"Are you okay Sarah? You look exhausted?" asked Jane.

"Actually Jane, I am but now isn't the time for resting. Someone I know very well just told me that," I said as Jane smirked back at me.

"Listen! Let's turn the taxi around and head back to Dad's place. You and Isabella can stay the night and we'll all head back to the prison tomorrow and hit them with all you've got. Come home with me and have a nice meal and let's celebrate your return and of course, Isabella. What do you think?" said an excited Jane.

"That's the best offer I've had in a very long time, Jane. You're on, sister."

The idea of a delicious meal and somewhere safe and warm to stay was too good to pass up.

On Jane's orders, the Warden came home early and seemed happy to have a full house. We all pitched in to cook, shared a bottle of wine and finished off with a delicious dessert that the Warden picked up on his way home. After dinner, I put Isabella to sleep on the couch next to us and we chatted for hours, discussing everything from Aliens to convents. It was the best night we had all experienced in a very long time and it certainly brought us all closer together and the Warden a little wiser as I had time to explain to him the whole process with Jane at my side.

"There is something I've been meaning to tell you Dad," said Jane.

"This sounds serious," the Warden said concerned.

"Do you remember those dreams I used to have when I was growing up and I used to tell you about them?" said Jane.

"How could I forget! They were always so bizarre and then low and behold they would come true. Don't tell me. You've had one of those dreams again?"

"Yes, I have and it's really important... I need to tell you because it's about Sarah. Everything she has told you Dad is true. I know it's so hard to get your head around but it's all true. She has been chosen by a dying race of intelligent beings to bring together women to act as surrogates for their species and it's true there is another more hostile species desperate to take over our planet. These hybrid children could help us if we just agree to help their species and become impregnated."

"You had all that in a dream and you have no doubts at all?" questioned the Warden.

"It's crystal clear, Dad. They picked Sarah."

"Sorry, Dad. I know how weird this all is and how hard it is to believe. I have been meaning to tell you but knew I had to pick my moment," Jane said.

"I'm sorry, Sarah, for not listening more when you tried to tell me... it's just a lot to take in," the Warden said, scratching his head.

"I know Warden. If it wasn't happening to me, I wouldn't believe it," I replied.

"That makes three of us," Jane chipped in.

"Well, it's getting late and I would love to keep talking but I have a huge task ahead of me tomorrow. So if it's okay with you good people I need to give my brain some downtime and get some sleep?" I said, yawning.

"You're kidding me, Is that the time? Wow, one glass of wine and you can't shut me up. It's my bedtime, too," said Jane.

"Well, I have a lot to process now, thanks, Jane. I'm going to have a nightcap or two. I'll see you girls in the morning. Sleep tight," said the Warden, topping up his glass.

I picked up Isabella and followed Jane as she showed us to our room.

"I'll leave the hall light on and I've left some PJ's on the bed for you. Everything you may need is in the bathroom. It's all my stuff, so help yourself," Jane said, "sweet dreams," she gave us a big hug and went to her room.

I finally fell into bed and I let out a big sigh as I cuddled up with Isabella. It was relief to be off my feet for the day but the weight of tomorrow's task sat heavy on my mind.

It wasn't a surprise that I woke up early after a restless night's sleep. The prospect of my next talk to the inmates kept me up most of the night. I just couldn't shut it out, as hard as I tried.

I got Isabella ready and made our way to the kitchen. I could smell something cooking and it was good.

"Omelettes with smoked salmon, shallots and spinach delicately arranged on toast with avocado butter, anyone?" Jane proudly announced as we arrived in the kitchen.

"Wow, yes please, Jane. This smells amazing," I said.

She encouraged us to start and said the Warden would be out shortly. No sooner had I sat down, a mug of freshly brewed coffee was placed in front of me.

"I'm in heaven, Wow! Jane Walsh. This is the most delicious breakfast I have ever laid my eyes on and this coffee is to die for. You're amazing!"

"She is indeed," the Warden said, taking his seat at the table.

"Good morning ladies and Isabella. How are you all on this fine morning?" said a chipper Warden.

Jane placed her Dad's breakfast in front of him, followed by his coffee.

"You know a man could get used to this, Jane?" he said as he winked at me.

"Dream on, Dad!" as we all had a chuckle.

Then there was blissful silence as we all enjoyed every mouthful of our breakfast.

"Well, all I can say is, that was the perfect way to start the day. Yes siree."

The Warden winked at Isabella sitting on my lap, who once again nuzzled into me.

"So, is it alright if I get a lift with you Warden to the prison?" I asked.

"Ooh, I don't know. Now you're pushing it. What do you think, Jane?" as he smiled at Isabella again.

"Oh, stop teasing, Dad!"

"That's what I love about you, Jane. Never could keep a joke going. I wasn't hurting anyone, now was I Sarah?" he quipped.

"No, not at all Dad," I said, butting in, as I turned to Jane and we both laughed at the expression on the Warden's face.

"Well, okay then. If you're going to be like that, then you can... you can... hell, I don't even know what I'm talking about," the Warden said bemused.

After breakfast and showering, we gathered up our belongings and made our way to the prison.

As we got closer to the prison, the mood seemed to turn more serious. Everyone was quiet. I could see the Warden constantly checking in his rear-view mirror as he drove but he wasn't checking traffic. He was checking on me as I was lost in thought. I wondered whether this day would really make any difference to how the women will react.

"Are you okay Sarah?" he asked from the driver's seat as he glanced in the rear vision mirror once again.

"Ah, as ready as I'll ever be, I guess. What's the old saying, 'you can lead the horse to water but you can't make it drink'. Is that how it goes?" I replied as I gazed out the window observing the passing landscape.

"Well, I don't think it should be your job to make them drink the water, Sarah. I have to say though, I'm proud of both of you. You get in there and give it your best shot Sarah and remember, you're not responsible for how they vote," the Warden said with conviction.

"Thanks, Warden. I appreciate your support."

My voice was croaky from being so tired after the poor night's sleep. Isabella feeling my vulnerability, cuddled into me.

"Sarah, I pressured Jane to tell me everything she knew about you. I make it my business to know everyone who comes into my prison," the Warden said as he watched for my reaction in the rear-view mirror.

"No surprises there," I said annoyed, as I glanced at Jane.

"I'm sorry Sarah, he just wouldn't let up" as Jane placed her hand on my lap.

"I'm bloody good at reading people Sarah and in the short time I have known you and by the way you have conducted yourself through all this adversity, you're one incredible young lady and the first woman to bring a hybrid full term," he continued to glance back at me the whole time to see if I was taking it all in.

"Thank you Warden but in truth I'm still just a teenager! What can I possibly say to these women who are way older and have been through a lot more compared to me?"

"You've been chosen for a reason but if you don't believe that, you won't convince the women. You have to believe right in here," he said, as he punched his heart with his fist.

"Thanks Warden but my confidence has taken a hit from the last attempt."

"Have these aliens appeared in front of anyone else Sarah?"

"Ah, not that I know of," I replied.

"You're a natural leader but you just don't see it yet. Question is,will you take the throne and help them? Let me tell you, Sarah, we are never ready. You make yourself ready by seizing the opportunity. Don't live with regrets; you can do it. Grab this opportunity with both hands. We believe in you!"

As he spoke, I glanced around to see Jane nodding, who then gave me a huge smile.

As he finished, we arrived at the prison. If the Warden's words weren't making me uncomfortable enough, the sight of the prison certainly did. It's now or never. I was over-thinking this. My father's voice popped in my head. *Don't over-think things, Samantha, don't over-analyse.* I could somehow almost feel his presence.

We made our way inside, where the Warden was greeted by several of the guards. They seemed to respect this man. Jane had said that he always had the prisoners' best interests at heart and it showed through his actions.

Jane excused herself. "I'll be with you in a jiffy," she said as she disappeared behind the door marked Staff Toilets.

We walked into the Warden's office as I held Isabella in my arms.

"So where to from here, Sarah?" asked the Warden.

"Well, third time lucky hey. I need to do this before I change my mind," I said.

He acknowledged with a nod of his head as he picked up his phone,

"Barbara, can you get Hames to assemble all the inmates in the main hall in five minutes? Thank you."

"Warden, I just want to say thank you for everything you said earlier. I know I doubt myself so much. You've given me confidence with your wise words, so thank you."

"I meant every word, Sarah. Well, they're ready and waiting, go get 'em," the Warden said, smiling at me.

As we made our way to the main hall, with Isabella snuggled into me, I'm sure she could sense my anticipation.

Once again, the mood in the room was heavy and the energy was much the same as I left it yesterday. The prisoners stood there against their will, arms folded in front of their chests and a pissed off look on their face. I wasted no time and began to speak but before I got one word out, the heckling started.

"Oh, not this again. We've heard it all before. We ain't interested, why won't you listen... get someone else to do your dirty work."

I didn't let them finish.

"Ladies... I know how hard this has been on you and some of you don't want to be here right now. I totally understand but please hear me out. I know you find this difficult to believe and once again I completely understand that too. I'm not here to judge you."

I paused as the group began to break up and leave, shaking their heads in disapproval and mumbling to one another. I felt disappointed they chose to leave. Then the strangest thing happened. Isabella, who was hiding behind me, walked off into the group of prisoners.

"Isabella... stop... please stop. Come back here," I shouted and I started to go after her. She turned around and looked at me as she continued to head off into the group. I could hear her thoughts clearly. It was like a muscle in my brain. The more I opened up and allowed, the easier it became to listen to what she was telling me. She explained to me that Lexus had asked her to help me and told her what to do.

The room became quiet and the women who were about to leave were mysteriously drawn back into the room, with a curious expression on their face, staring at Isabella the whole time. I took a deep breath and continued, as Jane entered the room and stood by my side. As I began to talk again, I was distracted by Isabella who walked amongst the prisoners and making contact with each of them by touching their hands. After touching Isabella, the women rubbed the sides of their heads and became quiet. It's as if she had downloaded them and they were processing the information.

"Yesterday, I explained why you became pregnant and then miscarried. They did it for the survival of their species. They did not mean us any harm. We would do the same, maybe even worse."

The women were chatting amongst themselves about what Isabella was doing and slowly became even quieter as Isabella continued to move through them. I continued.

"There is something I have not told you yet. I have been made aware there is another species out there and they are hostile. You have seen glimpses of this species through the person who was hung here a couple of days ago. She was a Thraxion, from the planet Thraxus. Her sole purpose was to kill as many Luveian hybrids as possible and she was very successful, as you know. Jane's baby was her last termination. She was right when she told you, they will come after us. It is the Thraxions that have nearly decimated Isabella's race and now they are attempting to hybridise their species with ours in order to survive on Earth. There is no other way for them. In short, if we don't come on board with the Luveians, we will be targeted by these Thraxions to hybridise with their species. Make no mistake they are coming, they are violent and they are ruthless. If

Thraxions impregnate you, your fear will feed the fetus. They thrive on fear and between our fear and their hostility, you have the makings of an absolute monster. I hope you can begin to understand how serious this is?"

The prisoners who had not been touched by Isabella continued to shout out their concerns.

"How do we know you're telling us the truth? And how do you know all this stuff anyway?"

I raised my hands in the air asking for quiet and a chance to reply.

"I have spoken with a Luveian," I paused, waiting for the ridicule, "they are from a planet called Luve and they are referred to as Luveians."

There was only a handful of women who had not made contact with Isabella and still protested.

"Bullshit! We don't believe you. You're full of shit. Prove it!" an inmate shouted.

"Aliens, my arse! Get outta here," another yelled.

Then the heckling finished and the women just stood there with blank expressions on their faces. I didn't even know if they were listening anymore. I was tired, frustrated and out of patience. Isabella had finished doing what she was doing and when she returned, I took her hand and started walking back to the Warden's office. There was no more I could say or do. You cannot force someone to believe. We walked past a group of prisoners who looked dazed and we proceeded to leave the room. We were nearly out the door when I heard Jane shout,

"Sarah, Stop! Please stop! Just wait!"

I turned around to see Jane raise her hands up and begin to speak to the whole group in a loud, pleading voice, I paused to listen to what she had to say.

"Listen... please listen. Everything Sarah has told you today is true. Everything! I have only known Sarah O'Connor for a short time but I would trust her with my life. Most of you don't know this but before coming here, I was staying at a convent as a nun, quite some distance from here. Exactly the same thing has happened there. Nuns became pregnant without having sex. Can you imagine the shock and humiliation for the nuns? We had no idea how it was happening and we could not stop it. You can see this child is different. You can see she is not fully human and what is going on here is also going on at the convent. Sarah is here to help us and she believes them. Okay, I haven't met them but I have never felt so much love as when I was pregnant by them. They are peaceful beings and they are trying to help us because they know what is going to happen. Sure, they want to survive, but they want us to survive as well and keep our home, our beautiful planet. I have witnessed firsthand what the evil Thraxion species can do. They don't want prisoners. They don't want to help us and they definitely don't care about us. They need our planet, not us.

This is not about helping Sarah; it's about us stepping up and playing our part together to save our family, our friends and our homes. You need to look at the bigger picture. You are strong, brave women and some of you may never leave this place and your whole life might not count for anything. Is that the legacy of the life you want to be remembered for? Or do you want a chance to be remembered as the mothers of the hybrids who saved our planet, our way of life and our existence?

Then one of the inmates spoke. Her tone sounded different. She asked a question in a calm and interested manner.

"O'Connor! You said you spoke with them... what did they say?"

I walked back with Isabella to where Jane was still standing and replied, "They said they were sorry. Sorry for all the pain and stress they had caused us. Sorry for all the shame and confusion. At first, they were just taking tissue samples from us while we were asleep, so they didn't frighten us. But as their numbers fell dangerously low due to the Thraxions, they had no choice but to try and hybridise with us as soon as possible."

I paused and gazed around the room staring at the women who were now listening intently to everything I was saying.

"From their research they knew this dynamic could be powerful against the Thraxions. They were carefully selecting women with specific DNA to give the hybrid the best chance of survival. Traits and characteristics were also important for this hybrid race. That is the reason why we have been impregnated. They knew it was probably too late for them but they believed they could at least help us."

The energy in the room was now calm and quiet. You could literally see their minds processing all the information they had received and they were digesting it.

"The Luveians saw a grim future and the ripple effects that would occur throughout the galaxy, if they did not help us and themselves. In the end ladies, this is still your decision. Remember this... we need each other."

I was done. I could not say another word. I picked up Isabella and walked back to the Warden's office with Jane following behind me.

The Warden's door was open and we walked straight in.

"Well? How did it go? You don't look so happy?" the Warden asked us.

"To be honest... I don't know. I really don't know. It's like a hung jury, so we'll just have to wait for the verdict," I replied in a frustrated tone.

"That's it? That's all you got. Let me go and talk to them. I'll put a bomb up their backsides that will send them into next year," the Warden shouted.

"That's not how the Luveians want it," I said firmly.

"I don't care what they want! What about what we want?"

"Listen, I can't wait here any longer Warden, we haven't got time. Jane, we need to go to the convent and talk to the nuns and see what's going on over there. These women will need time to process this information. It's a lot to think about."

"Well, I'm glad you warmed up on the inmates because if you thought they were hard work, you have no idea what you are about to walk into!" Jane said with absolute certainty.

"Well then, I guess it's time to find out. Time for the encore."

"Okay, we're heading over to the convent Dad. Will you be okay?" asked Jane.

"Yes. Yes, go! Don't you be worrying about this old bastard. I'll be fine. I'll survive in spite of myself."

"Goodbye to you, little Isabella. See you soon," said the Warden, giving her a little wave.

Isabella squirmed out of my arms and walked up to the Warden and gave him a hug.

"Well, thank you, darlin'," he said.

The Warden seemed surprised and a little overcome with emotion. I think he really missed his family and you could tell he yearned for more love and connection in his life.

After the hug, Isabella ran back to me and we waved goodbye. The Warden was emotional and staring at Isabella. She had made quite an impact.

Chapter Eighteen: Holy Retribution

Our taxi arrived at the convent and after paying the driver, we grabbed our belongings and made our way to the entrance gates.

"I meant what I said back there Sarah, Mother Superior will test you to your core. Brace yourself for the worst," warned Jane.

"I'm under no illusions, trust me. I'm only here to keep my word to the Luveians," I replied.

Jane was surprised that the outside gates were closed. You could no longer just walk in. Jane rang a bell and we waited for a response. After several minutes someone replied.

"Yes... who is it? What is your business here?"

"Ah! it's Jane Walsh, formerly Sister Mary Ellen. I wish to speak with Mother Superior please?"

The nun on the speaker voice must have recognised Jane's voice as her cautious tone changed quickly to one of excitement.

"Oh, Jane! Yes, yes. Just a minute!"

We waited patiently. The large, wooden door to the side of the main gates slowly opened.

We were greeted by an excited nun in her full habit.

"Oh, Sister Mary Ellen, I mean Miss Walsh! It's so good to see you again. We have missed you terribly here."

"It's wonderful to see you again Sister Beatrice," said Jane warmly.

Jane and Sister Beatrice embraced in a warm hug and rubbed each other's back up and down with their hands slowly, in a warm loving gesture.

"Oh, Sister Beatrice, this is my good friend, Sarah O'Connor and her beautiful baby, Isabella. They are travelling with me. I need to see Mother superior. Is she available? It's very important," Jane asked.

"Ohh! Um, I'm not sure bringing you inside is such a good idea. Mother Superior is worse than ever Jane. She hasn't been herself for some time," Sister Beatrice moved in closer to Jane and whispered something.

"Don't worry about Mother Superior. I'll will be fine Sister."

"Oh dear! I have knots in my stomach already, Sister. I mean, Jane. Oh! I have a bad feeling about this... I really do."

"It'll be fine, Sister. You'll see," Jane said to reassure her.

"Okay if you think its best, please follow me, I'll take you to the main meeting room. I have to call her from there to let her know you're here. Oh dear, I really do have an uneasy feeling about this, Jane."

We followed behind Sister Beatrice. As we walked, I touched Jane's hand to get her attention. She looked at me and I whispered,

"What did the sister whisper to you?"

"It is as though Mother Superior was possessed," Jane said looking distressed.

I began feeling uneasy and sick. I could sense a thick blanket of dense energy in the air. It sat on my shoulders like an invisible weight, like an entity. It made me want to shake my body several times to free myself from it.

We climbed several flights of stairs and with Isabella in my arms, we had to pause several times to catch our breath. We continued down a long balcony following Sister Beatrice as I gazed out and caught the views of the landscaped grounds which looked spectacular.

We were halfway down the balcony when a door burst open in front of us, startling us all. A nun was leaving her room and was just as surprised to see us.

"Well, well, well. What do we have here? If it isn't the pregnant little slut. Oh no, please don't tell me you've dragged an innocent child into your mess. God forgive them." The words were tainted with venom. I didn't need to second guess who this was and the uneasy look on Jane's face confirmed who this was.

"I heard you were a nasty piece of work! You certainly don't disappoint," I fired back, flying to Jane's defence.

"Ahhh... you must be the masculine one in the relationship! Of course, you are! Walsh was always the weak one and pathetically weak at that," scorned Mother Superior. Jane remained silent.

"You know what? I reckon there must be something missing from those holy clothes you hide behind! A set of horns and a tail perhaps?"

"Sarah, please! You'll only make things worse," Jane pleaded.

"No! That's where you are wrong, Jane. You can't reason with brainwashed hypocrites like her. It's a waste of time. She lost her soul and can't recall where she left it!" I said looking up and down her habit.

"You're not welcome here; I have no idea why you came here but I will not have you corrupting the holy women that reside here. I want you both gone now, including your devil spawned child," as she scowled at Isabella.

Isabella could sense and feel her evil energy and was clinging to my leg desperately.

"Holy! But they're being led by Satan herself. This entire place needs to be exorcised, starting with you!"

"I'd watch your mouth from now on, you dirty little tramp or I'll have you forcibly removed and returned to the hole you crawled out from!" Mother Superior replied forcibly.

"Just try it, you hypocrite!" I shouted looking straight into her eyes.

She pushed my buttons and brought a side out of me I didn't know existed. I was so angry. I could not begin to imagine how she has mistreated all these women over the years. I've only known her for minutes and I want to kill her. She was a monster. My intuition seemed to go into overdrive and I could feel Isabella tightening her grip on my hand. I looked down at her to comfort her but instead, I was suddenly uploaded... shit... Scarface wasn't the only Thraxion. Mother Superior was one too. It gave her every opportunity to kill the hybrids at the convent.

"Sarah, please! She is not worth it. Trust me. It's the other nuns we need to save," Jane said with urgency.

"You've come here to save these nuns? That's funny, it's not the nuns that need saving and what makes you think they will listen to you anyway?"

Mother Superior was urging on the slanging match but I was running out of patience. I was assessing all my options as we stood there now staring each other down. I had to do something soon. We didn't stand a chance while she remained here. She had all the nuns in a trance and they were terrified of her. She was conditioning these nuns for hybridisation, keeping them in a fearful state, day and night. The perfect breeding ground for Thraxions.

"Jane tells me you never got pregnant. No surprises there. I'll bet you've never seen any action, even long before you became a nun. No man was ever gonna touch you. Touch? What am I talking about? I'll bet they never even looked at you. Is that why you became a nun?"

I was stalling while I hatched a plan. I needed to know how I was going to execute this. As I stared down Mother Superior I was drawn to her eyes. They had become black. Her entire eyes were black and every now and then they rolled back into her head. It was the creepiest thing I had ever seen and now I was really worried about Jane.

"Is that your lame attempt to get under my skin? Ohhh, you're going to have to do better than that, you little bastard farmer. Why not be just like Jane? Weak and stupid!"

"Don't speak to my friend like that, you old witch!"

"Friend? Is that what she is? Jane was always pretending to be someone's friend. She has always been a reject you know. Didn't even make it as a nun. Why she couldn't even do the laundry correctly! I'll bet she would have even failed at cleaning the toilets. That's all I had left for her to screw up. No one wanted her, you know. How should I put this? That's it! She was a stain on humanity. I knew it the minute we took her in."

"You bitch! Show some compassion, you hypocrite! Isn't that what you're supposed to preach here?" I went to take a step forward as Isabella again tightened her grip warning me.

"Compassion, to her? You must be insane girl?"

"That's right, you're not capable of compassion... are you?" I fired back.

"I see you didn't keep your baby, Jane. No surprise there now. Poor Jane. What are we going to do with you?"

"Don't listen to her, Jane. She is a Thraxion! They are trying to control you through her. Don't listen to her. Do you hear me, Jane?"

I quickly glanced around to see Jane. She had her hands over her ears trying to block out Mother Superior's cruel taunts but I could she was vulnerable. Her walls were down and there was nowhere to hide.

"Oh, have I upset you, sweet Jane? Oh, I'm sorry! It's just that the truth hurts sometimes. There's nothing we can do about that now, is there? Never mind! The convent clown... there's an idea; maybe we can find you a job in a circus. Yes! Perfect!"

She knew she was tearing Jane into shreds and getting to me as well. I was doing my best to distract Jane. It hurt me to see her in pain, she had already been through so much.

"Jane! Don't listen, you hear me? Just don't listen to this monster," I was pleading with her now. I could feel that Mother Superior was gaining more control over Jane. I was really concerned. Jane wasn't responding to me.

I glanced around again, momentarily taking my eyes off Mother Superior, to check on Jane. Her hands were down by her sides and she looked like she was in a trance. It wasn't just the cruel things being said it was as though she was controlling her mind.

She stood there slumped and appeared vacant. Now I was really worried about her but I couldn't take my eyes off the old witch for more than a second. She would do her best to take me out. She wanted me out of the way as much as I wanted her gone.

"Jane! I want to hear your voice. Talk to me!" I placed my hand on Jane's shoulder and shook it.

"Jane... Jane... talk to me."

By getting to Jane, she was distracting me, to catch me off guard. From the corner of my eye, I could see Mother Superior slip her hand in her pocket. All the while still protecting Isabella, who was behind me clinging on to my clothes.

"Jane! I want to hear your voice. Talk to me." I yelled desperately trying to get Janes attention. It was too quiet. I had a sick feeling in my stomach.

"Tell me, Jane! How does it feel to always be a reject, not good enough? You know, you just don't make the grade. A loser. That must feel like hell. I think hell would be kinder than this place, Don't you, Jane?" Mother Superior continued her attack on Jane.

Almost robotically, Jane responded in a very weird manner.

"Yes, it would be."

"If you don't shut that evil mouth of yours, I'll shut it for you! You know that's not true Jane!" I said begging for a response. When I glanced again, she was just standing there frozen, with no expression on her face.

Jane is way too kind and sensitive for this world. Her soft gentle nature made her an easy target and after losing her baby she was vulnerable and easy to manipulate. Jane simply wasn't strong enough to take on this evil Thraxion.

Suddenly Mother Superior pulled out a knife and was wielding it around in front of me as the shiny metal blade flashed in the sunlight, forcing me to squint.

"Lookie! Lookie! What do I have here? I wonder where that came from?" proudly showing off her weapon. I stepped back shielding Isabella.

"I wasn't expecting you to play fair! Satan is alive and well!"

"Stop being such a spoilsport! Come play with me child. Let's dance? What do you say?" she said coaxing me into fighting with her.

She continued jabbing the knife recklessly towards me. I moved back further and went to move Isabella with me but she was no longer behind me. As she lunged at me with quick jabs. I ducked one way then another to avoid her jabs but then something felt different. Isabella wasn't clinging onto my clothes anymore.

"Isabella!" I screamed in a panic.

Mother Superior had manoeuvred her way over to Jane and had forcibly grabbed her hand and appeared to be uploading her with information and at the same time, still managed to lunge at me with the knife in her other hand. I could only manage fleeting glances as I continued to step away from the quick and constant lunging jabs from Mother Superior. I was horrified as Isabella now came into view; she was by Jane's side. It appeared as if Isabella knew Jane was in trouble and she was attempting to break the Thraxion trance-like hold on her.

The witch had now let go of Jane's hand and moved freely again as she flashed the sharp blade around furiously at me as if she knew she had to strike now.

I hadn't heard Jane's voice in a while and I felt sick in my stomach but I could not take my eyes off Mother Superior as she danced around like a young woman weaving left and right and lunging at me trying to force the knife into me as I darted from side to side to avoid her. I continued to jump quickly fending off her attacks but then in my peripheral vision, I saw a figure move and blur out of sight. I glanced quickly to see Isabella was standing on her own looking over the edge of the balcony railing.

"Isabella!" I screamed at the top of my voice running over to where she was standing.

"She's no good at flying either," Mother Superior said, laughing as she took off down the corridor and disappeared out of sight.

I grabbed Isabella and hugged her and placed her away from the railing as I looked over the edge to see for myself. Four floors down Jane's lifeless body lay with her legs bent in different directions. I grabbed Isabella and bolted down the stairs as fast as I could. Breathless and full of adrenalin I reached the bottom of the stairs panting and out of breath. I carefully put Isabella down and we made our way over to where Jane's body had fallen.

I tried to remain strong especially for Isabella but I felt myself becoming overwhelmed.

I knelt down beside her, unable to hold back my emotions, as my tears welled up and then dropped to the ground. I wiped my eyes so I could see Jane and I was now sobbing uncontrollably with Isabella now by my side and nuns gathering around us. Isabella knew death now.

"Don't just stand there!" I shouted angrily! "Call an ambulance."

In a cruel twist of fate, another good friend was gone. I wiped the tears from my face again and pulled Isabella into me and hugging her tightly. But as I stood there staring at Jane with my wet eyes my body was overcome with anger and I wanted revenge. I wanted to tear that witch apart, piece by piece and make her suffer slowly. I was also angry at myself for getting involved in this stupid argument in the first place. Maybe Jane would still be alive now, had I not reacted?

I took charge, "Please, Sister! Take care of my baby until I get back."

I handed Isabella over to a kind-looking nun despite Isabella's protests and ran back up the stairs full of anger. I wanted to end what the bitch had started.

I could hear the nun doing her best to distract Isabella, as they both quickly walked away from the grim scene. Isabella was in good hands.

Fuelled by anger I wanted to avenge Jane's death. My heart was racing in anticipation of what I was going to do. I set off in search of Mother Superior, running up the stairs and along corridors searching everywhere for her. It was a maze. I kept running and searching all the while thinking how much power and control Mother Superior had over Jane. It was as though she could pull Jane's strings like a puppet and willed her to go over the edge.

I turned and went up another flight of stairs, running along the balcony but I couldn't find her and I was getting so frustrated as well as out of breath.

"Here I am you evil witch," I shouted, "I'm the one you really want. We both know that. Come and get me! I'm all yours!" trying to coax her out of hiding.

I continued to search the building frantically, opening door after door and still no sign of her. Had she gone, vanished without a trace.

Still searching, I came across the chapel and intuitively knew to go inside. Upon entering, I closed the door quietly. I walked towards the altar, looking down each row of seats. No one was here. I turned back towards the doors and was immediately blinded by a magnificent bright light. As the light subsided, I could make out a figure. It was him... Lexus.

"Now you show up! I never see you when I need you. Why didn't you stop that! You could have saved Jane's life," I spat out with no regard to where I was.

Lexus remained silent at first and then replied.

"We understand your anger and your frustration Sarah."

"No, I don't think you do. In fact, I'm done! Finished! Do you hear me? I'm done with your stupid cause. I mean did you really think we stood a chance against them?" I shouted.

"You are angry and have good reason to be. We too have lost many of our people, just like you Sarah. We feel your pain."

"You feel my pain?" I scoffed at him.

"You have achieved so much and we are very grateful. There are situations, contracts that are in play throughout the universe however sometimes things don't always appear to be what they seem."

"Every person I get close to dies. I can't keep doing this. There has been so much death and now Isabella has already witnessed death at her age."

"We know and unfortunately this is only the start. They will try and take everything and everyone you love Sarah and they will not stop until it's all theirs. We understand if you have decided you can no longer continue. It was always going to be difficult especially for you to rely on others to engage in this fight. But your involvement is crucial to the success of our plan. We all need you."

"Did you know that nun was a Thraxion?" I asked.

He came up close to me and his eyes worked their magic on me once again. His energy melted away any anger I had felt towards him, I was under his spell again. I loved being around his energy. I loved him and wanted to be with him. He placed his hands on my shoulders which sent tingles right down my body.

"Yes, Sarah, we did and this means they have advanced faster than we first thought," he said seriously.

"They are a very clever and deceitful species, as we told you and they have taken us by surprise again. They will do anything to gain control. Anything!"

"You need to understand, Lexus, I've just lost another close friend. I tried to get the prisoners to agree. I honestly thought it would work and I now realise there's no way the nuns will agree. People find this all too much, especially telling them about Aliens and invasions. Human beings don't change easily, you know that. We keep making the same mistakes over and over again until it's too late. It's all there in our history. God, I mean come on! Who was I trying to kid! If the prisoners didn't listen why would the nuns? I'm truly sorry. I have failed you," I said, staring into his compassionate eyes.

"But you haven't failed us, Sarah. We are facilitating the pregnancies at the prison now. The prisoners have agreed to be surrogates."

"Really? They agreed? Are you serious?" I said gobsmacked.

"Yes, Sarah. Isabella raised their vibration and downloaded them at the same time, to help them remember their life contracts, what they came in to do and help understand what you were explaining to them. You succeeded Sarah but there is still so much work ahead," Lexus explained caringly.

"Wow! Didn't see that coming. Do you still need the nuns?"

"Yes, we do. We carefully researched and found earthlings that have the DNA, personalities, and characteristics to help rebuild our species. The women we selected are our best chance of survival. The hybrids will need to be of high intelligence, be strong and extremely resilient and show love and compassion towards their fellow hybrids and Luveians. Our research showed the nuns have the DNA and characteristics that we seek and will prove very beneficial for our species, in the future."

"So we need to convince the nuns as well?" I questioned again.

"Yes," he said firmly.

He leant into me and kissed me slowly. His lips caressed mine softly and I could feel his love flowing into me, I was overwhelmed. My tears flowed freely as his hands softly touched each side of my head. As he kissed me, time stopped still, I floated on air as my body tingled all over and I began to feel flustered, "Please let me go back with you?"

Moving back a little, he gently said, "Sarah, I must go now my light is fading. One last thing... you will never fail me, Sarah."

As quickly as he had appeared, he was gone again. I could still feel him, sense him but I felt so empty when he left like he took a piece of me with him. Lexus may lose his light but he has no idea how he lights me up!

I sat down in one of the pews still tingling. Somehow there was a sense of all-knowing. I couldn't explain it but now trusted that everything was happening as it should, perhaps even what happened to Jane. Was this one of the gifts Lexus had referred to. I felt a feeling of peace wash over me. My attention was drawn to the large cross with Jesus on it above the altar.

I knelt and began to pray for strength and inspiration to keep going with this cause. I also prayed for Mum and Dad, what harm could it do. Right now, I needed all the help I could possibly get. I barely got started when I heard the door open and someone enter.

It was a nun who walked right past me, barely noticing me. She looked young, in the process of becoming a nun, I think. She wasn't wearing a full habit but a simple grey tunic and her black hair had been cut short, very short.

As she made her way to the altar she stopped and made the sign of the crucifix, knelt and began to pray. I could hear her crying softly at the same time. I didn't think it was a good time to move so I sat quietly and took a moment to continue my prayer. After a few moments, I looked up and noticed she had finished praying and was now arranging some flowers at the altar. She was still crying and wiping tears from her face.

She stood back from the altar to check the new flower arrangement. Pleased with her work, she stepped back further, bowed before the cross and began to leave. As she walked past, I noticed she was startled, no doubt surprised to see someone.

"Oh, my God! Maria! Maria, It's me, Sarah," I said surprised.

"Sarah! What are you doing here? I thought I would never see you again."

"That's a long story... oh, Maria! It's so good to see you again," I said as I wrapped my arms around her, nearly throwing us off balance.

"You're a nun now?" I asked stepping back to look at her.

"Yes! Well, in the process of becoming one actually," said Maria.

"I would never have picked you to become a nun," I smiled.

"And I would have never picked myself to be pregnant at 15 either!"

"I can't argue with that. God, it's good to see you again. So, you moved on from the hostel... how did you end up here?"

"The short story is, after you left, I had another two miscarriages. I felt so lost and empty inside and fell into a deep depression. Eventually, I picked myself up, got on a bus and I was drawn to this town. I came here to pray one day and ended up staying... here I am."

"I've heard this story before," I said.

"I don't understand, what do you mean, Sarah?"

"There's a lot I need to tell you, so much has happened but right now I need to find Mother Superior. She just killed my beautiful friend.

"Oh! I'm so sorry, Sarah. I heard there was a tragic accident of some sort. That's so horrible, I'm so sorry for your friend. I actually came here to pray for her."

"It was no accident, Maria. Mother Superior murdered her. She is pure evil."

"They're strong accusations Sarah... are you sure..."

I interrupted Maria abruptly.

"Shit! Isabella!" I had been so concerned with finding Mother Superior, then Lexus appeared, I'd forgotten all about her.

"Isabella? Who is Isabella?" questioned Maria.

"Come with me and I'll show you. She's very special, Maria."

We left the chapel and quickly made our way back down the stairs. I was doing my best to shut out the visual of Jane lying on the pavement.

"Why are we going so fast, Sarah? What's the panic?"

"Maria, I haven't even told you half of it! Just trust me."

As we got to the bottom of the stairs, we saw the ambulance leaving the grounds. They had taken Jane's body away and a group of nuns were cleaning up the pool of blood left behind. I ran around nervously looking for Isabella, with Maria right behind me. Then from the corner of my eye, I caught a glimpse of a group of nuns. I ran over to the group, trying to catch my breath. Isabella was still with the nun I left her with. I panicked for no reason.

"Thank you, Sisters," I paused still panting, "I'll take her now. Thank you."

Isabella's face lit up upon seeing me and she leapt into my arms. We walked away from the group of nuns to chat in private.

"This must be Isabella. She is adorable, Sarah," Maria said softly.

"She is my daughter Maria," I said, cuddling her into me.

"Oh, Sarah she is so beautiful. So does that mean? Is she?"

I interrupted, "Yes she is. She is alien and human, a hybrid" I said slowly.

"This is what I could have given birth to? Instead of those things I kept on aborting... I don't understand Sarah," said Maria confused.

"Maria, I promise I'll explain everything to you shortly," I looked at Maria and asked, "have you had much to do with that witch Mother Superior?"

"Sarah Shhh! The others will hear you. No I haven't had much to do with her. It is the other nuns who have guided me but I had heard she was mean and recently I overheard the other nuns say that she has become even meaner lately... like she's possessed."

"That's an understatement," I snapped back quickly.

I moved away from Maria temporarily and gazed up into the sky, to regain my focus. The Luveians had been right all along, we needed more surrogates but I have my doubts about the nuns. I must trust the Luveains. I decided now would be a good time to talk with the nuns and hopefully, I could find out the location of Mother Superior's lair.

"Maria, can you do me a favour please?" I asked, "can you get all the nuns together in one place?"

"What's going on, Sarah? Why are you really here?"

"I'll explain everything soon. Please, can you do that for me? Now!"

"I'll try but what about Mother Superior? She won't allow it?" Maria said concerned.

"I'll take care of Mother Superior, okay? Besides, she is nowhere to be seen. I need you to tell me if anyone has seen her or knows where she is."

"Okay, only for you Sarah. Give me 10 minutes. I'll ask everyone to meet in the main hall down that corridor," she said, pointing, "I'll tell them Mother Superior ordered this meeting."

"Great! I'll be waiting there with Isabella."

I followed Maria's directions and found the hall. Thick stone walls with more stunning stained -glass windows and really high ceilings. It was a well-lit room and looked like a giant indoor courtyard. It must have been where Mother Superior addresses the nuns as there were lots of chairs laid out in neat rows.

I walked around the room, pacing up and down, reciting what I would say this time. I wasn't sure how they would receive the news that their beloved Mother Superior was an evil alien. Perhaps I should spare them that bit. I'm not even sure they are going to believe anything I had to say. Some of the nuns must be well over 50. Why would they even want to fall pregnant at this age, even if they weren't nuns? It just didn't make any sense to me at all. My mind was filling with doubt again.

Then I remembered Isabella's gifts and what she did at the prison. Isabella bounced around in my arms, as I continued to pace. I was deep in my revision, going over all the key points and how I could persuade the nuns to come on board when the nuns began filing into the hall. Some came in by themselves, while others came in small groups. Finally, Maria came up to me to let me know they were all present.

"This is it? Seriously! There aren't any others?" I asked surprised.

"No, that's it, Sarah, apart from Mother Superior."

I did a quick headcount and came up with about 20. I don't know why but I was expecting a lot more. Well, if this is all we have, so be it. Unlike the prison, there was no constant noise or chatter or heckling. They sat in silence with their hands on their knees and waited to hear why they had been summoned.

"Ladies, Sisters! Thank you all for coming. My name is Sarah. Sarah O'Connor and this is my child, Isabella, who some of you have already met. I am a friend of Maria's, I said, smiling at Maria and Jane's, or Sister Mary Ellen as you knew her, who tragically died this morning."

I began by explaining my personal journey, of leaving home after miscarrying at 15 and no one believing me. Being on the run alone, scared and trying to find answers. I told them about the other young girls I met, who were also falling pregnant and then miscarrying. I went through in detail what happened at the prison and how no one could explain it or knew what to do. It was a mystery that caused so much confusion and chaos and no one had any answers. I gently told them I knew what had been happening at the convent, regarding the pregnancies and how I sympathised with them for how embarrassed and ashamed they must have felt. I reassured them, they were not alone and that this was happening to other women. I explained to them, what was causing the miscarriages and how I had managed to work through it. I told them about the birth of Isabella and how the Luveians cared and looked after me through the whole process. I paused several times as the Nuns began whispering to one another. Some rolled their eyes back while others were shaking their heads in disgust or refusing to believe a word I was saying.

I continued to explain they had nothing to fear and that these beings were peaceful and that I now know that these gentle beings were responsible for the pregnancies and not their Holy Spirit, which clearly upset them.

As predicted, the room broke out in much louder whispers and controlled arguing.

"Sarah! What are you saying? Have you gone mad?" Maria said in a loud, embarrassed whisper who was standing close by.

"It's the truth and you know it. Don't go into denial around me Maria, or were you conceived by the holy spirit?"

I put my arms in the air calling for calm and quiet. It took a few minutes until they stopped arguing with one another and began to listen to me again.

I picked up Isabella and continued, explaining she is a hybrid being and half Luveian.

The room burst into noisy discussion as I placed Isabella down. She walked off into the group of nuns, glancing back at me and explaining what she was doing. I nodded back, letting her know that I understood, as she began to greet the nuns by touching their hands. She explained to me Lexus had instructed her to clear some old energy from them because their thought processes were severely engrained and she had to download them with some Luveian energy, otherwise they will never understand anything I was going to say. Lexus said, it will be like a reboot on a computer but they will need time to process all this information.

I continued slowly, giving Isabella time to work with the nuns, carefully explaining that their species is nearly extinct and that they need our help to survive. I watched their faces grappling with all this information, which was a shock to them and a lot to take in.

The hush in the room reassured me they were listening, albeit they were struggling to comprehend. I kept an eye on Isabella as she continued greeting the nuns and I watched them rubbing their temples with their hands after she made contact with them. I continued to talk slowly, allowing Isabella to reach as many nuns as possible, so they would receive the information I was telling them and for the bombshell that was coming.

I went into great detail of how ruthless and deceitful the Thraxions are and how they could walk right amongst you and you would never know. I told them a Thraxion had killed several impregnated hybrids still in the womb, the last being Sister Mary Ellen's, who came with me to inspire you to help us and how upset she was about it. Finally, I warned them that what I was about to say to them, would come as a shock. Mother Superior had become a Thraxion and had killed Jane, Sister Mary Ellen and I saw it with my own eyes. I told them she had changed into something evil and she was not the same person anymore.

The nuns sat there with stony faces glaring straight at me, creating a lot of tension and a long period of silence. I was expecting loud angry outbursts and finger-pointing at me for disgracing their holy leader. Some began to stand up and walk out. Others remained seated. All I kept thinking was if I had any credibility, I've probably just lost it.

"I can't believe you just said that! Are you out of your mind?" shouted Maria with her face screwed up in anger.

"That Mother Superior is responsible for Jane's death or they weren't immaculate conceptions Maria."

We both stared at each for a while in silence.

"Judge me however you wish but this is far bigger than you and me. Jane knew it, I know it and your precious Mother Superior knows it. Where is she hiding Maria?"

"I don't know where she is! I'm not her keeper!" she said, getting defensive.

"I was right there when it happened, Maria. Mother Superior killed Jane!" I said angrily, knowing she was defending Mother Superior.

"I only have your word for that, Sarah; you're telling the story."

"Are you calling me a liar?! Is that it! You think I've just made all this up."

"Don't be so dramatic, Sarah! Calm down."

"Calm down, dramatic! Are you for real? You have been brainwashed here, Maria, completely brainwashed. Do you know that? I'm living in the real world, not living in fantasy land doing a whole lot of wishing, hoping and praying. How's that working out for you, by the way?"

"You have changed, Sarah. Who are you?"

"Damn right I've changed Maria and you haven't and that scares me."

"What have you become? Who have you become?"

"The person I was always supposed to become Maria. Not some mushroom protected by holy clothes and brainwashed by Mother Superior."

"Perhaps it's best if you go. I don't think you're welcome here anymore."

"I'll go when I'm good and ready! Perhaps it's time you went and said some more prayers. God help you all, you're going to need it!"

With that, she shook her head in disgust and left the room mumbling under her breath.

With Maria gone I felt compelled to continue talking to the few remaining nuns who were still seated and appeared to be thinking about what I had said, telling them even though they may not like or agree with what was said, to give it a great deal of thought, because we are all in danger.

Then to my surprise, one of the remaining nuns calmly said, "How do you know all this? These beings you speak about?"

I paused, knowing my answer could upset them.

"Because I have spoken to one," I said quietly.

"What are they like?" she responded in a soft curious tone.

I described them as gentle, peaceful beings and that's why they want to help us. I told them how far we are behind intellectually and on a conscious level which is why I get the same response every time I talk about them. I challenged them by stating they could believe in God without seeing him and I could call them crazy but went on to state, I had seen them, spoken with them and that they are very real and was hoping by seeing Isabella in person, that it would have been proof enough for them to believe what I was saying was the truth.

I made myself available should they wish to speak with me or had any more questions. I thanked them for listening and watched them stand up and file out of the hall in deep thought, contemplating the circumstances they now found themselves in.

When I observed the nuns, it appeared the older nuns would be loyal to Mother Superior no matter what. They appeared to be groomed by her over the years to follow and obey their Superior and over time their questioning minds had been tamed to just follow, not question her.

However, the others who were a little younger, I believe still had questions and natural curiosities that kept them a little more open and maybe a little more flexible. Maybe they had become tired of her cruel and demeaning ways and questioned what was really happening here and disapproved of her punishing dictatorship. They were also very fond of Sister Mary Ellen and didn't like the way she was mistreated by Mother Superior. If they believed Mother Superior killed Sister Mary Ellen, there would be no loyalty shown to her now.

Was it a mistake coming here and have I paid the ultimate price, losing Jane? To make matters worse, Mother Superior knows I have been successful giving birth to a hybrid and will do anything in her power now to stop me. She is out there somewhere planning how to take me down. I know we haven't seen the last of each other, not by any means.

I am dreading telling the Warden what happened to Jane. He has been so happy lately and he will need someone to support him through this tragedy. My dilemma is leaving here. It's not what the nuns will decide, I have no control over that. It's Mother Superior. Where has she gone? Did she over-hear me talk about the prison? I am sure we didn't talk about that in front of her. She might be over there now, finishing off Scarface's work, taking out as many hybrids as she can. But if I leave here and the nuns agree to be impregnated, then what? She may just be waiting for me to leave, to take them out when I leave.

I found peace and serenity in the chapel and decided to go back there. I picked up Isabella and made my way back up the stairs and into the chapel. Short of breath and feeling stressed, I found the peace and solitude of the chapel comforting.

"Lexus, if you can hear me, I need your help. I'm stuck here and I don't know what to do. The nuns are in deep in prayer about what to do and now I'm very concerned about the prison. I have a bad feeling and it's getting stronger by the minute. My intuition is telling me she is on her way there to do damage, but the nuns need help and reassurance here."

There was no one in the chapel which gave me the freedom to talk openly and out loud.

"Why do I feel so alone in all this? You're supposed to have my back! You're supposed to be helping me."

I waited for several minutes and then the brilliant came through. I closed my eyes for a few seconds and then opened them up to see Lexus in front of me.

"We feel the heavy burden you carry on your shoulders Sarah. You serve your species admirably and we are eternally grateful for the chance you are giving us, the hope that keeps our species alive, the chance that we may survive. None of this would have been possible without you. Please know Isabella is here to help you. There are strong Luveian traits that have appeared to come through her DNA and she will need time for these to develop and mature but they will prove invaluable in time."

"Yes, I know she has already been a great help. I can hear her thoughts now."

"We have information for you. We carried out research on the body of the one you call Scarface. She is not a hybrid. The good news is they have not found a way to successfully hybridise yet. They know we have succeeded and will stop at nothing to find out how and copy us. They will continue to destroy the hybrids at every chance. They are using walk-ins. This is how they are surviving on earth; however, they only have a limited time in the chosen host's body.

"Woah! Woah! Woah! Slow down! You are going way too fast for me Lexus. Chosen body! Walk-ins? I have no idea what you are talking about," I said, confused.

"This is difficult to explain. Every soul needs a physical body for a vehicle on earth. Are you with me so far Sarah?"

"Yeahhh… I think so. You mean they like just take over the body," I said, still a little confused.

"Yes, that is a basic understanding," replied Lexus.

"The soul has an agreement with its chosen body at birth. If that agreement expires with the soul, The Thraxions can walk into that body but can only survive in that host body for a short time. Their behaviour will be completely different as it's not the original person or being in that body."

"Keep going. I'm keeping up!" it was starting to make sense, "please continue."

"The Thraxions still need permission before they enter. If a soul on earth goes through intense personal problems or trauma, they are vulnerable for an exchange to take place. That's a simple explanation. Do you understand?"

"Yes, I think so. It's a bit out there. But yes, I think I do," I replied.

"The Thraxions are picking vulnerable souls, bargaining their way onto earth so to speak. The other soul passes over, so their personality changes instantly. It will be obvious to their loved ones. Those with suicidal tendencies make an easy transition for walk-ins. Open mind, Sarah! I hope you understand as you must return to the prison."

"You are stretching me way out of my comfort zone here! Way out. If this is so, why aren't there more of them already?"

"They need very selective hosts. There still has to be an agreement made, remember. Most souls are still not ready to leave. They are fearful and try to abort the agreement. It can be a very stressful experience. You are correct; the hybrids at the prison are now in danger. You must leave someone in charge here and go now. I have not told you this before, but every time I come here to earth, I lose precious life force. Sarah, I am fading fast. I may not be able to return next time," his head dropped slightly.

"Why didn't you tell me earlier? I wouldn't have called on you so much, Lexus, you should have told me."

"I had only come when you needed help and guidance. I was trying to conserve my life force to always be there for you, Sarah. However, the contact does have consequences."

"Lexus! What are you saying? Are you dying? Will you be back?" I was becoming frantic.

"Sarah, I am weak and must return home now. I have so much love for you and Isabella. I will always be with you both."

"This is how you're going to leave me? Lexus, please!"

With that, he was gone again. The bright light faded and the light that was shining through into the chapel picked up the slow, descending particles that gradually fell like snow. My heart was breaking. I could see he was struggling this time; something was different about him. He looked tired and weak. My eyes welled up and tears fell down my cheeks. I sat there quietly and began to pick up his thoughts,

Sarah I can feel your heartbreak...please don't be upset...I'll always be with you...you have much to do and little time...I'll be fine, please don't worry about me.

It brought a smile to my face as I wiped away the tears. I heard a voice behind me which ruined my moment. Maria had come looking for me and found me in the chapel, saving me the trip to find her. She was my obvious choice to take charge and watch the nuns.

"Sarah, I thought I might find you here. I'm so sorry for storming out earlier. I came to apologise. How can I make it up to you?"

"Actually, Maria. I need to ask you something."

"Yes, of course. What is it?"

"I have to return to the prison now. I need you to watch the nuns and keep them safe if Mother Superior returns."

"Me? They won't listen to me! And why are you so sure Mother Superior is behind all this?"

"I don't have time to argue, Maria. You asked me how to make it up to me and this is it. Just trust me and watch the convent. We need all the hybrids we can get, so please keep them all safe."

"And how do I do that?"

"Keep Mother Superior out. Don't let her back in. When I go, lock all the outside gates. No one is allowed to enter. No one! I don't care if it's the Pope! You got it?"

"I'm not sure I know what to do. There are other older nuns better equipped to deal with this than me."

"No! No, it has to be you, Maria. I trust you. I need you to do this for me."

Chapter Nineteen: The Chosen One

Isabella and I arrived back at Benson Prison and I had a strong gut feeling I was walking straight into a trap. Something feels wrong, I can sense it.

After speaking to the guards at the prison entrance and confirming the Warden's name, we were allowed to enter. I hadn't seen those guards before which also raised my suspicions. On arrival at the reception area I asked again to meet with the Warden.

"Your name, please?" questioned the guard.

"Sarah O'Connor."

"Yes, he is expecting you."

"Expecting me? I didn't tell him I was coming!"

"The prison guards will take you up to see him now," then she signalled them over to escort us up to the Warden's office.

I held Isabella's hand tightly and kept her close to my side. Isabella had grown dramatically in such a short time; it was kind of scary.

We arrived outside the Warden's office, Barbara was on the phone, busy tending to the Warden's affairs. She waved at us after finishing her call, hung up the phone and then greeted us.

"Hello, Sarah! How are you? Oh my God! Isabella! You can't have grown that fast so soon, good gracious," which sent Isabella ducking for cover around my legs.

"Hi, Barbara. I believe the Warden is expecting me?"

"Yes, dear, that's right. Just go right on in."

I smiled back as I walked past her desk and opened the door to the Warden's office and walked into my worst nightmare.

"Well, well! You finally made it back here, Sarah. I believe you have met Mother Superior. She has been telling me all about your little visit to her convent," said the Warden.

I glared at her with a death stare.

"That's nice. Yes, we have met," I said with a fake smile.

"We have indeed, oh and look at your precious little angel!" Isabella tucked in tight behind me.

"Warden, can we talk in private, please? I really need to tell you something very important and urgently," I pleaded.

"Oh, please! No secrets here, Sarah. I've already brought the Warden up to speed with all of your evil misdoings as well as all the facts, isn't that right Warden?" Mother Superior gloated.

"As a matter of fact she has and I feel so betrayed by you Sarah. I believed everything you told me. So many lies and like a fool I believed you. You've made me the laughingstock of this prison."

"Warden! What's going on? What's got into you? Why are you behaving like this? She's the one lying. You have to believe me," I shouted in desperation.

"Guards! Lock her up in solitary. Mother Superior would you mind watching this little one till I work out what to do with her."

"You took the words right out of my mouth Warden. I couldn't think of anything I'd like more. I would love to care for this precious little one," said Mother Superior.

The guards grabbed me. I managed to break free and yell to the Warden.

"She killed your daughter right in front of my eyes and you don't even care! Why are you doing this? She's the one lying that's why I came here, to warn you. You have to believe me, Warden," I shouted.

"I must say you're very convincing Sarah but we both know you were the only one with Jane and Red when they died and have tried to blame it on someone else. Are you calling Mother Superior, a holy respected nun who has dedicated her entire life to God, a liar?" asked the Warden.

"Why on earth would the Warden listen to a lying little tart like yourself who clearly enjoys a little fun on the side? Young girls today Warden, no morals at all. It's disgusting how you behave and it doesn't surprise me you have been in prison before."

"Absolutely right, Mother Superior. Pyke solitary now! I won't ask again," demanded the Warden.

"Warden, you're making a big mistake. Please don't take Isabella from me. I beg you! Please, Warden! I beg you!" I said as I pushed my feet into the floor to stop myself from being dragged forward.

"Oh, stop being so dramatic, child. You do love a bit of drama, don't you? The child will be fine with us. Wont you sweetie?"

I watched on in disbelief as the old witch forcibly grabbed Isabella and the guards began to drag me out of the office. I turned my head to see Isabella screaming at her as they continued to drag me out of the Wardens office. I began fighting with all my might. I kicked one of the guards in the shin and just as I thought to grab Isabella I was placed in a headlock by one of the guards.

"I'll be back real soon, you'll see sweetie. I love you, Isabella," I said with tears rolling down my face.

"You will pay for what you did to my daughter O' Connor. I promise you that!" the Warden said, glaring at me with an evil stare.

"How many times do I have to tell you I didn't do it, Warden. She's lying! She is lying!" I shouted desperately.

The door to his office was now closed. As they dragged me past Barbara, who looked on horrified.

"Oh, Sarah! What have you done? Oh, goodness."

I was thrown into solitary. I wasn't fearful. I was furious. All I could think about was keeping Isabella safe and as they shut my cell door, I pleaded with the guard.

"Pyke, you have to listen to me. Something very bad is going to happen here. That old witch has brainwashed the Warden. She is evil!"

She wasn't listening. After closing my cell door and locking it, she walked out. I watched as she swiped her card on another gate and continued walking down the long corridor.

That witch has won. She has Isabella and the Warden in her pocket and possibly control of the entire prison, including all the unborn hybrids. The Warden actually believes I killed Jane. Is he being irrational after losing his daughter? If he does believe I killed Jane, why wasn't he angrier than that? Mother Superior has Isabella and because she's the first hybrid to be born she will want to find out how the Luveians have been successful and I'm trapped in a cell unable to protect her and I can't call on Lexus, he's too fragile.

Time passed slowly, giving me plenty of time to beat myself up for not been able to protect Isabella and failing the Luveians because I was in a hurry to tell the Warden and protect the hybrids. I sat on the prison bed with my head in my hands as I covered my face in despair and that's when I heard her thoughts.

Mummy please help me... The mean woman who killed Jane. She is pulling my arm and hurting me, saying she is going to hurt me if I don't tell her things... please come and get me Mummy.

I burst into tears, unable to help Isabella and then I heard someone whistling as they approached me.

"Your lunch is here princess, come and get it!"

I jumped up off the bed and grabbed the cell bars on the gate.

"Please can you help me, please!" I begged.

"Hey, aren't you the kid whose been banging on about the dooo doooo dooo dooo alien stuff?"

"Yes that's right! Please I've got to get outta here now! I don't have time to explain!"

"Well good luck with that kid. Things don't work like that around here."

I began getting sharp pains around my temples and placed my hands on the sides of my face, I was getting a message and I wasn't listening.

"You're Tellson... Ison... no... no... wait, it's Tyson. Oh my god you're Tyson! You're Red's Mother!" I shouted.

"How the fuck did you know that? Who are you?" Tyson replied stunned.

"Oh my God! Red was my friend, we hung out together. I was with her when that bitch killed her!" I said quickly.

"You knew Red? You were there when she died? What was she like? I never got to know her," her head dropped as she spoke.

"Okay Tyson. Listen, I can't do the 20 questions right now but I promise you I'll tell you all about Red later... but first you have to help me, please, I don't have much time. The same monster that killed Jane now has my daughter and will probably do the same to her. The Warden has been brainwashed by that witch and now she has my kid. She's convinced the Warden that I killed Jane and Red!" I spat out the words out so fast I wasn't sure Tyson had kept up.

She stared back at me and said,

"Jane's dead? We didn't know that. She's only just lost her kid. How did she die?"

I rolled my eyes frustrated at the questions being asked.

"Sorry kid, if you want my help, I need to know you're telling me the truth."

"Yes, yes I know Tyson but I don't have time to go into details now. Fuck! Okay, listen, Jane and I went to the convent to have the same talk we did here... that monster fucked with Jane's head and willed her off the side of the building while she held me at knifepoint and I wasn't able to stop her. The Warden won't believe me and now she's going to kill Isabella. She is a fuckin' psychopath Tyson, do you follow... do you believe me? I've got to get out of here, now!"

"Hell, yeah! I know you would never hurt Jane. You two were like sisters and a friend of Red's is a friend of mine. Come to think about it, the Warden has been acting strange lately. It's like he's not the same person anymore. He's become really angry and violent like... yah know wadda mean. Okay I'm in kid, what do you want me to do?" Tyson asked.

"Can you get me out of this cell?" I asked.

"The best I can do is get you a shank. Then you're kinda on your own kid."

"Okay then just do it. Get me the fuckin knife... Tyson! I don't have time!"

"Okay, okay! Hold onto your horses! I'll be back soon. Hang tight and best you come up with a plan while I'm gone."

She disappeared as I sat back on the bed, placing my hands on the sides of my head, trying to connect with Isabella.

Isabella can you hear me... please hear me sweetie... Isabella what information does that nasty woman want from you?" I waited patiently for a reply. My legs were bouncing up and down with nervous energy and beside myself worrying what she might do to Isabella and then she replied,

Mummy she wants to know how the Luveians have managed to hybridise and she is threatening to hurt me if I don't talk... please come and get me... please Mummy.

My eyes teared up again and ran down my face, frustrated at not being able to help Isabella and now I was furious at Mother Superior.

Tyson returned about an hour later.

"I believe you needed some extra linen, mam? Be careful though, the ironing is done so well around here, it can be sharp," she

winked at me and held the bundle in her arms as she called out to
the guard.

"Pyke, I have fresh linen for the new prisoner. Can you help me
out here?"

Pyke came forward and opened the small sliding door on the
cell gate. Tyson passed the bundle through, winked at me again and
then left whistling a tune.

"Pyke before you go, can you please give the Warden a message
for me?" I asked.

"That would be?" Pyke replied.

"Could you tell him I have information for Mother Superior
about successful hybridisation. She'll know what I mean."

Pyke shook her head thinking I was some kind of whack job
and then left. I found what I was looking for carefully concealed in
the bundle of linen. I had no intentions of hurting a guard unless, of
course, they try and stop me from protecting Isabella. I need to get
Mother Superior on her own. If I can take her out, maybe I can get
through to the Warden and undo all her poisonous lies.

"Mother Superior! I have a message from young Sarah for you,"
said the Warden.

"Oh really and what would that message be?" scowled Mother
Superior.

"She says she has information on successful hybridisation,"
explained the Warden.

"Does she now. Well I'm happy to oblige and pay her a visit
Warden."

"You'll need some guards with you Mother Superior."

"Oh no! That won't be necessary, no guards please Warden. I'm
sure I can take care of this myself. I've done just fine up until now.
She is in a cell, unarmed and we have her daughter. I do not foresee
any trouble now, do you Warden? Mind you, she might need some
protection from me! Jane and I were very close you know, such a
beautiful soul, a pleasure to mentor," she said on her way out,
smiling to the Warden.

"Don't get too close Mother Superior. You can't trust these inmates at any time. Perhaps I should go with you myself, you can never be too careful!"

Mother Superior turned back, "Warden, you're a busy man and I will not take you away from your work. I'll be fine. I have handled a lot worse over the years, I can assure you."

"You be careful, Mother Superior. She's a smart cookie, that one."

"Oh, don't you worry, I know she is. It'll be fine. Now, off to do my duty and help another lost soul."

I heard footsteps approaching me. As it got closer I could see it was Mother Superior and two guards. The guards led her into the solitary block and then left us, just as I had hoped. I know she wants to take me out and this is her best chance.

"Well, we meet again, you little trollop," hissed Mother Superior.

"You bitch. That was quite an act you put on up there for your man."

"Now... now... sticks and stones. I do believe you have some information for me."

"If you hurt one hair on my daughter's head I swear, I'll kill you."

"Really? And how do you propose to do that? You don't seem to be in a very good position to be making threats, now do you?"

"If only he knew the truth! How did you poison him so quickly?"

"Enough of the small talk, child. Now, I believe you have something for me, is that correct?"

"Yes, as a matter of fact I do." I said standing at the front of the cell bars.

"Go on, child, I haven't got all day. I'm supposed to watching your little brat... men they haven't got a clue. I was just in the process of teaching her some manners you know."

I knew I had to bité my tongue and ignore her as she tried to get under my skin. My heart was beating so fast, in anticipation of what I was about to do. I was trying not to sound anxious.

"Well come on now, spit it out child."

"It's a complicated process so here I have written it all down for you. You can read, can't you?" I said sarcastically.

"Don't play games with me you little upstart. Give me the information or I'll get it out of that little brat of yours," she said annoyed.

"You look so helpless in there, no one to fight your battles, poor little Sarah. I'm told they can't hear a thing outside these walls. Because the scum that's put in here, scream and cry all day and all night for someone to help get them out of here. Drives the guards batty, that's why they make them soundproof. So, when I end your pathetic little life and take your crossbreed back for testing, no one will hear a thing. So sad, don't you think? Just so sad," as she talked she moved closer and closer, knowing I wouldn't be armed.

I reached into my pocket and grabbed a note, putting my hand through the bars pretending to pass it to her.

"I've written everything down, all the information you need is here, now promise me you will be release my daughter. You'll get this when I see her."

As she stepped forward to snatch the note. She dropped her guard, just long enough for me to grab the knife and jab it quickly and deep into her heart area. I pulled it out and stabbed it in again and again furiously. I wouldn't get a second chance. I couldn't fail.

Her face lit up in shock as her eyes bulged out in horror and she collapsed into the bars of the cell. Blood gushed onto the floor and into my cell. She grabbed the bars for support with one hand and tried to stop the bleeding from her heart with the other.

Gasping for air and coughing up blood, her throat gurgled from choking on her own blood. She looked at me in total shock, her stern, wrinkled face was horrified at the thought of being outsmarted by me. I looked down at the floor and saw the thick red puddle spreading all around her.

She stood slumped against the bars, fighting for her life. I thought of what she did to Jane, pulled the knife out once more and with one more forceful stab, shouted, "This one's for Jane you bitch!"

She fell to the floor, choking and still squirming in pain as she looked up at me for the final time, her face pale as her head slumped to the floor. I pulled the knife out of her, wiping it clean onto her clothes and hid it in my pocket, knowing I would probably need it again.

Adrenalin was pumping furiously through my body as I stood panting loudly, shaking all over. I looked down at her. I had just killed someone. My body **was** so overrun with adrenalin it made me feel sick. I quickly turned away from her, heaving all over the floor. I knew I had no other option but who had I become?

Mother Superior's lifeless body had now been picked up on the security cameras and the sliding doors were quickly opened as the guards burst into my cell block. They dragged her away from my cell and into the corridor. The Warden came barging in and barking out orders at the guards.

"Get her to the infirmary and get this blood cleaned up immediately!"

"Warden she came in here and went psycho and tried to stab me. I managed to overthrow her and defend myself," it sounded even weaker when I said it but it was the only excuse I could come up with quickly.

"You really expect me to believe that, O'Connor? I wasn't born yesterday. You'll have to do better than that," said the Warden infuriated.

"Is Isabella safe? Is she okay? Please tell me you're looking after her Warden?" I pleaded.

"I've heard enough of your lies, O'Connor, I know you killed Jane. You took her away so I couldn't protect her and no one would see you. Very clever, only this time your numbers up O' Connor!"

"I hate being taken for a fool. Guards! Cuff her and take her into the general area," ordered the Warden.

Two guards nodded and carried out their orders, while another two stretchered Mother Superior straight down to the infirmary.

"Where are you taking me Warden?" I said concerned.

"How about you just shut up? You'll find out soon enough," he snapped back.

We arrived at the general assembly area where the inmates gathered for news and any other special occasion.

"Pyke! Get all the prisoners out here now," yelled the Warden in a very direct voice.

"Yes sir!"

As we waited, I was getting an uneasy feeling. Something felt really off and it was getting worse by the second.

The inmates filed into the main assembly area, shocked to see me in cuffs which sparked lots of questions. Then my intuition kicked in strongly and I felt like Joan of Arc, about to be tied to a stake and burnt alive in front of an angry mob.

As I gazed around at the inmates, I noticed their energy was different, they appeared softer. Except Tyson, who began to shout abuse at the Warden and the guards.

"Why she cuffed? Let her go... you cocksuckers! Let her go!" Tyson shouted looking agitated and very angry.

"My daughter and her baby were murdered by this person and I have evidence now linking her to Red's death as well. You killed the wrong person Tyson," the Warden shouted.

The energy in the room was tense, you could sense something really bad was about to happen. Tyson continued to vent her disapproval at the way I was being treated.

"Prove it! We don't believe you! You're lying you bastard!"

The inmates became agitated.

The Warden moved in close to me and whispered in my ear, "I would love to finish you off myself, O'Connor, but then I thought what better way than to be killed by the people you begged for their help and then betrayed. It's got a nice ring to it, don't you think?"

Bam then it hit me. How could I have been so blindsided. The clues were all there but I didn't pick up on them. The Warden had been taken over. It makes perfect sense. He is a Thraxion and finishing off what Mother Superior's started, to take me out and stop me helping with the hybridisation at the prison.

"Are you familiar with the phrase, 'If you give someone enough rope, they eventually hang themselves O'Connor'... Hames, go get the brat. She can watch this too. She can see mummy strung up for the liar and murderer she is!"

"Warden! What are you doing? What's got into you? This isn't like you," said Pyke with a distraught look on her face.

"Warden, I beg you, please don't bring Isabella out here... please!" I said shouting desperately.

"Warden, I don't feel comfortable about this at all. I don't want any part of this. We are a prison not an execution facility," argued Pyke.

"One of you bitches go and get the rope or you'll both be sacked. I'm sick of repeating myself to you clowns. Now go!" shouted the Warden.

Then to my surprise Pyke put her hands up in the air, as if to say she didn't want any part of this and walked out of the assembly area and shortly after, the other guard followed her.

"Come back here now! I order you! Right! Your fired... both of you, effective immediately!" the Warden shouted with so much anger you could see the veins on his neck bulging out. His voice went so deep, it made him sound almost inhuman.

With the guards gone the inmates circled closer around the Warden as he grabbed my arm, "She has played us all for fools. She deserves to die for what she did to my Jane, to her baby and Red. You have my permission to kill her! Or... I will do it myself."

I shouted as loud as I could, "He's lying! I didn't do it. I swear!"

The inmates looked at one another seemingly confused, not knowing who to believe and began arguing and yelling amongst themselves.

I watched as Hames brought Isabella into the room, her little eyes darted around desperately looking for me. She eventually found me and I could see how upset she was. She knew the Warden was hurting me but didn't know how to stop it. Hames stood still after noticing the other guards had left the assembly area. She let go of Isabella's hand and then also left the area quickly. The energy in the room was really dark, as Isabella made her way over to me. How did this go so horribly wrong, so quickly?

The Warden betrayed by his guards and now on his own was agitated and angry.

"Well O'Connor... as they say, if you want the job done properly... you've got to do it yourself," as he pulled out a gun from its holster, "besides this is a lot faster and easier."

He pointed the gun at me and forced me to the centre of the room. The inmates watched on helplessly as the Warden waved the gun around while yelling abuse at them,

"Look at you scumbags... you pathetic pieces of shit. I've spent my whole life looking after you and for what."

My heart was now beating furiously as I stared at Isabella who
had squeezed past the prisoners to make her way to the front of the
circle. The Warden kept on ranting to the prisoners.

I looked at Isabella, *I love you sweetie... I will always love you.*
Tears ran down her little cheeks as she stood there, dwarfed by the
inmates who stood all around her.

The Warden in his crazed state pointed the weapon at my
temple and cocked the gun. My heart was beating so fast and so loud
as I braced myself for the inevitable.

*Mummy I love you, please don't die... please don't leave me... I
love you mummy.*

I stood there powerless as tears streamed down my face. My
heart was breaking as I looked up to the ceiling, imagining it was the
sky, as tense seconds passed by slowly, I agonisingly awaited my
fate.

*I love you Lexus... I'm sorry for failing you and your people.
Please watch over Isabella and guide her to finish what we started. I
love you Lexus.*

"You didn't really think you would get away with it now, did
you O'Connor? To be outsmarted by a teenager. How could we? I've
got to say though, you are good. God damn you are good. Getting all
these cons to believe you... trying to convince old nuns to be
surrogates at their age... wow!"

I glanced down at Isabella knowing it would be the last time.
She had this intense stare, her hand was raised in the air and with
her palm directed at the Warden's head.

He began screaming in pain and he dropped the gun. He had
both his hands over his ears as he dropped to the floor in agony. My
heart was still beating furiously, adrenalin was pumping wildly into
my veins as I gasped in shock escaping death and instinctively
grabbed the gun with my cuffed hands.

"Tyson, grab the keys off him and throw him in a cell!" I
shouted.

Tyson and her gang grabbed him, still screaming in pain,
dragged him into a cell and locked the gate as I watched on.

"Get these cuffs off me, quick! Hurry! We don't have much
time," I yelled at Tyson.

"Right, Tyson! We need to secure the prison. From now on, no
one enters without my permission, got it? We need to overthrow the

guards and lock them in cells. Take as many inmates as you need and take the gun. You may need it. Be careful Tyson, they will come at you hard. Without any bloodshed if possible," then I had a thought, "wait up Tyson," I yelled.

Isabella, what you just did to the Warden... can you do that to all the guards at once? I asked, waiting for her response.

Yes of course mummy. Do you want me to do it now? She looked up at me curiously.

I placed my hands on her shoulders and looked her straight in the eye.

Yes Isabella, please do it now.

I watched on as she stood still and then raised her hand in the air with her palm facing in the direction of the guards. Her eyes stared intensely as she focussed her energy at the guards. We could hear the guards begin yelling in pain, a short distance away in an area sectioned off from us.

"Tyson go... go now quick while they are down," I yelled eager to strike without any bloodshed. Tyson ran off with ten or more inmates to disarm the guards and lock them up in cells.

I remained with Isabella until they returned, working out what to do next while the rest of the inmates just stood there in amazement, watching it all unfold. Tyson returned with her gang a short time later short of breath and panting.

"Okay they're all behind bars Sarah but you need to get someone on the security gates and the cameras, ASAP!" Tyson said still panting.

"Okay, Tyson! Place your best girls on security. They watch the outside world and report to me on anything that moves out there. I'm going to leave you in charge of rostering your girls on security. We need to deal with Barbara and the rest of the staff," I asked as Tyson nodded in approval, still trying to catch her breath.

With Tyson's gang, we managed to get all the prison staff in cells and now had full control of the prison.

"Listen up ladies. I need a bus driver and some volunteers," I shouted into the circle of inmates, who seemed excited to see what was going to happen next. An inmate came forward, followed by another and Tyson also volunteered.

"No Tyson I need you here with me. Ladies I need more volunteers, I can't do this without you," I waited patiently.

Then another stepped forward followed by another. Before long I had a group of ten volunteers. I wasn't sure why they were so reluctant. Maybe they had been so institutionalised for so long now, that they were now too intimidated by the outside world.

"Thank you. Okay, I need someone to drive the prison van to a convent about twenty miles from here. I want you to get every nun and bring them back here. I don't care if they don't want to come! Just get them in that bus and back here. Ask for Maria and tell her Sarah sent you. Got it! Straight there and straight back. You are safe in here, not out there. Remember that! Good luck girls."

I knew I couldn't keep an eye out on the nuns from here and I certainly wasn't going back there again. I could at least keep them safe here and it felt right. Isabella was pulling at my jeans and would not stop until she got my attention.

Yes, Bella? What is it? What's wrong?

There are a group of girls at the homeless shelter. We need them here. The open minded and the highly intelligent and then we are complete. Lexus said it's vitally important that those young women make it here. We need their DNA.

"Okay I got it. Thanks, Bella."

"Okay... listen up! I need some more volunteers to pick up a group of young girls from a homeless shelter about 15 miles north of here."

Four big and burly women stepped forward as a group.

"Yeah, we can do that, just give us the directions," one of them said.

"Can I count on you coming back?" I said with a smirk on my face.

"Yeah, of course. I'm not having no alien baby by myself," she said, shaking her head.

"Okay, now listen. It's absolutely vital, they come here. Got it? I don't care if you drag them here kicking and screaming! Just bring them back here. Do you need some more help? Now is the time to let me know."

"No! We're good. One look at these ugly, scary bitches and they'll come running, promise yah!" one of the group shouted.

The other inmates close by, broke into laughter.

"Okay, great! Here are the directions. Good luck and get back here as soon as you can. By the way, the woman running the place, Mrs Henderson, she can be a little bit overprotective of the girls, go easy with her, she's a good person. Tell her Sarah sent you and that I promise I will look after these girls," I explained carefully.

"By the way, can one of you drive a bus?"

"Yeah! I can. Or least I used to be able to," shouted an inmate.

"Oh shit! I feel so safe now," replied one of the other inmates.

"Okay, sugar tits, you drive then."

"Settle down. I was just jiving with cha. Chill out a little sugar. We're leaving this concrete hell... yee hah," she screamed out loudly.

Tyson and all her girls had come through. We were in control of the prison and the guards hadn't been harmed and were now all in separate cells. There was 10 of them in total. They weren't happy but it could have been a lot worse. I needed them for insurance, in case there was trouble with the outside world.

"Just giving you the heads-up ladies! We have a group of nuns and young homeless girls coming to stay here for the next few weeks. They will probably want to stay in their groups, to be close to each other. So, I'm suggesting we divide the groups into three blocks. I'm advising you to move all your things into the block you prefer to stay in. Now, I know this will piss some of you off but unfortunately it's going to be uncomfortable for everyone else too. I don't want any trouble, so let's do the best we can and suck up the bits we don't like. Choose wisely If you don't want to sleep next to praying nuns or loud teenagers."

They began to discuss the idea with one another and some nodded their heads in approval while others had a problem with it.

"The other solution is you can sleep outside in the grounds and keep watch all night."

I waited patiently for the buses to return, anxious to see how the inmates went with bringing the nuns and girls back to the prison. No doubt they did drag some kicking and screaming. There's going to be a lot of tension inside these walls, which made me then realise, I needed my own guards.

"Tyson! You got a sec?" she was my most trusted person in here right now and I had to put my faith in her.

"Yeah, sure kid, what's up?"

"Listen, I've been thinking. When the others arrive back here, there may be some trouble. I may need backup, those who will follow an order without hesitation and without questioning me in front of the others. You know what I'm talking about?"

"Loud and clear," said Tyson.

"Can I count on you then Tyson?" I questioned.

"Absolutely. It's a lonesome job at the top. You have no friends, it's stressful and it's a whole lot of hard work. It's all yours."

"I hear you loud and clear. I'm only doing it because I promised someone."

"You're the best leader for this group, no doubt in my mind whatsoever. Let me get my crew together, you can trust them, Sarah, I'll go give 'em the heads up."

"Before you go Tyson, I need you to be my eyes and ears in this place. I know you've done it all before and I need all the help I can get right now."

"You're doing just fine, Sarah. I've got yah back," she winked at me and then ran to gather her crew.

The bus with the nuns was the first to arrive. I was warned by my new security crew, who then waved them through. The bus drove around the back and into the compound. As it stopped, I waited near the door, curious to see how many nuns came back. I could see Maria was the first to get off and she didn't look happy.

"What do you think you're doing?" Maria said fuming as she got off the bus.

"Nice to see you too, Maria... sisters, welcome to Benson Prison Facility. I hope you enjoy your stay here," I said in a loud voice as the nuns continued to get off the bus.

"You trying to be funny now?" said Maria angrily.

"No, Maria! Just welcoming."

I counted 19 in total, including Maria.

"Are they all here?" I asked one of the volunteers.

"Every single one of them," an inmate replied as they filed off like a line of penguins, each carrying their own suitcase containing all they could take with them.

"Sisters, please follow me. You will be safe here. We're waiting for another bus and when that arrives, I will explain everything to you, I promise."

I knew this would be challenging for them but there was no other option. There was a lot of disapproving faces.

"So why did we have to leave? That was our home, our church. We don't belong here, child!" said one of the nuns.

"I will explain everything soon. Please, trust me Sister.

"If it helps there is a chapel here too. Tyson! Can you show the nuns where they are staying and show them around a little please?"

The last bus arrived an hour later. It parked and the girls got off looking tired and were complaining and whinging.

"Girls, welcome and please follow me. You will be safe here and please hold your questions for now. I will explain everything shortly," I said firmly, cutting off a barrage of questions.

"Why are we here?" one said yawning.

"Who are you? and what the hell are we doing in a prison?" demanded another.

"Hold your questions, please. I will answer them shortly. Thank you, girls," I said loudly.

They came inside and adjusted their eyes to the bright lights inside the prison. They arrived late, around midnight. They stood in a group no doubt a little intimidated by the inmates and their surroundings. I asked the nuns to join us who had also kept their distance and remained together in a tight group.

The inmates were busy checking out the new arrivals and with all three groups together, it made for an interesting picture. The prisoners in their orange overalls, the nuns in their penguin suits and a group of young, homeless girls dressed in array of colours.

"For those of you who don't know who I am, my name is Sarah and if you have any questions about anything at all, please come and see me and I'll do my best to explain what's going on. Sisters you have already heard this, so bear with me."

I explained carefully to the young girls all about the Luveians and Thraxions, pregnancies and miscarriages and brought them up to date with everything, including why they were here now. I introduced Isabella to the young girls and as I continued to explain the situation, she made contact with them and downloaded them with lots of information, making my job so much easier. I received the usual heckling and protests but as Isabella worked through the group, the heckling and arguing subsided.

"We all need to work together here to make this work and unfortunately time is against us. As I said, if you have any questions, I will do my best to answer them. Thank you for listening."

"Why nuns?" a young girl asked.

"They have been picked for their faith and compassion," I replied quickly.

"Why criminals? What are they good for? I don't wanna work with them?" another asked, sheepishly hiding behind one of the girls at the front.

"Well, you're brave, for starters, I'll give you that. You'll be living with these criminals for the next ten weeks, so you might want to tone it down a little. They are strong and resilient," I answered quickly.

"What about these whiny, whingy cry-babies?" yelled an inmate which got the prisoners laughing out loud.

"They're here for their high intelligence and being open minded."

"God! We're all doomed! Shoot me now!" shouted an inmate.

"Okay, okay, it's a strange mix, I get it but we need to make this work and I'm here to make sure it does. We can't afford any trouble, so let's get this done but for now let's get some sleep and come back together in the morning." I said loud and firmly. With that they walked back into their respective blocks and preferred cells to settle in for the night. Tyson took the girls from the shelter and helped them settle into their block and surroundings.

Isabella! Can you send a message to Lexus for me, please?

She nodded.

Tell him they are here and ready. Can you do that for me, sweetie?

Lexus said they will be impregnated tonight and he said thank you.

I gave her a big hug and squeezed her tight.

I felt for the guards, the staff and Barbara, they were being held against their will but they were safe and not harmed. I had to stay focussed on the bigger picture. The surrogates were here and the hatches were battened down. All was in place for the dawn of the hybrids. With help from the Luveians, I will ensure the hybrids are ready and are prepared as best as I can, for the imminent Thraxion invasion.

After making sure everyone was settled in, Tyson joined me.

"Well that went better than expected," she said.

"Better than I thought. I couldn't have done it without you Tyson," I replied.

"Yeah that's cool. Listen, I swung around to check on the guards and that freak. I never got to tell you but I was the one who hung Scarface and as she was dying her body was flashing images of scales all over her. Like some kinda reptile. It scared the shit out of us but I didn't let on in front of the others. It was really freaky."

"No you never told me about that but why are you telling me now?" I asked.

"Well when I went past the Warden's cell, I noticed he was pacing around like some wild animal and as I glanced at him and I saw those same images again, just not as bright. It gave me the creeps," she said as she shook her body all over.

"Yeah I don't like who he has turned into and that's why he's locked up in a cell."

"What are you going to do with him and the guards?" Tyson asked.

"I'm making this up as I go along but if you have some great plan, I'm all ears," I replied.

Tyson screwed up her face and shrugged her shoulders at me.

"I'll take that as a no. Listen Tyson, I want you to keep the gun and if anything happens with the Warden, don't hesitate, take him out. Promise me you'll do that?" I pleaded.

"Yeah, okay and don't worry, I know how to use this," she replied.

The next two days went by without any major incidents. There was lots of complaining but nothing serious, everyone appeared to be getting on with it.

"Tyson have you seen Isabella anywhere," I asked.

"No I haven't. I'll go and have a look around."

I had become so busy running the entire prison, Isabella had not been my main focus. She was growing up fast and becoming more adventurous so I trusted her to spend some more time on her own.

I was becoming frantic after searching for her everywhere and not being able to find her. Then I stopped still and centred myself, trying to pick up what she was thinking. Her thoughts became so loud it was giving me a headache.

Help me mummy he's hurting me… please hurry I can't breathe mummy…

I immediately knew where she was. I yelled at an inmate to find Tyson and send her up to where the Warden's cell was. I ran as fast as I could to his cell, to find him with his arms through the cell bars and holding Isabella by the throat, strangling her. I could swear the Warden had grown ten feet tall and in my mind I saw Godzilla holding a rag doll.

"Let her go now or I'll kill you… put her down!" I screamed at the top of my voice.

"This little mutant is the reason I'm in here and you're out there. I should have done this when I had the chance before Mother Superior wanted to get information out of her," the Warden said.

Isabella was choking and her little legs were kicking wildly as she looked around at me terrified.

Mummy he's killing me do something quick.

"Tyson where the fuck are you!" I shouted at the top of my voice, "Tyson!"

Her legs had stopped kicking and she stopped making the choking noises. Desperate, I ran up to him and started punching his arms with my fists, trying to break his hold. I wanted to kick him but he was behind the bars as I watched his body intermittently flash images of the Thraxion scales on his body which was now full of rage. He looked and sounded like a monster.

"Isabella! Isabella!" I screamed.

Tyson came running up to the cell and in a split second pulled out the gun I gave her. I jumped back from the cell as Tyson fired several times at the Warden hitting him in the legs, so she didn't hit Isabella who was dangling in front of him. The Warden dropped to the floor releasing Isabella. I pulled her away and placed her on the floor and instinctively began performing CPR on her. After tense seconds of pumping her little chest and breathing into her lungs she gasped a breath of air. Relieved and overwhelmed with emotion I scooped her up into my arms and held her tight. I didn't want to let her go, hugging her tightly and crying, overcome with emotion. The Warden was writhing around on the floor in agony demanding to be helped.

I erupted in anger.

"Tyson I want to show all the women what we are dealing with. I don't think they realise how serious this is and how dangerous these things are. I want you to give him the same treatment you gave Scarface."

Tyson looked at me and nodded, "Consider it done."

I asked the inmates to bring the nuns and homeless girls into the main assembly area where the large overhead beam was, with the rope still in place from where Scarface was hung. The Warden let Tyson leave it there as a reminder of the dangerous person who killed Red.

Within minutes the women had gathered in a large circle.

"What's going on and why are we out here?" asked a young girl from the shelter.

"We were in the middle of prayer," complained a nun.

"Someone told me recently we can keep explaining things to you but it's not until you experience it for yourself you will truly understand. He was right and it was the fastest way to explain what he was trying to tell me. It's time you had the same experience. This monster nearly killed Isabella," I shouted as I pointed to Isabella's neck covered in bruises.

"Maria can you take Isabella to the infirmary, please?" I asked.

"Sarah what's going on? Why are we out here?" Maria asked.

"Maria, please, just do as I ask! I don't want her to see this!"

Maria shook her head annoyed. After staring at me for a few seconds, she took Isabella's hand and they walked away. The group watched on, as Tyson was grappling with the rope and preparing the knot for the Warden's demise. When the Nuns realised what I was going to do they became extremely uncomfortable, gasping in shock while the young girls were looking on stunned, staring in disbelief at the very thought. They watched on as Tyson then walked over to the Warden in his bloodied cell, still moaning in pain.

"Sarah please don't do this. I'll cut you a deal... let's just talk about it. I've not been myself since Jane was killed. You know that. C'mon please," the Warden pleaded. Tyson ordered two of her

strongest girls to drag the Warden out of his cell and drop him where
I was standing. As they dragged him across the floor they left a
bloody trail. He had lost a lot of blood by now and you could see he
was weak. I could feel myself getting anxious in anticipation of what
we were about to do. The energy in the room was tense. Everyone
was on edge.

"We do not wish to witness this brutal, barbaric behaviour
child," said one of the nuns as she turned and began to walk away.
Others began to follow her.

"No one is leaving sister! Tyson get your girls to circle the group
and make sure no one leaves," I demanded, as Tyson nodded to her
girls.

"Please this is so wrong, we don't want to watch either, we
believe you now, please let us go," cried one of the girls from the
shelter.

"I know this seems brutal to you all but trust me, you need to
see this monster for yourself. They show themselves when their lives
are threatened and this is the only way I can show you. Trust me, I'm
keeping you safe by killing this thing," I looked over at Tyson and
gave her the nod to do it.

"Sarah let's talk about this I know we can talk things
through... please," the Warden begged.

Tyson opened up the knot and placed it over the Wardens neck
and then pulled it tight, as the young girls began screaming loudly.

"Showtime girls... take it away," Tyson yelled.

'Like tug of war,' they each grabbed the rope tightly and
heaved together straining as they hoisted him in the air, as Tyson
then tied off the end of the rope to a large pillar nearby.

The Warden's legs kicked frantically, pumping more blood out
of his wounds and onto the floor, pooling in a puddle below his feet.
He clutched at the rope around his neck trying to release the
pressure but to no avail. All you could hear was the Warden choking
and the young girls screaming, as they looked on horrified. Images of
scaly thorny like protrusions on his body flashed, making the young
girls scream even louder, some were now hysterical while the nuns
had now turned their backs and were facing the opposite way with
their eyes closed, praying.

The energy in the room was intense as we watched his legs
slowly stop kicking, his arms dropping to his sides from his hold on
the rope around his neck and his head finally slumped to the side.

The nuns were now praying out loud in unison, trying to drown out the screaming from the terrified young girls. The homeless girls were holding onto each other for support in tears and shocked, stunned after witnessing the brutal hanging.

An inmate shouted to me, trying to get my attention.

"Sarah there is a female outside the prison. She says she knows you and is asking for you by name."

I was still in a daze and feeling sick for having to be part of the hanging.

"Sarah do you want me to let her in?" shouted the inmate again.

"Sorry let who in?" I replied.

"There's a young woman asking to come inside the prison and she is asking for you by name," she shouted back.

I stood there thinking about what she said and who it could be. Then I realised someone I was expecting, was not on the buses that arrived at the prison.

"Shit, it must be Tina. Let her in," I ordered.

I asked Tyson to walk down to the entrance to greet Tina. I remained standing with the group surrounding the Warden.

"I know what you just witnessed was ugly and I'm sorry for that. I wish there was another way I could have shown you what we're all up against but if you don't help the Luveians, you will be targeted by these monsters."

I watched as the silhouette of Tyson and Tina walked up the long corridor from the entrance and up to the group and into full view.

"Jane... Jane is that you... I thought you were... what the fuck?" I stood there in disbelief.

"Sarah... is that? Oh my God... what have you done to my...?"

ABOUT THE AUTHOR:

Jerome is one of ten siblings and from very humble beginnings. He was born and raised in Perth, Western Australia. He began to rebuild his life again at forty, after his marriage of ten years ended and a failed business venture which sent him broke. Years later he married the love of his life, and following his Mother's advice he started to write, combining his love of movies and great storytelling with his love of spirituality. Six years later, he self-published Dawn of the Hybrids, the first book of the trilogy.

Thank you for reading my first book. I am very humbled by the great feedback I am receiving. If you enjoyed reading my book, would you be so kind as to write a review for me. This will help me launch my new writing career. I would be very grateful and wish you many blessings in advance.

Thank you,

Jerome

www.ingramcontent.com/pod-product-compliance
Lightning Source LLC
Chambersburg PA
CBHW020132120726

47903CB00007B/2226